SKELMERSDALE

2 2 NOV 2012

D0809984

Wv

The Slugs might not be able to see us.

But so far we had certainly not seen them. "Switch to semi-auto. At least until they show themselves."

Since we couldn't see them, our rifles went silent.

My heart pounded in my ears.

Cordite smoke fogged my vision.

The fog swirled.

The swirls resolved into solid objects.

Black, armored shapes slid through the gloom toward us.

Boom-boom-boom!

I shuddered at the memory. Slug warriors on the attack beat their weapons against their armor, in unison; the sound still came to me in nightmares.

Brumby whispered, "Hello again, you little bastards."

ORPHAN'S DESTINY

ROBERT BUETTNER

www.orbitbooks.net

ORBIT

First published in Great Britain in 2008 by Orbit

Copyright © 2005 by Robert Buettner
Excerpt from *Orphan's Journey* © 2008 Robert Buettner

The moral right of the author has been asserted.

A CIP catalogue record for this book
is available from the British Library.

ISBN 978-1-84149-755-6

Typeset in Times

Printed and bound in Great Britain by
CPI Mackays, Chatham, ME5 8TD

Papers used by Orbit are natural, renewable and recyclable
products made from wood grown in sustainable forests and certified
in accordance with the rules of the Forest Stewardship Council.

Mixed Sources
Product group from well-managed
forests and other controlled sources
www.fsc.org Cert no. SGS-COC-004081
© 1996 Forest Stewardship Council

FSC

Orbit
An imprint of
Little, Brown Book Group
100 Victoria Embankment
London EC4Y 0DY

An Hachette Livre UK Company
www.hachettelivre.co.uk

www.orbitbooks.net

For Warrant Officer Robert Kreilick Buettner and
USO Hostess Annette Catherine Buettner, whose
contribution to this book cannot be overstated

"A Confederate sharpshooter's ball slew our drummer today, as he took breakfast on a fair July morning. The lad joined up when his parents died, and had not passed fourteen. They say it is a soldier's lot to die young and unexpectedly. Or to live and forever question God why he was spared. For me, should I live, I shall ask what cruel God makes death an orphan's destiny."

— True Occurrences During
    the Great Battle at Gettysburg:
    Recountings of a Soldier of the
    Sixty-first Ohio Infantry

ONE

"ANYBODY OUT THERE? OVER."

Static, not a human voice, cackles back through my earpiece.

Sssss. Pop.

Ten feet across this egg-shaped chamber, the hull-plate barricade I've thrown across the entry glows red. The Slugs are burning through their own ship to finish me. Roasted metal's tang singes my nostrils. Two minutes, tops, then Slugs will surge through their opening like man-sized, armored maggots.

I reverse the pistol in my hand to use it as a club. The gesture measures my resolve. The pistol's empty magazine well measures its futility.

I sigh and my breath worms out and glows purple in Slug interior lighting. Before my heart can beat, my helmet ventilator wicks away the condensation like a stolen soul.

My legs sprawl across the quaking Slug metal-blue decking and I thump my numb, armored left thigh with a gloved fist. Leg infantry needs two good legs. I could limp if I had to. But to where?

I let my back sink into the rescue-me yellow mattress of the Polytane hull-breach plug. That's how we boarded this monstrosity, like pirates in Eternad armor, but the hull breach is no way out for me. Behind it stretches vacuum, the emptiness that fills space between Earth and the moon.

My visor display freezes the year in emerald digits at 2043. The timer, though, rushes down to four minutes and keeps falling.

When those timer digits spin down to zero, the human race will live or die. I die either way. I'm Jason Wander. For now, history's youngest and screwed-est major general. For a while, a twenty-four-year-old lieutenant. For eternity, Infantry.

I'm also the human speed bump between the Slugs and Brumby. A mile beneath me in this beast's belly, he may blow this invasion transport into rutabagas and both of us with it. If I can buy seconds here at the price of my life.

If we fail, Slugs by the millions will overrun Earth in slimy waves. Mankind will struggle, of course, with a brick-by-brick tenacity that will make Stalingrad look like a pie fight. The Slugs don't know mankind yet, not when it's defending its own turf.

The oval that outlines the Slugs' emerging doorway glows white. We didn't know they could do that. We know even less about them than they know about us. Soon, we may both know too much.

One minute left before they break through, just over three minutes until detonation, if ever.

My shoulders sag under my armor.

It has, all things considered, been a fine twenty-four years. I knew my parents, though not for so long as I would have liked. I grew up. I met good people. The best, in fact. I experienced the one great love of my life, albeit for just 616 days. I had a godson I came to love like my own child. Oh, and, depending on which version of history one read, I saved the world.

My 'puter beeps. Three minutes.

They say contemplation of death comes in phases: denial, anger, some other stuff, then, finally, acceptance.

Maybe that was the thing I had been luckiest about, compared to the other orphans I had known. A soldier's destiny is to die young and unexpectedly. Soldiers often die nobly. Soldiers often die for others' hubris or stupidity. But it is rarely a soldier's destiny to have the time to accept his death.

The first molten metal plops, then sizzles, on deck plates as the Slugs burn through. I grip my spent pistol tighter.

In some alternate reality, there may be truth in the soldierly deception that war is bloodshed that brings life. I cock my head. That is, word for word, what the woman who bore my godson said when I delivered him in a cave on Jupiter's largest moon.

That's where this started for me, three years ago.

TWO

"YOU COULD BLEED TO DEATH!" I swiveled my head from the obstetrics instruction holo flickering to my left to the unladylike thigh-sprawl I knelt between. The field lantern's Eternad-battery light cut crumpled shadows on the cave's rock walls and ceiling. Zero Centigrade artificial atmosphere, manufactured by the Slugs we kicked off this rock seven months ago, numbed my fingers, slick with amniotic fluid and blood. A cave on Ganymede makes an awful birthing suite.

"No, Jason, this bloodshed brings life. Can you see the head, yet?" Corporal Sharia Munshara-Metzger puffed like a four-foot-eleven locomotive.

"Yeah. I think it's crowning, Munchkin." Whatever crowning meant. Four years ago I joined the infantry as a specialist fourth class, to stay out of jail. Fate and shrapnel had left me the acting commanding general of the seven hundred human survivors of the Battle of Ganymede. Obstetrics I knew like Esperanto.

I slid my eyes back to the holo. Bad enough to report the gynecological play-by-play without staring into the genitals of my best friend's widow.

Through clenched teeth, Munchkin spat Arabic that I was pretty sure compared me, her acting commanding general, to something excreted by a camel. Eight hours' labor erodes military courtesy.

She pressed her palms to her temples and thrashed her head side to side. Sweat droplets arced away from bangs plastered to her forehead, zero degrees or not. Her cheeks, olive and flawless, swelled as she puffed and blew. She focused her big brown eyes on me. "Why did we do this, Jason?"

Who we? What this? Women omit pronouns' antecedents like aspen drop leaves in fall. But woe betide the man who fails to mind-read. I guessed. "Because the Slugs sat out here bombing the human race to extinction?"

She snarled. "I mean, why did Metzger and I have this child?"

I rolled my eyes at a question I had asked myself a hundred times during Munchkin's pregnancy. United Nations Space Ship *Hope* had carried ten thousand male and female light infantry troops and five hundred Space Force crew for six hundred days from Earth to the orbit of Jupiter. The politicians weeded six million volunteers down to us lucky orphans who had lost entire families to the Slugs: "The Orphan's Crusade."

Even for orphans, unwanted pregnancy was a last-century relic, unheard-of since After-Pills. Yet only *my* best friend, the commander of the mile-long spaceship on which humankind had bet its future, and *my* gunner, after *I* introduced them, managed to break every imaginable regulation and conjure up a little nipper amid interplanetary combat.

Troubles find me like buzzards find roadkill. The Battle of Ganymede had been no exception.

A contraction stabbed Munchkin. "I must push."

I shifted my eyes between the holo cube and her crotch. Munchkin's Egyptian-pixie pelvis needed another centimeter's dilation to pass a watermelon-sized human. I shook my head. "Not yet."

The look Munchkin shot me made me glad it didn't come from behind the sights of our M-60, but she didn't push. For reasons I'll never understand, the worse things get, the more people think I have answers.

I suppose that's why I got field-promoted. As a specialist fourth class, I wasn't even in charge of the machine gun I loaded for Munchkin. Now I was commander of this disaster. The politicians didn't call it a disaster. They pronounced the battle a miraculous victory. The Battle of Ganymede will never be miraculous to us seven hundred survivors who buried ten thousand comrades beneath this moon's cold stones. But the alternative was the extinction of the human race, so it was miraculous.

Before we lost Earth-uplink five months ago, the legislatures of our various nations sprinkled us with medals and promotions in absentia and promised us relief was on the way.

So, as acting commander, I was thinking up stuff for my remnant division to do while the cavalry rode four hundred million miles.

"Sir? Major Hibble on Command Net." A shadow flicked across my view as my acting division sergeant major ducked into the cave behind me.

"Busy, here, Brumby." I shifted my torso between Brumby and Munchkin's privates. Stretched to nine centimeters, drained by eight hours' labor, however, Munchkin could have cared less if she was appearing live on the frontscreen of the *New York Times*.

"They found something, sir."

I turned. "What?" There were no more live Slugs. Certain of that, I had sent half of our force, including our surviving medic—the bastard had assured me Munchkin's due date was two weeks away—with Howard Hibble to search for clues to what had made our now-extinct enemy tick.

To date we knew that Slugs had been a communal organism that originated somewhere outside the Solar System and turned up four years ago on Ganymede, using it as an advance base to bomb the human race out of existence city by city. We assumed the Slugs were galactic nomads, traveling in their entirety from planetary system to planetary system, sucking each system dry, then moving on.

The Slugs never confirmed or denied anything, they just killed people.

Every Slug warrior fought like hell until killed or cornered, then dropped dead to avoid capture. We'd been outsmarted, outnumbered, and slaughtered.

We won only because Metzger sent his crew to the lifeboats, then kamikazed *Hope* into the Slugs' base in an impact so violent that Howard's astroseismologists said Ganymede still twitched seven months later.

I'd agreed with Howard to march troops halfway around Ganymede not to find live Slugs. Metzger had killed them all off and wrecked their cloning incubators and destroyed their central brain. It—Howard insisted on referring to the Slugs as "It," a single organism with physically disparate parts—was gone, over, obliterated.

Howard thought some of their hardware might have survived the impact. Somehow, these glorified garden snails had known how to air-condition a planet-sized moon, fly between star systems, and raise armies of infinite size and perfect discipline. They understood everything they needed to defeat us.

Except the perverse propensity of separate, individual humans to sacrifice ourselves for one another, by which Metzger had turned defeat into victory, for the price of his own life.

Brumby waved the handset at me, strawberry-blond eyebrows raised. Brumby looked like a freckled neoclone of a cowboy marionette I saw on a history chip, from the pre-holo TV days, named Doody Howdy or something. "TOT-uplink's gone in two minutes, sir."

I glanced at Munchkin. She lay still between contractions and nodded. Her husband had given his life to win this war. She understood that managing the peace was my job.

Brumby was twenty-four but combat had left him with a grandmother's twitches. His fingers quivered while I swept my hands with a Sterilette, then pressed the handset to my ear. "This is Juliet, over."

A blink's hesitance separated question from answer as the signal relayed through the Tactical Observation Transport hovering line-of-sight-high between us.

"Jason, we found an artifact."

I raised my eyebrows. Intact Slug machinery might hold the key to their technology. To date, we had recovered nothing but metal bits, plus Slug carcasses, personal weapons, and body armor. "What is it?"

"A metallic, oblate spheroid. Fourteen inches long."

"A tin football?" For a grunt, I had high verbal SATs.

"Sixty pounds, Earth weight."

"What's it do?"

"Lies in a hole in the ground, so far."

I squeezed the handset. "Howard, it's undetonated ordnance! Get your people away from it!"

"We've never seen any indication that the Pseudo-cephalopod employed explosive weapons. It favored kinetic-energy projectiles. The engineers haven't sniffed any explosives."

"A human wouldn't know a Slug bomb if it got stuffed up his nose!"

"We've already crated it. My hunch is it was a Pseudo-cephalopod remote-sensing device."

The Army put up with Howard because his professorial hunches were usually right.

I sighed, then shook my head. "Howard, get your ass back here!" Our mission had never been to Lewis-and-Clark Ganymede. It was to destroy the Pseudocephalopod ability to make war on Earth from Ganymede. We had done that. Now, my job as commanding officer was to get my troops home, safe. If the Slugs had left behind a remote sensor, they might have left behind time bombs, Anthrax, or bad poetry. If there was a chance in a million that the Slugs remained a threat I didn't want my force split like Chelmsford's at Isandlwhana. Howard's archaeological expedition was a dumb idea. "And leave that goddamn bomb right where it is!"

Static hissed back.

Brumby said, "We've lost 'em 'til the TOT repositions above the horizon, sir."

Brumby retrieved the handset and trotted back to HQ, as gangling as the stringless puppet he resembled. Brumby had left Earth a high school senior with a genius for creating stink bombs and a belligerent propensity for setting them off in high school cafeterias. That had made him a combat engineer.

He would return to Earth, if we ever returned, an acting division sergeant major with post-combat yips.

"Now?" Munchkin growled through clenched teeth.

The instruction holo said that if I coached her to push too early, before she was fully dilated, she would exhaust herself. I hadn't gotten to the part of the holo explaining what I had to do then, but I was afraid Dr. Jason would have to reach in there and pry the little rascal out. Or cut Munchkin open. I shuddered.

Sharia Munshara-Metzger was the closest thing to family I had. But as one soldier looking after another, I had seen her bleed before. And I had the remains of an infantry division waiting on my orders while I midwifed. What the hell. "Push, Munchkin."

Ten minutes of screaming—by both of us—passed. Then I held my godson, as healthy as any squalling, purple prune with a cord growing from his navel. I swabbed mucus from his mouth and nostrils, then laid him across Munchkin's belly.

While I tied off, then cut, the umbilical cord, I asked, "Did you pick a name?" I knew she had, because every time I had asked her over the last seven months she looked away. Munchkin had a Muslim superstitious streak as wide as the Nile. I figured she was afraid she'd jinx the kid if she said a name.

"Jason." Munchkin's smile glowed through the subterranean twilight.

"What?" I swallowed a lump in my throat, even though I'd half guessed the name. Munchkin, Metzger, and I were all war orphans. Ganymede was our orphanage and we were our own family.

"Jason Udey Metzger. My father was Udey."

I adjusted my surgical mask, so I could wipe my eyes without seeming to. "People will call him Jude."

People would call him more than that. The Son of the Savior of the Human Race. The Spawn of the Exterminator of the Universe's other intelligent species. The only Earthling conceived and born in outer space. The Freak.

"Jason, this is the best day of my life." Tears streamed down Munchkin's cheeks and she sobbed so hard that Jude Metzger bounced on his mother's belly like he was rafting class-three whitewater.

I understood. But I thought that for me the best day would be the day we all left Ganymede.

I was wrong.

THREE

ON THE MORNING OF OUR 224TH DAY on Ganymede, measured in Earth days, Jude Metzger celebrated his one-week birthday under Jovian skies. But the *Ganymede Gazette,* the daily paper my guys published on the backs of old ration wrappers, had a bigger headline.

For 223 days Ganymede's skies didn't change. The daily, orbit-induced windstorms whirled golden dust above the mountains. Beyond their peaks and the dust clouds shone stars and Jupiter's visible lesser moons, Europa, Io, and Callisto, some days pink, some days pearlescent or violet against space's indigo. Over all loomed ever-orange Jupiter, at each rise and set magnified by the artificial atmosphere's lens so the gas giant filled the horizon.

We all watched the sky every one of those days. Not because it was beautiful but because there lay home.

On the morning of day 224, at five-zero-three Ganymede Standard Time, Brumby burst into the mess cave, binocular range finder in one freckled hand, the other pointing back over his shoulder.

Brumby didn't have to speak. Only one thing would excite any of us interplanetary castaways like that.

Egg-scrambled (concentrated) tubes and therm cups clattered to the frozen lava floor. Before the echoes stopped rebounding off the cave walls and ceiling, three hundred combat-boot pairs thundered out into pale twilight.

I let the men clear out, then followed them onto the rocky terrace that Brumby and the surviving engineers had blasted out of the mountainside. Architecture on Ganymede involved blowing things up, since we had three building materials to work with: rock, rock, and rock.

By the time I got outside, someone, not Brumby who stood alongside me to avoid trampling, had picked it out. I simply let my eyes follow the pointing fingers.

Just a luminous fly crawling toward us across the deep purple ceiling of our world, but the prettiest sight I had ever seen. The relief ship. Maybe.

Brumby turned to me. "Sir, how long you figure before the first of us gets off the rock?"

"First question is how we make sure we *all* get off, Brumby. Order alert status."

Brumby stiffened. "Sir? Alert?" Brumby and seven hundred cold, exhausted, lonely GIs figured it was party time, not jump-in-our-holes time.

It may be no coincidence that "General" and "Grinch" begin with "G." Alert status meant the troops dispersed to fighting positions. "Disperse" meant walk, crawl, and climb. Three things GIs had bitched about since Troy.

Well, there were, historically, two schools of military thought here. Concentration of force, like the Romans huddling in phalanxes, shoulder-to-shoulder and shield-to-shield, or dispersal, spreading troops out so one grenade

couldn't get a whole squad. Short, the general in charge of
the Army Air Corps at Pearl Harbor a hundred years ago,
huddled all his aircraft together so they would be easier to
guard. And created perfect targets for Japanese bombs.

So I was a dispersal man, myself. Even if my grunts
hated it. The sooner we fled this rock the sooner I could
shed the stars on my shoulders and slide back to being a
grunt, myself. Oh, I hoped they'd let me keep a lieutenant's bar. But presiding by default over an accident had
made me no general officer.

"Brumby, all we know is that speck is *somebody* coming. Might be relief. Might be Slugs. Pass the word to the
battalion COs." The Ganymede Expeditionary Force's
surviving "battalions" weren't much more than platoon-
sized, maybe fifty soldiers each. Word-passing would take
Brumby sixty seconds.

Brumby half shook his head, denying the possibility
that there might still be Slugs, more than questioning my
order.

"Brumby, if it's our guys, they'll be in field-strength
radio range in a couple hours." Generals—even field-
promoted spec fours—didn't need to justify orders to
their aides. Maybe it was my way of telling him I wanted
that speck to be our guys, too. "The men can break out the
potato vodka then."

Brumby's jaw sagged. Surely he had realized I knew
about the still? During the six-hundred-day voyage out
here from Earth, one of Howard's lab techs had hidden his
booze-making equipment and his potato raw material in a
Hope escape pod, never expecting he, the pod, and his still
would wind up dirtside, stranded among the embarked-
division survivors.

Brumby grinned, then saluted. "Yes, sir."

While Brumby passed the word, I cupped a hand over one ear and radioed Howard. "Hotel, this is Juliet. Say your estimated time of arrival and position. Over." Dispersal didn't mean having half your force miles away.

"Jason, it's Howard. We'll be back there in an hour. At least that's what they tell me. I'm not sure where we are. Did you see it?"

Howard land-navigated like a blind Cub Scout but I should have known he would have spotted anything that moved in space. I said, "You think it's our guys? What if it's Slugs?"

"The Pseudocephalopod displaced between conventionally mapped spatial locations by transiting temporal-fabric folds."

"In English, Howard."

"Slugs jumped through worm holes that join points where space folds back on itself."

"Another hunch?"

"It had to be that way. Stars with planetary systems are too far apart to be reached by conventional travel at sub-light speeds. Even if It lived a long time."

"Okay. So?"

Howard continued. "So, if It still existed, for which we have no credible intelligence, It would most likely appear to us in a way we never expected, not by replicating tactics that failed It before."

"Why not? Human armies repeat mistakes all the time. Even the intelligent ones."

"It wasn't a human intelligence."

I nodded, handset to my ear. Howard might be a

professor but prudent soldiers didn't survive by underestimating their opponents.

"Jason, that's *Excalibur* up there."

"*Excalibur?*"

"*Hope*'s sister ship. She was under construction when we left home thirty-one months ago. I thought you knew."

Howard thought nothing of the kind. He might be a professor at heart but as an Intelligence officer he had bought into all the Spook need-to-know crap. The Spook rationale would have been that if none of the rest of us knew there was a follow-on assault ship, we couldn't spill the beans if the Slugs captured us.

"The trip from Earth takes almost two years with chemical-fuel technology. How do you think *Excalibur* got here seven months behind us if she didn't leave while we were still under way?"

I drew a breath, then let it leak out like I was about to squeeze off a round. No point scolding. Especially when the news was good. "Okay, Howard. That ship's not Slugs."

"That would be obvious to any schoolchild. But one of my staff officers actually suggested we go on alert. Isn't that ridiculous?"

"I guess."

Two Earth days later Howard Hibble and I stood alongside a hand-cleared, two-mile-long runway. Another of Brumby's better-living-through-explosives projects, he had sliced and relocated mountains with a diamond cutter's precision, using plastique that looked as benign as cookie dough.

We watched *Excalibur*'s first relief ship carve a red friction streak as it dropped across the sky from orbit. By the time it drew close enough to be bigger than a speck, its skin had cooled from the thousand degrees Fahrenheit of a ten-thousand-mile-per-hour descent. The ship spun a contrail like spider silk as it arced down through the artificial atmosphere.

The relief ship touched down on Ganymede at two hundred miles per hour, then boomed down our runway past us. Our shoulders hunched, we turned and watched its landing run-out, as much to shelter from the wind-wash the ship sucked behind it as to see it.

It looked like an old-fashioned clothes iron, squashed and with the handle cut off, a taupe wedge 128 feet long and just as wide, sprouting angled fins from its rear end.

My jaw hung open and my stomach churned. "Howard, that heap is just a dropship!" We had assaulted Ganymede from orbit in dropships identical to the one that now shrank as it sped down our runway in a moon-dust cloud. Dropships were gliders. This tub couldn't take off! Hell, our own dropships hadn't even brought us *down* successfully. Every one had crash-landed.

Howard patted my arm. "The original design was for a reusable space plane to shuttle down *and* up to low Earth orbit. It got shelved in 2001. The dropships had troop transport compartments in place of fuel tanks and engines. These ships are powered. This variant will carry fewer troops but it'll take us up to the mother ship fine."

Adrenaline tingled my fingers. That was just one more thing the Army told Howard the Intelligence Spook but hadn't told us grunts. One more thing we couldn't have revealed if captured. Operational security makes perfect sense but I still hate being lied to.

The relief ship reached the end of its run-out and pivoted to taxi back in our direction. As if to prove Howard's point that it was powered, its engines gunned and our creaky ticket home churned dust as it rolled back toward us.

The Slug War had forced humankind to pick up manned spaceflight where it had left off back when cars burned gasoline, in the late 1990s. The seventy-year hiatus had given humanity budget enough to solve lots of social problems and time enough to pat itself on the back for achieving decades of world peace. Great accomplishments. They looked less great to an infantryman like me who had to ride into battle against the most destructive enemy in the universe in last-century antiques.

The ship rolled up to us and braked, nosing down on her landing gear, engines whining and heat still rolling off her skin. Mean midday temperature on Ganymede still only rose to two degrees Fahrenheit, so that warmth felt good. Block-lettered "UNSF" decorated the ship's fuselage in United Nations powder-blue. Designs on the friction-scorched vertical stabilizers looked like a black-and-white squirrel with an S-shaped tail. Below it I made out the lettering "Pride of the Skunk Works."

I pointed at the insignia and made head-scratching motions at Howard.

Howard cupped his hands around his mouth and shouted, "It's a Lockheed-Martin Venture Star."

The engines died.

Howard dropped his voice. "In the last half of the twentieth century, we hid an aircraft factory in the Nevada desert. The 'Skunk Works.'"

I raised my eyebrows. "Nixon hid the defense plants from the hippies?"

Howard smiled. "No. From the Russians, during the

Cold War. The hippies melted into the mainstream after Vietnam. The Venture Star died on the drawing board in the early 2000s. Amilitarism fizzled the Skunk Works."

I nodded. I had spent my free time the last seven months completing downloaded correspondence courses toward bachelor's and master's degrees in military history. Americans made war only too well once we set our minds to it. But we resisted getting into wars, from Woodrow Wilson to Charles Lindbergh to Arnaud Welkie and the No-bots in the 2030s. And as soon as Americans could, we turned away from our wars to benign—or self-indulgent—pursuits. America had flipped between pacifist and gung ho for 150 years, now.

The relief ship shuddered on wheeled landing gear, fuselage ten feet above Ganymede, then hydraulics whined and a ramp unfolded from its belly.

The ramp reassured me that this ship represented a two-way ticket. Our dropships had been single-use assault vessels. The ships disembarked us by splitting apart like pea pods, blown open by explosive bolts, never again usable. A ramp was not only red-carpet treatment, it meant this ship was capable of flying us up to the mother ship and, in turn, home.

I don't know who I expected to see descend the ramp but it was never Division Sergeant Major DeArthur Ord.

Ord's Eternad body armor shone immaculate crimson, and he strode down that ramp as sharp and measured as machinery, helmet tucked under one arm, fingers wrapped precisely across the laser-designator bulge, embassy-duty style.

His hair, what little Uncle Sam let him show, was as

gray as gunmetal and so were his eyes, unchanged since I first met him, as my senior drill sergeant in Infantry Basic.

Ord halted in front of me and saluted so crisply that his hand quivered. "Sir, Rear Admiral Brace extends his compliments."

I returned the salute. Ord's eyes would never do anything so unmilitary as to twinkle, so let's just say he must have polished them. My heart leapt. Ord was actually proud of me. It wasn't every day a drill sergeant rescued a smart-ass enlistee from the court-martial scrap heap, then saw that enlistee go on to command the division that won the most desperate battle in the history of the human race.

A Signal Corps holographer, who had followed Ord down the ramp, captured the scene for history with a Palmcorder.

It swelled my heart when I saw Ord stride down that ramp. But when I thought about it I cocked my head. Ord was plenty senior enough to be first down that ramp. Noncommissioned officers ran every army. Division sergeant majors sat at the left hand of God.

But Ord should report to the embarked-division commander, who would be an Army two-star. It sounded like *Excalibur*'s commander, a Navy-style rear admiral, was top dog, which was odd. But whoever was in charge, if that career officer was a political animal, and few officers made flag rank who weren't, he would have led his troops down to Ganymede with holocams rolling. Admiral Brace had dodged a holo opportunity that carried no apparent risk. Why?

Ord continued. "As do the Secretary-General of United Nations and the President of the United States."

I smiled. "I bet she does!" The Ganymede Expeditionary Force had paid a terrible price but the President, our commander-in-chief, had to feel the same gratitude toward my soldiers that America and the world did.

Ord blinked. "He, sir."

"Huh?" Not a general-like response but Ord's remark made no sense.

"The President resigned before her term expired. It is President Lewis who sends his greetings."

"Resigned?" No American President had resigned in nearly a century. The Palmcorder technician played his lens across us. The V-Star's cooling fuselage creaked.

"Things changed while you were up here, sir."

Beneath my helmet, hair stood on my neck.

FOUR

TWO DAYS LATER Howard and I again stood side by side on the Ganymede plains watching a V-Star fly. But this one was bound skyward. It jacked itself vertical on hydraulic struts angling from its belly, then Ganymede quaked as the V-Star's engines lit and rumbled.

Howard shouted in my ear, "That's fourteen, Jason."

The most expensive hundred miles in the universe are from dirt to low planetary orbit. Ganymede's gravity was more like the moon's than Earth's, but these V-Stars still packed lots of fuel. That meant there was room for only fifty GIs in each upship. Gliding down without engines or fuel tanks seven months ago, the same-size air frames had carried four hundred troops each.

Munchkin and Jude had ridden upship number one, along with the other medicals. As CO, I waited for the last ship off the rock, upship number fifteen. Howard, Brumby, and a half-dozen staff, stoop-shouldered from potato-vodka hangovers, waited with me.

I was younger than most of them and at least as fond of getting zogged. But I had hoisted one cup with them, then excused myself like a good CO, so they could party like it was 2099 while I sacked early. Command is sobering. Literally.

Today, except for Howard, they sat cross-legged in a circle, reclining on their packs and playing cards. Brumby sat on a neoplast crate packed with Howard's precious Slug Football.

Howard claimed he hadn't heard me tell him to leave it, but he probably would have brought it anyway. Howard argued it was the single most extraordinary artifact recovered in world history. But the reason I let him keep his Slug-metal stray puppy was that it hadn't shown any propensity to bite anybody.

The V-Star gathered speed and dwindled to a speck. It would rendezvous with *Excalibur* one hundred miles above us, then the last V-Star, refueled and refreshed, would scream down to pluck us from this most foreign place. Ganymede once again would host no living things.

In the sudden silence, Howard adjusted old-fashioned glasses on his wrinkled face, read his wrist 'puter, then caught me looking back, over my shoulder, at the low crags behind us. "We only have three hours. You're not going back over the rim?"

The landing strip and takeoff apron were built across solid rock and water-ice, on a plain beyond the rim of the crater where GEF had arrived on Ganymede. That flat crater floor had proven to be volcanic dust deep enough to swallow dropships whole. Hundreds of soldiers got buried alive without the chance to fire a shot. In the days that followed, thousands more fell in combat.

Landing Zone Alpha, beyond the jagged hills behind Howard and me, was a graveyard. Hallowed and consecrated by unanimous act of the General Assembly of the

United Nations and by the blood of nine thousand orphans. My only family.

I nodded at Howard. "I can make it over the rim and back in an hour."

Howard had known I couldn't leave this place without saying good-bye.

I Ganymede-galloped toward the crater rim, covering twenty paces with each low-gravity stride.

Howard shouted after me, "It's a long wait 'til the next bus!"

I scrambled to the crater-rim crest in fifteen minutes and paused to let my heart slow down. Howard's warning was sound advice, but even Space Force blue-suit weenies would hardly leave behind the stud-duck acting commanding general.

I dialed up my oxygen generator. Ganymede's artificial, Slug-generated atmosphere had grown to four percent oxygen. But Earth-normal was over twenty percent. And this atmosphere was still as thin as the air at Everest's summit.

Beyond the opposite crater rim, through the surface dust already rising from late-afternoon winds, the sun flickered like a distant porch light, fifteen degrees above the jagged horizon. I looked out across the crater floor to the impact-rebound structure at its center. The peak rose two thousand feet, like a medieval castle. It had been our fortress when Slugs and GIs had battled to control its parapets.

I picked my way, still puffing, across rock fields and down to the crater floor.

Ganymede had been a terrible place to fight a war. It was a more terrible place to bury the woman I loved.

I slipped and slid the last hundred vertical feet, then caught my breath again. Beneath my boots began a six-mile-long, eight-foot-wide causeway. Jury-rigged from pre-fabricated fiberglass shelter panels, it bridged the volcanic-dust sea.

The dust plain remained flat and featureless. If a tombstone rose here for each Slug warrior that had died and sunk beneath the dust, LZ Alpha would have made Arlington Cemetery look as empty as a village churchyard. The Slugs had charged us in waves, fifty thousand at a time. A man would sink in the dust as though into quicksand, but the Slug warriors glided across it like flat pebbles across pond water. Until we killed them. Then they sank like stones.

And kill them we had. At first, impersonally with precision-guided munitions. Then with rifles. Then with our bayonets. Then, finally, with our rifles again, swung stock-first like clubs until they shattered.

Our own dead now clustered near and upon the distant central peak, where the dropships crash-landed.

I checked my 'puter while I paused for a blow, then turned back and scanned the sky, perpetually twilight under one-thirtieth of Earth's sunlight. It was still hours before the upship would even *arrive*.

I should just have stood still a moment, remembered them all, then turned back. Instead, I bounded onto the causeway.

I paused halfway to the mountain at a makeshift gravestone, constructed from torso shells of Eternad body armor, lashed to the causeway's edge three miles distant from the central peak. Eternad armor stops assault-rifle rounds, but it weighs no more than cardboard, so the shells twitched in the rising wind. A plaque hammered from duralumin ammunition boxes and riveted to a chestplate read, "Two hundred feet beneath this monument rest four hundred men and women of the Combat Engineer Battalion, Ganymede Expeditionary Force, and the crew of United Nations Space Force Assault Ship Two. Killed in Action Third April, 2040."

With the nearest living soldier ten miles away I allowed myself to draw a breath and blink back tears. They died. I lived. Why me?

"Action" in the gung-ho sense hadn't even killed them. Simple human error had. Intel hadn't dropped probes on the LZ to preserve surprise—they thought. The flat lava plain that Earth's best minds believed they recognized from millions of miles away had proven to be volcanic dust as deep as the sea. Those kids, most older than I was, died as unaware of their fate as us grunts in the follow-on dropships had been.

Someone wrote that war is an orphanage and the soldiers with whom you fight become your only family. The GEF troop-selection process, picking only from among those who had lost entire families to the Slugs, meant we were literal orphans, as well.

The Battle of Ganymede had orphaned me for the second time.

I shuffled the rest of the way to the mountain's base, more from respect for the fallen than from fear of falling.

I had barely met most of them. I ached not for lifetimes unlived but for anecdotes unfinished, jokes untold.

Ten minutes later I drew alongside the carcass of UNSF Assault Ship One, its skin tiles charred to charcoal by atmospheric friction. The ship's wedge shape remained intact, though plowed into knee-deep dust.

I never knew the copilot. I would never again know anyone like the pilot.

Priscilla Olivia Hart had stood barely five feet tall even when she swaggered. And the self-proclaimed world's best pilot always swaggered.

So the stones beneath which she lay made a grave as small as a child's, compared to the sea of others. We had all come in here as children. Sometimes it seemed those who never had to grow up were the lucky ones.

I tugged off a mitten and touched the stones, so cold they burned my flesh. But I kept my hand there. Once I drew my hand away from her, away from this place, away from these people, I would be alone again. Being alone is the worst part of being an orphan. "Why, Pooh? Why you? Why me?"

I reached inside my armor's yoke, unpinned my collar brass, and laid the stars across her grave. I needed to leave something of myself, something so she wouldn't be alone. I couldn't leave the ring because I hadn't kept it. The ring she refused from me because my job was too risky and I would widow her when I did something noble and stupid and died.

I leaned against her grave and let myself weep.

When I looked up, Sol's pale dot hung just above the crater rim. I read my 'puter as I tugged my mitten over numb fingers. Had I really stood here that long?

It only then occurred to me that a Space Force pilot would be more concerned about protecting his ship and crew by staying in his launch window than about whether he left one AWOL dirt-grubber behind, regardless of that grubber's acting rank. Had I really been stupid enough to think the last ship would wait for me? At midday, minutes meant little. But Ganymede's sunset brings artificial atmosphere contraction and hurricane-plus wind.

To that pilot, every minute's delay meant stronger launch crosswinds. After his mission, his first responsibility was his ship, just as my troops were mine. If I stood in that pilot's boots I would leave me behind in a heartbeat.

Crap!

I bounded back along the causeway, got blown over by the crosswind, and nearly turned an ankle. That slowed me to a shuffle.

In the distant sky crawled the firefly that was the last upship, inbound at eleven thousand miles per hour. Crap, crap, crap. I sped up.

By the time I crested the crater rim, the V-Star touched down in the distance. I stopped watching it and concentrated on dodging boulders as I descended.

When I rounded the last house-sized boulder between me and the takeoff apron, nothing remained on the apron but footprints and the V-Star. Its elevation-pylon doors whined open as it prepared to jack itself vertical for launch.

I sucked air like a vacuum 'bot set for deep-pile synwool as I ran. Sweat soaked the long johns beneath my armor. Seventy-mile-per-hour wind sizzled dust against my helmet visor.

I looked up at the V-Star and saw Howard's helmeted head poking out of the hatch like a bespectacled hunting trophy nailed on a wall. He waved me toward him.

I sprinted and leapt through the hatch. Pneumatics hissed and it slammed and locked twenty seconds later.

My earpiece beeped as the V-Star pilot spoke to Howard. Her voice rasped over the Command Net, heard only by Howard, her copilot, and me. "If waiting for your general costs us this ship, I'll make hell a lot hotter for that asshole, Hibble!"

I smiled. Pilots.

Panting, heart pounding, I strapped in alongside Howard and realized that my panicked dash had saved me a broken heart. I'm not sure I could have left them all if I had had to think about it as I marched away. I wondered whether I had lingered on purpose. The ache of loneliness sank into my chest even as GI breathing fogged the air around me.

Hydraulics whined as the V-Star pointed its nose to the sky and I sank into my seat back. The Space Force troop bay technician across the aisle had touched his boots to Ganymede for all of ten minutes. All his buddies, all his family, were where he was going, not where he had been.

The fuselage shuddered as pumps fueled the engines. The technician glanced at my harness, to be sure I was strapped in, then nodded at me, one soldier to another.

The space between our eyes was thirty inches. But the gulf between our lives was light-years.

Then I settled back into my seat and felt like I had just shrugged out of a field pack. The irate pilot had called me "General," but now, in the nurturing womb of a ship somebody else was driving, I would be free to be just a GI. I would shed the temporary rank that forced me to be the daddy of soldiers older than I was. I would be slid back to a lieutenancy, where I belonged.

The intercom squawked. "Ignition!"

I closed my eyes and let the grumpy pilot fly me toward home. My worries were over.

I thought.

FIVE

V-STAR TROOP BAYS LACK WINDOWS but the troop bay technician had duct-taped a cheap plasma flatscreen to the forward bulkhead, then hard-wired it. Therefore, we saw the
same feed as the pilot's camera while she slid our upship
alongside *Excalibur*'s majestically rotating, mile-long bulk,
like a snowflake landing on a polar bear.

Excalibur looked like *Hope,* except for the addition of
defensive weapons systems that were, like *Excalibur* herself, mere surplus, now that Slugs were extinct.

I lay back in my seat until the last of my men were
safely through the lock, then unbuckled. I stood in that
odd centrifugal-force gravity I had never expected to feel
again and faced the exit hatch.

"General? May I have a word, please?" The pilot's
Texanese twanged through the intercom.

I turned and stared toward the flight deck. The V-Star
flight deck connects to the troop bays through a shoulder-
width tube that corkscrews through the avionics. Negoti-
ating the tube requires some delightfully unladylike
contortions, so female pilots usually entered and exited
while the troop bay was empty of GIs.

Pooh had told me the pilots were acutely aware they were putting on a show for their passengers. She had also told me she would demonstrate the flight-deck worm for me privately, anytime I wanted.

I swallowed back tears even as I smiled.

From emotion, not good manners, I turned my head away as the rasp of this pilot's synlon flight suit against aluminum echoed in the bay. Finally, her boots tapped the deck plates.

"Politeness doesn't make infantry less stupid."

Smart-ass was even more a pilot trait than a Texan one. I turned back to face her, then looked around for the Texan pilot.

The woman who stood, feet planted shoulder-width apart, in front of the flight-deck hatch, was tiny and as Japanese as cherry blossoms. Her eyes were enormous, brown almonds set in porcelain. Her hair was ebony silk and she combed it with her fingers, taming helmet-head spikes. Almonds or not, her eyes burned at me.

I flicked my eyes across the shoulder loops of her flight suit. I didn't really feel like I outranked a doorman, but part of being an officer is demanding military courtesy. I tried to burn my eyes back at her. "Major, did the Space Force teach you the difference between Stars and an Oak Leaf?" Every zoomie should be required to spend a month with a real drill sergeant.

"General, we're still aboard my ship. Hero of the Battle of Ganymede or not, you endangered my ship and my crew. I don't care cowshit what's on your shoulders."

I paused. I'd kind-of skipped over the military justice part of my correspondence courses. There was something somewhere about a vessel master's absolute authority.

The name tape stitched to her flight suit, over her heart, read Ozawa.

The name tape was the second thing I noticed.

Pilot attire had changed while I was gone. Pooh's flight suit had been UN powder-blue, floppy coveralls. Major Ozawa's was diagonal-striped rescue-me orange and yellow. More significantly, it was stretch synlon, tight enough that there wasn't much question about how Major Ozawa would look without it. And the answer to that question was "terrific."

It's not like I hadn't seen a woman for seven months. Munchkin wasn't the only surviving female soldier in GEF, and a few of them were cream. But an officer doesn't think about his soldiers that way. They say it's professional detachment, like being a gynecologist. But Major Ozawa wasn't even in the Army, so I felt undetached stirrings.

"Whenever you've seen enough, General."

I jerked my eyes back up to hers. "Uh."

I blinked and felt myself flush. It is just barely possible that I might have been staring.

She folded her arms across her chest. "I held this ship twenty minutes for you. Relive your glory. Strand yourself and your Medal of Honor if you want. But you jeopardized my ship."

She was right. "You don't understand—"

She chopped the air with a hand as delicate as a sparrow's wing. "I understand hundred-knot crosswinds! Do you? You almost killed fifteen of your own people!"

I blinked back tears and swallowed. Then I whispered, "I already killed nine thousand of them."

Her mouth froze open like a pink Cheerio.

We stood like fence posts until a boot scraped metal and Sergeant Major Ord poked his head through the exit hatch. "General Wander? Admiral Brace requests to welcome you aboard, sir!"

Ozawa avoided my eyes, craning her neck at gauges and recording end-of-mission data on a Chipboard.

Ord led me through the lock into brightness, warmth, and the womblike thrum of ship machinery for the first time in seven months.

In the embarkation corridor, Brumby dismissed the men and whispered, "Shower!" It sounded like a four-letter word. In point-six gravity, it would be more a sponge bath, but anticipation of warm, soapy water cascading over my skin made it tingle. An orderly led my troops off to clean fatigues and showers and cheeseburgers while I followed Division Sergeant Major Ord toward *Excalibur*'s bridge.

Excalibur's layout seemed just like *Hope*'s, where I had lived for nearly two years. I probably could have found my own way through the onion-peel deck layers to the bridge. But traveling behind Ord had entertainment value. We reached a stairwell, what the swabbies called a ladder. A pair of starched, enlisted Space Force ratings knelt on the deck plates, blocking the ladder, while they polished away grime that had been imaginary for the last hundred million miles.

"Make a hole!" Ord's command bellow seemed to physically blow the swabbies to stand at attention. The female was cute. As we passed them, their backs plastered against the bulkhead, her eyes were wide but her nose wrinkled. I became acutely aware of the Ganymede grit packed into every wrinkle in my uniform and every crevasse of my body. Seven months in the same armor was no way to impress a lady and generals didn't date enlisted ratings.

If Ozawa was any indication, women were going to be a problem. Like any twenty-two-year-old male het, a nerve as thick as a jumper cable linked my eyeballs to my groin. But moments after I looked at an eligible female, the thought of being with any woman other than Pooh Hart washed over my brain like a stain.

I sighed and just followed Ord as our bootsteps echoed along one corridor, then another.

Ten minutes later we got piped onto *Excalibur*'s bridge. *Hope*'s bosun had just keyed an electronic recording—*Excalibur*'s bosun actually blew a little silver whistle. Either way, it was for me as a general officer.

The bridge was the size of a low-ceilinged schoolroom, dim-lit in red so the flatscreen wall displays glowed brighter. In front of the screens, twenty swabbies sat at twenty consoles, each whispering data and instructions to the ship through cherry-stem microphones.

The master holo, *Excalibur* in iridescent miniature, floated centered amid the pilots and contollers like a translucent giant squid. The ship's pressurized payload and fuel-storage sections were forward and the propulsion booms trailed aft like tentacles. All along the master holo, colored-light streaks and blips winked on, crawled, then faded up and down the holo as the ship's vital signs changed. Every elevator that moved, every hatch that opened or closed, made a spark that a seasoned vessel commander could read like a living, three-dimensional book.

The holo would have dominated the room, except for

the figure who stood staring into it, head bowed, feet spread shoulder width apart, hands clasped in the small of his back.

Rear Admiral Atwater N. Brace had chosen Class-A uniform for this day, Space Force powder-blue and more coverall than suit. A service-ribbon rainbow plated the space over his heart. Not a combat decoration among them. His chin thrust forward as outsized and steel-smooth as an aircraft carrier's bow. His skin shone crimson, reflecting the master holo's glow.

Ord and I waited at attention, helmets tucked under our left arms, swallowing, blinking, and listening while the console operators' whispers made elevator music on the great ship's bridge.

I counted to three hundred while Brace let us dangle. His ship, his rules.

Brace raised his head and faced us. Ord and I saluted. Brace returned a crisp one. Space Force officers who came up through any country's Air Force saluted with that fly-boy limp wrist. Brace had to have been wet-Navy.

"Sir, Acting Major General Wander commanding United Nations Expeditionary Force Ganymede requests permission to come aboard."

"Granted, Acting General."

Brace forgot to give Ord and me "At ease." But he didn't forget to emphasize "Acting."

I thought the console jockey seated nearest us inclined his head a millimeter to listen.

Brace stretched a smile, showing polished teeth. "We're cleaning up your troops, Wander."

Philistine grunts couldn't bathe themselves.

"Field hygiene was tough. The water down there's

been ice since the Pre-Cambrian." Bathing had been cold, ineffective, and just frequent enough to keep soldiers from getting sick.

Brace's small blue eyes squinted as they flicked up and down my body armor. The infrared-absorbent crimson coating had scuffed down to bare Neoplast at the wear points and the torso had taken a few Slug-round hits. Plenty to gig there.

"Obviously." He turned to Ord. "Sergeant Major, show Acting General Wander to his quarters."

Ord saluted. "Aye-aye, sir!"

Hearing Ord say "aye-aye" instead of "yes, sir" was like watching a rhino polka. Brace was driving this bus and even Ord knew it.

Ord led me down a short corridor to my quarters. Unlike aboard *Hope,* when I was a specialist, fourth class, I was billeted forward, in officer country.

"Is he always an asshole, Sergeant Major?"

"Who, sir?"

"Who? I'm not a Basic trainee anymore, Sergeant Major. I may not be in your chain of command. These stars may not stay on my collar past this evening's chow. But at this moment I command seven hundred GIs who've been through hell. For the next two years they're gonna slack off and feel sorry for themselves. They'll pick fights like six-year-olds with people on this ship who haven't watched nine thousand friends die. But they're my six-year-olds until somebody takes them away. I need to know what kind of ship Brace runs. I need candor from an NCO. From another combat infantryman."

Ord looked back at me as we walked. His eyes had

that twinkle again, like he was watching a baby's first stumbles.

"Admiral Brace was top-twenty at Annapolis, sir. That let him pick a Naval Aviation slot. He pulled temporary astronaut duty with old NASA, then back to wet-Navy carriers. Commanded the *Tehran*. He knows space and he knows how to manage big ships." Ord stopped at a stateroom door and laid his hand on the latch. "Your quarters, sir."

"And you know how to dodge questions, Sergeant Major."

The corners of Ord's mouth twitched up one millimeter, then he nodded. "He's one solid-brass asshole, twenty-four/seven, sir."

I stepped into a private room with my own shower for the first time since I was a suburban teenager with a living biological parent. Before the war, a million years ago. I motioned Ord to follow.

"Sit, Sergeant Major?" I was a general officer. He was a noncom. I didn't need to make it a question. But Ord was Ord and I was a kid.

Ord nodded, then sat, as though his back rested on bayonet points.

My officer cabin's wall had a built-in thermcab. Now, that was living wick! I pulled two coffee plastis, popped their therm tabs, then handed one, steaming and black, to Ord. No noncom turned down coffee. Few took it other than black.

Ord may have relaxed one millimeter.

"Sergeant Major, I've never met Brace before. What's his problem with me?"

Ord hooked his helmet over one armored knee. "Sir, technically, you outrank the admiral."

I sipped coffee, scalded my tongue, and nodded. "Even though I'm a kid who doesn't have the education to swab an Annapolis toilet?"

Ord swallowed coffee like it was a milkshake. "It's beyond that, sir. You've led troops in combat. Few contemporary officers have. As a military man, the admiral respects that. But as a man who's trained his whole life to do what you've done before you turned twenty-five, he's jealous, too."

"Grown-ups deal with that."

"Yes, sir. But the emotion's still there. The general needs to be aware of it. There's also a fundamental personality difference between successful infantry officers and technical-branch officers."

"You're telling me infantry doesn't have assholes?"

"Sir, there are many effective leadership styles. I'm saying you and the admiral have styles compatible with your missions and environment, but incompatible with each other."

I unsnapped my breastplate and let it slide to the deck, then shrugged out of my scuffed arm tubes and stretched.

Ord nodded at them. "Infantry functions in a less structured environment."

"Mud and chaos?"

Ord nodded. "Flexibility regarding uniform requirements and the like may strengthen an infantry commander's performance. But naval and flight officers benefit from more rigid attitudes."

"They sleep under sheets. But if they miss a checklist item, a nuke goes off. They follow the book."

Ord cocked his head and shrugged.

I pointed at his spotless armor. "You didn't teach us to be slobs in Basic."

"I'm not referring to baseline habits, sir. Their maintenance forms the backbone of military discipline. I'm talking about adaptability when they can't be maintained."

I nodded. "Okay. Thanks, Sergeant Major. Not just for the advice. For the baseline that got me back here."

Ord stood and slid his empty plasti into the disptube. "Sir, it's me, it's all of us, that should do the thanking. To you and the rest of GEF. You did good, sir." He saluted and I returned it as he faced about. Which was just as well. It wouldn't have done for him to see a general cry.

I showered, as much as you can in point-six Gee, until my skin pruned, then lay down on my bunk and felt warm sheets against my skin for the first time in memory, closed my eyes, and let *Excalibur*'s engine vibration massage me to sleep.

I had earned a sweet, boring six-hundred-day cruise home.

I didn't get it.

SIX

A MONTH AFTER *EXCALIBUR* BOOSTED OUT of Jupiter's orbit, Jude Metzger learned to roll over in point-six Gee. I cornered Ord again and learned things, too.

Artificial dawn dimmed empty training-deck corridors and my ankle-weights' slaps echoed as I jogged laps in point-six Gee. As awkward as those weights were, after months toting the burden of Eternad-armor battle-rattle, I felt as free as a falcon on an updraft. The red "Caution Firing" light alongside the Live-Fire Pistol Range glowed and I stopped, panting, hands on hips. It was Sunday, limited duty. Who would be firing pistols at oh-five-hundred, or even awake, except watch and crew?

The Caution light flicked black, so I pulled up my T-shirt hem, toweled off forehead sweat, and twisted through the hatch.

The range's sole occupant stood at one firing line booth, his back to me, silhouetted in gunsmoke fog painted red by range lighting. Ord's ear protectors were in place not, I supposed, because mere pistol fire could make him flinch but because protectors were regulation. Ord would sooner break his arm than regs.

I touched his starched utility sleeve and he turned his head, his pistol, empty with the slide locked back, still pointed downrange.

"Up early for Sunday, Sergeant Major."

He nodded at my sweaty shirt as he peeled off his ear protectors. "As is the general."

I looked at the pistol and cocked my head.

"Project of mine, sir."

It was an ancient, blocky automatic, a .45-caliber M-1903. Blue steel, with walnut custom grips.

"Been a while since that's been regulation." Not 150 years, though. A Service .45 was hell to aim, kicked like a mule, but it hit hard, so some specialized units had used it well into this century.

Ord passed his hand over the booth remote and his target groups popped onscreen three feet in front of us. The center of each Slug silhouette was completely shot away, but ragged pinpricks also ringed the hit zone.

Ord popped a round from the fresh magazine clipped to his shoulder holster and plopped it in my palm. Instead of the blunt, coppery bullet I expected, the cartridge's business end was a lengthwise-striated cylinder, like a brass wheat shock. I raised my eyebrows.

"Flechette round, sir." Ord pointed at the round's tip. "Ninety-five brass needles in a heat-intolerant matrix. The matrix vaporizes as the round travels down the barrel. At ten yards"—he traced the target's vanished center with his index finger—"the pattern spreads to eight inches wide. Effective at close quarters against massed Pseudo-cephalopods."

I shrugged. "Or it would have been." I fingered the pin-prick sprinkle that surrounded the grouping. "Good thing it's for shooting Slugs. One of these needles wouldn't stop a man."

"Exactly, sir. In close-quarters battle, GIs in Eternad armor wouldn't need to worry much about hitting one another, but Slug armor's glorified cardboard. Besides, sir, the kinetic energy in one of those needles at a .45's muzzle velocity is considerable. Small object, but high speed."

I trampolined the round in my palm. "Did we ever get flechette for the M-20?"

Ord nodded, then flicked the slide lever and broke the .45 into cleanable pieces. "The round wasn't ready when *Hope* embarked, but *our* division rifleman's basic load is flechette every fourth magazine. Once the chemists perfected the matrix, even a cook like me could hand-load rounds for other weapons like this."

I sighed. Professional soldiers like Ord actually liked guns. I had the same off-duty interest in designer bullets as I had in needlepoint. How could Judge March and Ord and General Cobb think I was born to be a soldier? "Sergeant Major, what do we do now?"

Ord stroked his baby with a bore brush. "I plan a bit more PT, a leisurely breakfast. An excellent holo remastery of *Sergeant York* begins at oh-nine-hundred on the recreation deck. And of course there's duty paperwork—"

I tossed my head at the ship all around us. "I mean all of us. Now that the war's over."

He cradled his .45 into its Neoplast travel box. "What soldiers always do, sir. Whatever our country needs."

"That's my point. There's no war. Who needs us? My troops feel it, too. Half of 'em have gained fifteen pounds, no matter how much PT we schedule. The other half have lost fifteen pounds."

Ord nodded. "The gainers are rewarding themselves for surviving. The losers are depressed, guilty that they survived when their buddies died. Some of the depressed ones will suffer long-term Post-Traumatic Stress Disorder." He eyed my T-shirt and arched an eyebrow. "The general has a foot in both camps."

I tugged my shirt hem down over my navel. "I've put on five." I also lay awake for hours wondering why I had survived, and self-flagellated with extra PT to punish myself for it, which was probably why I had only gained five pounds. But as a commander I hadn't discussed my angst with anyone. I frowned. Ord read minds. "So, what do I do with the guilty ones?"

"Keep them busy. This long crossing is a blessing. Most of them will get over their disorientation before they butt up against reality."

"And those who don't?"

Ord blinked. Then he stared at my blooming love handles. "If the general cares for company, we can double-time to the gym together."

Perhaps because he read trainees' minds, Ord always gave me credit for reading his. This time, as usual, it took me too long to catch his drift.

SEVEN

ONE TROOP I DIDN'T HAVE TO KEEP busy was Howard Hibble's. Not when his Spooks had more dead, frozen Slugs to poke and slice than Texas had chili.

We were ten months out from Jupiter. Jude Metzger had learned to stand, if he had something to lean on.

Howard and I shivered in a classroom-sized compartment, while I leaned against its stainless-steel plating. It was designed as a trauma center for the battlefield casualties that *Excalibur*'s embarked division had been spared. So we peered over cheekbone-high red rubber masks that filtered formaldehyde stink, as much as filtered any Slug germs, and through the chill fog of our own breath in the bright-lit, operating-room chill. In each compartment corner, a dead Slug lay on a stainless-steel morgue slab. Lab-coated, surgical-masked Spooks hunched over each corpse.

Howard led me to the closest one and spoke to a scalpel-wielding woman who bent over a Slug, slit open nose to tail, like a cleaned trout. Howard said, "What have you got this morning?"

She wiped her hands on a towel, then handed him a

Chipboard. I hoped she was wearing contact lenses because her pupils were neon orange. They matched her lip gloss. Soldiers didn't call Howard's Intelligence soldiers Spooks for nothing. He and his work lured people with unique skills to the military. The military, in turn, allowed him to manage them uniquely.

Tangerine Woman said, "This one was immature. If we can apply that terminology to new sub-parts of a Pseudocephalopod organism that was probably older than dinosaurs. First time we've really identified one fresh from the incubator. Nitric acid traces on the epidermis." She pointed at white glop on the Slug's skin. A slit-open tube, like a purple flower stem, wound through the green jelly of the Slug's innards.

Howard pointed. "Gut contents?"

"Ammonia. Nitrates."

He handed her back the Chipper. "Metabolic rate?"

"Fast. It must have taken a battalion of cooks to feed a Slug army."

Conversations at the other tables yielded similarly fascinating factoids about our extraterrestrial former neighbors.

Out in the companionway, Howard and I stripped off our synwool-lined lab coats and I rubbed cold from my fingers. "Anything interesting?"

Howard's eyes gleamed. "Well, the young one, as you would call it. That's fascinating."

"Oh, yeah. Ammonia. My curiosity knew no bounds. So what?"

"The Pseudocephalopod nurtured its new tissue in fertilizer."

"Slugs were plants?"

"Slugs, as you call It, were alien. The Linnean hierarchy

we use to categorize life on Earth may have no application elsewhere. Shoe-horning alien life-forms into our kingdoms and phyla is nonsense."

Not only nonsense but as useless for humanity's future as invertebrate paleontology. "What about your Slug Football?" Slug hardware might actually teach us something we could use. We knew the Slugs had technology that stifled our nukes. That's why we had to send infantry to Ganymede in the first place, instead of just smearing that rock with a few zillion megatons. Howard called what the Slugs did "neutron damping." Whatever.

Since the turn of the century, the spread of democracy had obsoleted terrorism. At least, the theory was that if citizens were free to finance minivans and Sony RoomHolos they would be too busy to blow up others. It had worked. But "one maniac with the wrong suitcase" still terrified any rational human. If The Football turned out to be a device we could replicate in every city, and neutralize nukes, now that would be worth The Brick.

Howard's lips curled like he'd sucked a lemon. "Hardware research jurisdiction is with Space Force. Brace had the crate stored. With the Pseudocephalopod gone, the artifact is beyond price."

I made my own sour face. "Howard, is it possible the Slugs aren't gone?"

"Oh, the Pseudocephalopod presence on Ganymede is eradicated, alright. Seven months of patrolling, satellite recon, and Tactical Observation Transport surveys are pretty conclusive."

"You know what I mean. This idea that in the whole galaxy there was just this one roving pack of slinking green worms and we exterminated them. That's crap."

Howard shrugged. "Science reacts to observable data. One hundred fifty years ago, geophysicists said the continents could never have drifted apart because there was no observable energy source big enough to have moved them. Any schoolchild who looked at the jigsaw puzzle on a classroom globe could see that was balderdash. But we lack any data that the Pseudocephalopod still exists. Pseudocephalopod extinction is a soothing faith. Like heaven. The memories of this war are enough nightmare for the next ten generations. Worrying about repeating it could paralyze reconstruction." Howard unwrapped a nicotine gum stick with shaking, yellowed fingers. Spouting a party line he didn't believe made Howard long for a cigarette. But he couldn't have one aboard a spaceship.

He chewed, then sighed. "Besides, we don't really have the tools aboard to examine The Football non-invasively. We'll do it Brace's way."

Aboard *Excalibur,* everybody did everything Brace's way.

Which brings me to Captain's Breakfast and my role in yet another court-martial. I attract those like lint.

EIGHT

If THERE WAS ONE THING Atwater Nimitz Brace valued more highly than his own reflection, it was tradition. So he had instituted Captain's Breakfast, a magnanimous social throwback. Brace invited all who signed up, even embarked enlisted infantry, to be his guests each Sunday morning for white-linen buffet brunch in the officers' mess. The officers' mess swabbie cooks were Brace's hand-picks, and they got first crack at stores. So, much as it pains an infantryman to admit it, Brace's Navy set the best table between Jupiter and the orbit of Mars.

However, GIs prize sack time above rubies and they could sleep in Sundays. There was just one reason that my troops had crowded the sign-up sheets for Captain's Breakfast at each of the fifty Sundays since we had left Jupiter.

Since the truly old times, not just before the hydrofoil Navy but before diesel oil, sailors traditionally received a daily rum ration.

The modern military had no truck with recreational drugs, injected, inhaled, or ingested. But booze is "different," and a ship's captain is a demigod. Brace was permitted "Captain's Stores," and he could dispense them as he pleased.

At Captain's Breakfast each diner hoisted two, no more, no less, thimblefuls of rum from the Captain's Stores in toasts to John Paul Jones or the Navy Goat or whatever naval icon took Brace's fancy that morning.

Trust the infantry to sniff out, within four hundred billion cubic miles of vacuum, the only open bar.

On that Sunday, I took advantage of the table reserved for the embarked-division commanding officers, me and the Third Division CO. The truth was us seven hundred survivors were baggage. The ten thousand undamaged troops of Third Division were the embarked division, but Third's CO played squash on Sunday mornings. The remaining two hundred gluttons crowding the officers' mess included my soldiers, Third Division troops, swabbies, and Brace with his staff.

And the lone civilian aboard, who stood less than three feet tall and drooled.

Jude Metzger may have been a civilian but that Sunday he was decked out in cut-down Space Force dress blues the quartermaster had sewn for him. Jude's little uniforms weren't some cradle-robbing military brainwash. The Toddler Department at Tykes-'r-Us was still a hundred million miles away. We improvised with what we had aboard.

With years of travel to fill, the quartermaster's tailors weren't Jude's only adoptive parents. Cooks baked him zwieback when he was teething and pureed carrots when he wasn't. Machinists mates fabricated little medal replicas for his uniforms. Munchkin stopped using those after Jude ate the Victoria Cross.

I suppose GIs dote on kids from guilt because our job is

to slaughter parents we've never met. Or we seek the child-
hood we lost.

My division commander's table sat four: Munchkin,
Howard, Jude in a high chair improvised from ladder rails,
and me.

I carried Munchkin's tray while she strapped Jude into
his chair. He made bubbles and looked around, unaware
that it was his first birthday.

At our table's center, the cooks had made Jude an elon-
gated cake, shaped like *Excalibur* herself done in chocolate.
He grabbed for it, more from curiosity than hunger, but
couldn't get within a foot. Meanwhile, his mother snapped
a bib around his neck and mashed vegetables for him with
her fork.

At the front of the buffet line a mess-jacketed string
quartet—holo, but such a good recording you couldn't spot
a flicker—played what Howard identified as Vivaldi.

Howard ignored them and his French toast. He leaned
forward and studied Jude, while my godson smeared mashed
peas across his cheeks, occasionally landing some in his
mouth.

Munchkin looked up from her omelette at Howard,
frowned, then punched his bicep. "Stop looking at him like
he's from another planet!"

Howard rubbed his arm and pouted. "He *is* from another
planet!"

"You know what I mean."

Howard wrinkled his forehead and pointed as Jude
caught a pea gob before it hit the tablecloth. "There's something about the way he moves."

Munchkin swung her fork like a broadsword. "Dammit,
Howard! He's a perfectly normal one-year-old! The ship's

surgeon sees Jude every week. He hasn't found any tentacles yet."

Howard sighed.

"If you act like he's a freak, he may grow up to be one!" Munchkin's lower lip thrust out.

I had learned that the Munshara-Metzger lip thrust preceded explosion. Time for a subject change.

My eyes darted around the room, then I pointed. "Look! Ozawa's here!" Major Ozawa, the pilot who had roasted me for being late on Ganymede, stepped into the buffet line.

Munchkin raised her eyebrows, while one hand cut sausage with a fork and the other wiped Jude's nose. "You like her?"

"Huh? No. I mean, I don't know her."

"You want to know her?"

It seemed to me that when I was ready to reenter the dating game after Pooh's death was my decision. However, a month before, Munchkin had shifted into sisterly matchmaker mode. There were thousands of females on this ship. Ozawa was one of the few left, it seemed to me, that Munchkin hadn't tried to fix me up with.

I could've turned the tables, I suppose. Push Munchkin back into circulation. Metzger died just days after Pooh. But the pain would have been worse for Munchkin. For me, too. She had lost a husband and her son's father. I had lost a lover.

Munchkin said, "We work out together. Fantastic body! Smart, too."

"Dammit, Munchkin! I'm not interested."

"Then why's your face red?" Munchkin stood and waved her hand. "Major! Mimi!"

Ozawa smiled and nodded, both hands on her tray.

I leaned toward Munchkin and whispered, "She hates me!"

Munchkin cocked her head. "Oh? I thought you didn't know her."

Ozawa set her tray down, then knelt beside Jude and flashed a smile that would melt Neoplast. "How's my big boy?"

Jude giggled and grabbed for the ribbons on her chest.

Babies are better hottie magnets than Maseratis. And Major Ozawa was some hottie. I thought she was pretty when I met her, helmet-head and all. In a dress uniform with everything in place, she sparkled.

Munchkin said, "Major Ozawa, you've met General Wander?"

Ozawa turned her big brown eyes on me and her smile cooled. "General."

Howard extended his hand. "I've wanted to meet you. The pilot who tested the VSFV. Amazing!"

Ozawa grinned at him. I fell into third place in attractiveness among males at this table, behind a guy with four teeth who ate with his fingers and a prune-faced geek who dressed like an unmade bed. No wonder Munchkin had trouble setting me up.

I made myself noticed. "What's a VSFV?" I winced. My snappy patter didn't make Munchkin's job easier.

Howard nodded at Ozawa. "Venture Star Fighter Variant. Before *Excalibur* left Earth, the major test-piloted a Venture Star fitted with a high-capacity thruster system. For space maneuver. The first space fighter."

I blinked. It was the sort of assignment Pooh Hart would have killed for.

Ozawa shrugged at Howard. "It looked like hell, hung

with all that plumbing, but it was a hoot to fly." She leaned toward Howard. "You're the Slug Spook!"

Howard shrugged back.

Everybody at this table seemed to have a purpose in their post-war life but me, the infantryman. A test pilot, a cryptozoologist, a mother, and a preschooler.

I pointed at the bacon alongside Ozawa's waffles. "I figured you'd be eating off the sushi bar."

She chipmunked her breakfast into a porcelain cheek. "Ozawas are fourth-generation Texan. Raw fish is bait."

We sat ten feet from the omelette station, at the end of the line. Brumby sidestepped down the line and arrived in front of the omelette station.

Three swabbies stood in line behind him, one a skinny, rat-nosed guy I recognized from somewhere. I pointed. "Who's the little guy?"

Mimi swiveled her head, swallowed bacon, then snorted. "Brace's valet." Mimi and Brace had astronauted together at NASA. About all they had in common was that they were both high achievers and they both took to me like a vegan to veal chops.

I snorted. Valet? Why the Navy and the Space Force felt that the more senior an officer got the less capable he was of laying out his own uniforms and shining his own shoes was beyond me.

Brumby held out his plate and it quivered. "Extra bacon, please, ma'am." Bacon was a premium item. Both Brumby and the mess steward he was wheedling were enlisted, so the "ma'am" was gratuitous. But wheedling cooks was every infantryman's secondary Military Occupational Specialty. In Brumby's case, so was a freckled grin.

The steward smiled back at Brumby and dumped her

entire remaining bacon reserve onto Brumby's eggs. That meant the rest of the lineup would have to settle for reconstituted sausage or soy-based fakon.

Brace's rat-nosed valet snorted, then stage-whispered, "You eating for the dead fuckers, too, blinky?"

Brumby stiffened and blinked as the steward slid the omelette onto his plate. As a corporal, Brumby's squad's position had been overrun by Slugs during the first major ground assault of the Battle of Ganymede. Brumby's leadership and valor had earned him the Distinguished Service Cross. But his bunkmate was decapitated by a Slug round.

In the lull after the first assault was beaten back, something disconnected in Brumby. He drifted into an aid station, eyes glazed, his headless bunkmate in a fireman's carry across his shoulders, the corpse's head in an ammunition bag. Brumby wanted the medics to sew his friend up.

Brumby had been wound like a quivering spring ever since. Rat-nose's whisper was shitty to say to any GEF survivor. To say it to Brumby was like pulling a grenade's pin.

Rat-nose flipped Brumby's plate with a finger. Buttered egg spattered Brumby's tunic. Brumby's left eyelid flicked.

I sprang from my chair and lunged for Brumby's elbow as he cocked his fist, but my fingers closed around recycled air.

Rat-nose sailed majestically backward across the officers' mess, his head snapped back by Brumby's punch. You'd be amazed how far a straight right hand can launch a man in point-six Gee. Tiny white objects arced on the same trajectory as Rat-nose's back-bowed body. Teeth.

Rat-nose might have sailed twenty feet, but after fifteen feet, he and his incisors hit the captain's table.

Brace's mouthy little valet crash-landed on a white-linen

runway and skidded shoulder-blades-down across the table-top. Ship's officers scattered, too slowly. Maple syrup exploded from pedestaled silver tureens. Boysenberry compote napalmed immaculate mess jackets. Sausage patties buzzed past my ear like shrapnel.

Munchkin snatched Jude from his high chair and ducked under our table.

In moments the place was still, except for cocoa dripping from a toppled china urn.

Brumby stood beside me, brushing eggs from his tunic with his left hand, shaking the sting from his right, and muttering, "Oh, fuck," over and over. His eyes blinked like old semaphore lanterns.

Two mess stewards had Brace's valet under the arms. His eyes were crossed, blood streamed from one nostril, and from the way his bleeding lip sagged it looked like the ship's dental officer had a new patient. Overall, it wasn't anything that hadn't happened a thousand times in bars outside military posts from Fort Benning to Luna Base.

"Sergeant"—Brace stalked from his end of the table, until he could poke his head forward and read Brumby's name tag—"Brumby! What the—?"

In the holos, the band stops during barroom brawls. Since Brace's quartet was just photons, Vivaldi whispered on.

Brace spun and stabbed a finger at the quartet. "Somebody shut that damn thing off!"

The band played on.

Brace snatched a sugar bowl from a table and pegged it at a bulkhead-mounted control panel. The bowl shattered, but the musicians faded to green silhouettes, then disappeared, leaving no sound to echo in the low-ceilinged room but raspy breathing. Brumby's, Brace's, and someone else's, which turned out to be mine.

Brace straightened and breathed deep, his quivering face purple. Pasted to his cheekbone with milk was a cornflake. Brace would probably put himself in for a Purple Heart for that. Victim of cereal killer.

I coughed into my hand to cover a snigger.

Brace turned his wrath on me. "Wander, you think brutal hooliganism is funny? Anybody heard of discipline aft of Ninety?" Infantry country began at bulkhead ninety-one.

I mustered a glare at Brumby. "I'll deal with my sergeant. I'll leave the seaman to the captain."

Brace looked over at Rat-nose. Somebody had propped Rat-nose up on a table edge, a napkin pressed to the lower half of his face, his eyes burning into Brumby. He was breathing through his mouth, and when he adjusted the napkin, I saw a black hole where his front teeth should have been. Rat-nose may have been a smart-mouthed coward, but he was *Brace's* coward. Until then Brace hadn't so much as glanced to see whether his man was alright.

Brace drew another breath, then frowned. He ran a finger across his cheek and scraped off the cornflake.

Somebody snorted.

"Wander"—Brace pointed a quivering finger at Brumby—"have him in my conference compartment in thirty minutes." He spun on his heel, then shot back over his shoulder. "You, too. And clean him up!"

Ten minutes later, while we awaited Brumby's return from aft in a fresh uniform, I sat with Howard in my cabin.

I rubbed a hand across my face. "I'm gonna have to throw the book at Brumby. You know that."

"I think he expects that, Jason."

"Brace's squid struck the first blow. But I'll have Brumby on extra duty for a hundred million miles."

Howard shrugged and unwrapped a nicotine-gum stick. "If it's up to you."

"Of course it's up to me. I'm Brumby's CO."

Howard rolled the gum stick like a little blanket and popped it in his mouth. "A ship's captain under way has absolute authority."

"That's crap, Howard." It wasn't crap. One of my correspondence courses had been Uniform Code of Military Justice, United Nations modification. Brace could take jurisdiction of any person on this ship, just by saying so. "Anyway, what's he gonna do? Make Brumby walk the plank?" Maybe. A ship captain's power extended to summary capital punishment if he felt his ship was in peril. Technically, we were still in combat, so rendering oneself unfit for duty, such as by breaking your knuckles on somebody else's nose, could even be construed as constructive desertion, a hanging offense. Well, dangling in point-six Gee, it would be more slow strangulation. I let my breath hiss between my teeth and shook my head.

The dull thud of flesh on metal interrupted as someone rapped on my cabin's hatch.

"Come, Brumby!"

It wasn't Brumby.

NINE

THE VISITOR WHO SIDESTEPPED through the hatch was Ord.

He hadn't been at Captain's Breakfast. And I knew he didn't attend divine services. Yet he was wearing a Class-A uniform on an off-duty Sunday morning. Not that he would have been caught in Levi's and flannel. Ord's idea of casual wasn't civvies, it was fatigues starched stiff enough to march by themselves.

I cocked my head toward his chest-full of formal decorations. "Going somewhere, Sergeant Major?"

"I heard about Brumby, sir. Would the general care to have me attend the upcoming proceedings?"

I narrowed my eyes. "Sergeant Major, whose side are you on, here, Admiral Brace's or the Infantry's?"

"Side, sir?" Ord made his eyes wide.

Exactly twenty-nine minutes after Brace's ultimatum I let Brumby rap on the bulkhead next to the closed hatch into Brace's conference room.

Brace let us stew in the companionway for six minutes and fifty seconds.

"Come!"

Brace sat, hands folded and jaw jutted out farther than

usual, at the end of the conference table. To his right sat a stiff Navy lieutenant wearing Judge Advocate General shoulder brass and to Brace's left sat Rat-nose, slumped in his chair and doing his best to look violated.

A circular, silver court Stenobot hummed, centered on the gleaming synwood table, sucking in a 360-degree holo of the proceedings.

Our team consisted of the freckle-faced accused, his CO, being me, and Howard, as a witness more than as anybody who had a clue about helping.

A discreet moment later, Ord slipped neutrally in, closed the hatch behind himself, then strode to the cabin center and planted himself at parade-rest, equidistant from both camps.

Brace cleared his throat and skewered Brumby with his eyes. "Acting Sergeant Major Brumby, as commanding officer of this vessel, I have considered the disposition of this matter. Having personally witnessed the inciting incident, I find that no preliminary inquiry is needed. A general court-martial will be convened at the earliest possible time to consider the charges."

Brace glanced at the JAG swabbie, who read legalese off a screen. Brace left out constructive desertion but unless Brumby beat the rap his military career was over. In the meantime, he would spend the remaining year of this voyage in the brig.

Brace asked Brumby, "How says the accused?"

Brumby swallowed and his head twitched left. "I'm sorry I hit him, sir. But if I plead guilty I'm screwed, right?"

Brace curled his lip. "Guilty or not guilty? If you're

incapable of a direct answer, ask someone else to speak for you!"

Silence.

Brace sighed. "In my capacity as master of this vessel I deem your statement a plea of 'not guilty.' The matter will be set for trial. In the interest of fairness—"

A half snort escaped me.

Brace shot me a look. "In the interest of fairness, the trial panel will be selected not from the accused's own unit nor from the unit of the assaulted individual."

In other words, the panel would come from the only other outfit within a few million miles, the Third United Nations Division, the follow-on force who shared *Excalibur* with us. They were experienced infantry, like Ord, drawn from all the world's services, not exclusively war orphans like GEF had been. They respected my survivors. The Third's soldiers resented them, too, because the politicians had passed over the Third's veterans for me and the rest of GEF's wet-behind-the-ears kids.

The JAG swabbie whispered something to his screen, then angled it so Brace could read the words.

Brace nodded. "A preliminary matter. The accused is a noncommissioned officer. As such he may elect to be tried before a panel of his noncommissioned peers or a panel of commissioned officers."

Brumby turned to me, palms upturned, cheek jerking.

I had learned the military justice system's practicalities the hard way. Majors and colonels didn't pull extra duty. Crap like court-martial panelist fell to junior officers. Junior officers were inexperienced kids, soft and sympathetic. Noncommissioned officers—sergeants—worked their way up by following the book. Everybody knew that in courts-martial, crusty sergeants regularly threw the rule book at the accused. The choice was obvious.

I almost said "Commissioned" by reflex, then I caught movement at the corner of my eye. Ord had twitched. I noticed only because I knew him, knew that at parade rest he wouldn't even twitch. I watched him. There it was again. A head shake.

Ord wanted Brumby judged by a hanging jury of grizzled sergeants, not squishy second lieutenants. That made no sense.

I hesitated. Ord was in our corner. Wasn't he?

Brace drummed his fingers on the synwood tabletop. The victim shifted in his chair, his cheeks gauze-packed, so he looked more like a blowfish than a rat. That was a more appropriate image for the little squid, anyway.

Brace cocked his head at me. "Well?"

The light clicked on for me. "The accused chooses a panel of his noncommissioned peers."

Brumby's jaw dropped.

The JAG swabbie ran a hand across his face to camouflage a smile.

Brace raised his eyebrows, then nodded. He stood and clicked off the screens. "Very well. The matter will be set for trial. We stand adjourned."

A minute later, Brumby and I headed aft to infantry country. He asked, brow furrowed, eyelids batting like windshield wipers in a downpour, "A noncom jury, sir? I hope you know what you're doing."

I turned to ask Ord to confirm that I had read him right when I had chosen Brumby's fate.

But Ord had left us alone.

TEN

BRUMBY'S TRIAL STARTED A WEEK LATER, in the converted operating room that was being used to dissect Slug KIAs. It stunk of formaldehyde. I wondered whether Brace chose the venue to signal that Brumby was dead meat. No, Brace didn't have a sense of humor enough for that.

A Space Policeman—the Space Force version of an MP—wearing a sidearm guarded the hatch, in case the accused made a run for vacuum, I supposed. Maybe he was there to quell outbreaks of infantry hooliganism, since both Brumby and I were present.

Eight panelists sat to the right, each wearing the Class-A sergeant's uniform of his or her original unit, not UN gear. All wore three chevrons up and three down. By the service record files I had read, all were not only senior NCOs, they were as frivolous as bricks. The witness chair was left of the hearing officer, a light colonel from Third Division who wasn't a lawyer but who had presided at courts-martial before. The JAG swabbie prosecutor sat at a Duralumin folding table facing the presiding officer. Brumby, his appointed counsel, and I sat at a table to the prosecutor's left.

Brumby's counsel was Army JAG, older than I was and a permanent captain. He hadn't been pleased that I chose a noncom panel or, for that matter, with his assignment to defend a sure-loser case.

The presentation of evidence wasn't contested since the incident was on surveillance holo. Over and over, in slow motion and at normal speed, a slightly translucent Brumby laid a beauty on a slightly flickering Rat-nose. The only trouble was Rat-nose's provoking comment was drowned out by the string quartet.

Mimi Ozawa appeared and testified to what Rat-nose had said. She took the stand starched and stiff in pilot's powder-blue. Of over eleven thousand people on this ship, only the twenty dropship pilots, twenty copilots, and a few spares were true astronauts. That, most soldiers aboard thought, made them more technocrats than warriors.

The JAG swabbie tapped a stylus on the top edge of his notescreen while he questioned her. "Major Ozawa, you testified that the alleged remarks directed toward Acting Sergeant Major Brumby provoked him."

"Yes." Ozawa nodded. She never seemed to make eye contact with Brace. Munchkin said the word was Ozawa and Brace had once been an item. That annoyed me. I suppose because the idea of Brace enjoying himself seemed so unrealistic.

It certainly couldn't have been jealousy about Ozawa. She was arrogance and dispassion wrapped in a pretty package.

"Similarly provoked, would you have reacted similarly?"

It seemed to my nonlegal mind that it didn't matter whether a petite female technocrat would have decked

Brace's little squid or not. Ozawa's job required her to control her emotions, to be icy calm at every moment. The truth, I had to admit, was that Brumby's job did, too. At least to the extent of not pounding the snot out of people during brunch. I leaned toward Brumby's counsel and whispered, "Object! She'll say she wouldn't have hit him!" The lawyer just whispered notes.

Ozawa had probably never punched anything more animate than a seat-harness release button in her life. She shifted in her chair. "No."

The JAG swabbie nodded and the corners of his mouth turned up.

She smiled at him like he had just asked her to the prom. "I would've broken the plate across his head."

I snuck a glance at the panel foreman, a female Transportation Corps topkick. I thought she smiled.

I had to cover my grin with my hand. Across the hearing room, Brace's knuckles whitened as he gripped a chairback in front of him.

Otherwise, our testimony lacked the, well, punch of watching Rat-nose's teeth splash down in Brace's teacup.

The mitigation phase consisted of me reading the recommendation I had written for Brumby's DSC and Purple Heart with cluster. One member of the panel shed a tear on his Marine gunnery sergeant olive lapel. Otherwise, I read no sympathy.

The restitution phase was new to the military. It made sense. If convicted, a wrongdoer had to make the wrong-ee whole. For our side, we found a Space Force dentist who testified that Rat-nose would actually have sounder, prettier teeth after the "assault incident." However, a prosecution shrink testified that the victim had been traumatized by the violence. Rat-nose's life would be "permanently impacted."

I leaned forward and tugged Brumby's lawyer's sleeve, "Ask him if Brumby might have been traumatized by having half his shoulder shot away! Ask him whether having friends die in your arms before they even got old enough to vote for President permanently impacts your life!"

The captain leaned back and covered his mouth with his hand. "Sir, Sergeant Major Brumby's service record was covered in your mitigation-phase testimony. The victim did not cause Sergeant Major Brumby's post-combat trauma."

"The hell he didn't! Brumby's career will be over if he's convicted. What kind of traumatized life do you think any combat soldier can have as a civilian?"

The presiding officer shot us a "pipe-down" look.

The captain refused my clever legal advice and the defense rested.

"Rest," my ass. My heart rattled in my chest and I breathed like a thoroughbred after six furlongs.

When the presiding officer had charged the panel, the eight stood as one and marched out to deliberate, like the by-the-book sergeants they were. Brace, who had sat behind the prosecutor, arms folded, for the whole proceeding, left. So did the prosecutor.

The presiding officer packed his 'puter case.

Brumby's JAG captain busied himself shuffling papers, distancing himself from a case he knew was lost before he ever got appointed.

I told Brumby, "This is gonna take a while. Let's get some coffee, Brumby."

Brumby sat still and asked me, "Sir, will I get a Dishonorable?"

It was no time to speak the truth. I tried to accentuate the positive. "We can appeal, Brumby. The fat lady hasn't sung."

Brumby's brow furrowed and his left eyelid twitched. "No, sir, she hasn't. I mean, the panel hasn't even returned a verdict."

Crap. Before I could stop myself, I winced. I was supposed to be positive. But by talking about appeal, I had revealed to Brumby that I had given up hope. Giving up hope is a luxury denied officers in command.

"Sir, why did you choose an enlisted panel?" Brumby hesitated. "I'm not being critical, sir. Just wondered."

I knew why. I thought I saw Ord twitch. I thought he had signaled me. I thought Ord was telling me to pick a panel of sergeants because they might think breaking regs was awful but they would also think that inter-service brawling was mere recreation. I didn't doubt Ord. Ord could never be wrong. But now I doubted whether I had read his mind correctly.

I opened my mouth to explain.

The hatch through which the panel had left opened and the panel foreman beckoned the presiding officer with a finger. My heart thumped.

The foreman cupped her hand over her mouth and whispered to the presiding officer. He shook his head.

Maybe they just wanted instructions on a point of law. Maybe they wanted coffee and doughnuts.

Brumby stared at the conversation, then at me. He whispered, "Sir, if they're back soon, that's bad, huh?"

Brumby's counsel overheard. He turned, lips pressed tight, and nodded.

Crap.

I patted Brumby's forearm. "They probably just want instructions. It can't be a verdict already."

The presiding officer straightened and called across the compartment to the Space Policeman. "Advise the prosecution that the panel has reached a verdict."

My heart sank. It had been just fifteen minutes since the panel retired. No eight rational people could agree on pizza toppings in just fifteen minutes. Eight individual sergeants couldn't decide a soldier's fate, his life, in fifteen minutes. Unless they were going to fry him.

I had read Ord wrong. I had stupidly chosen a panel of sergeants. Brumby was going to pay for my stupidity.

The longest ten minutes of my life dragged past, then Brace and the JAG swabbie and Rat-nose returned.

Everyone stood while the panel reentered from the deliberation room.

Brace glanced past me and Brumby, serene in the knowledge that Brumby was getting brig time and a dishonorable discharge. Just as good, I, the seat-of-the-pants accidental general, was getting embarrassed.

The presiding officer looked across the room. "Madam Foreman, has the panel reached a verdict?"

The Transportation Corps topkick stood. "We have." She didn't make eye contact with any of us at the defense table. That was supposed to be bad. The rest of the panel stared ahead, impassive as the veterans they were.

The presiding officer swiveled his head toward Brumby. "The accused will rise."

Brumby stood at attention, alongside his counsel. So did

I. Even without my blunder, Brumby probably would have been convicted. What I thought I had read in Ord's body language was that noncoms were used to brawls and Army noncoms were none too fond of prissy sailors. Bend a GI's career because he cold-cocked a squid? Better to award him a commendation! It seemed so obviously stupid now.

I ground my teeth while the foreman unfolded a paper slip. Did she really need to write it down?

She cleared her throat. "On the issue of restitution."

I rolled my eyes. Probably the last thing Brumby or I cared about was how much would come out of Brumby's pay and allowances each month to compensate the Space Force for fixing Brace's valet's teeth.

"We find the accused responsible for the deductible portion of the assaulted party's dental expenses." Service personnel paid a couple cents by payroll deduction every time we got medical treatment.

"However, we further find said responsibility to be offset by the assaulted party's responsibility for cleaning expenses for the accused's uniform. By virtue of the assaulted party's complicit behavior regarding the throwing of food onto the accused's uniform."

I had sat in on a couple of courts-martial. I had also been closer to participating as accused in more of them than I cared to. Empaneled NCOs generally knew little about the law but thought they knew lots. Of course, this restitution verdict meant vacuum, since they were going to throw Brumby out on his ear. After that, Brumby's pay and allowances would be zero. Why had they even bothered to cut Brumby a break on the issue? My heart leapt. Maybe . . .

I glanced at the JAG swabbie. He frowned and shifted in his seat.

The foreman paused, then continued. "On all other charges"—she smiled at Brumby—"we find the accused not guilty."

Breath exploded from my lips. I hadn't realized I'd been holding it. Brumby hugged his counsel, who looked bewildered as well as uncomfortable.

Then Brumby, grinning, hugged me. "Sir! You always knew!"

I shrugged. Acting like you always knew was part of being an officer.

By the time Brumby finally released his shoulder lock on me, the panel was gone. Across the room, the JAG swabbie stared down into his notescreen as he folded it away. That was, I suspected, because he had figured out that my choice of a noncom panel had cost him the case. Also, I suspected, he didn't want to look at Brace.

The JAG swabbie needn't have bothered. Brace stalked toward the hatch, then paused and pointed at me. "Wander, you have just perpetrated a gross injustice. I'll remember that."

He slammed the hatch behind him.

My fingers trembled with exhilaration.

As soon as the festivities here wound down, I would find Ord and share the news. I was as happy that I had figured out what Ord had been telling me, that I had read his mind, as I was with the substantive result. Ord would turn handsprings.

Not exactly.

ELEVEN

I FOUND ORD TWENTY DECKS AFT of the court-martial, on a busman's holiday from his divisional paperwork. A Third Division platoon sat cross-legged on their platoon bay deck as Ord stood before them brandishing an M-20. Across each soldier's knees lay a similar rifle. They all wore utilities, but also bulky, red Eternad gloves. From the gun oil I saw on the gloves and smelled in the air, they had been at this a while.

Ord said, "The training-manual-established optimal time to field-strip and reassemble the vacuum-adapted M-20 Assault Rifle is one minute, fifty seconds. That time, however, was established for Space Force personnel. Can any squid field-strip the basic infantry weapon faster than an infantry soldier?"

"No, Sergeant Major!" Fifty voices bellowed and shook the deck plates.

I smiled. Timed field-stripping in Eternads? Eternad gloves were supple enough that a soldier wearing them could pluck a coin off a tabletop, but it was vintage Ord to demand that troops meet field-manual standards while wearing them. Especially troops bound for home and not into combat.

Ord glanced at his wrist 'puter. "Begin!"

Fifty rifles clattered and drowned conversation. I touched Ord's shoulder, then leaned close. "Brumby was acquitted."

Ord nodded.

"You should have seen the look on Brace's face!" I grinned.

Ord frowned and turned his attention to his 'puter.

I cocked my head. Even from Ord I expected a thumbs-up, or at least a smile.

A private held up her reassembled rifle in triumph. Ord bent, checked it, and nodded. Seconds later, the fiftieth soldier thrust his reassembled weapon toward the low ceiling. Ord pressed his 'puter's stop button, raised his eyebrows, then turned the dial toward me so I could read it.

The platoon stared at me.

I looked up, as poker-faced as I could, and waited a heartbeat. "One." I smiled. "Forty-four!"

The soldiers whooped and slapped high-fives.

When the cheering trickled away, Ord said, "Outstanding! However, I heard a Marine platoon completed the exercise in one thirty-nine. Practice, ladies and gentlemen. We'll try it again in ten."

Ord led me around the corner into a platoon sergeant's empty cabin, while the stunned platoon began breaking down their rifles yet again.

I said, "We never would have beat Brace if you hadn't told me to pick noncoms, Sergeant Major. That was brilliant!"

Ord closed the hatch, then crossed his arms. He didn't match my grin. "May I speak frankly to the general?"

Huh? "I wouldn't want the sergeant major to speak any other way."

Ord's brow furrowed. "Beating Admiral Brace was not my objective. Nor should it have been yours. That tactic wasn't brilliant. It was obvious! To any officer with a grain of sense and a few years' experience! I *think* you have the grain of sense. Sir. I gave you the clue because you don't have the experience, which isn't your fault."

"But Brace—"

"Admiral Brace should have seen it coming, too. But he's a technocrat. Besides, he couldn't have kept you from choosing noncoms."

"You expected me to do it!"

Ord nodded. "I did, sir. Then I expected you to take the admiral aside, explain what the outcome would be, then use your advantage to work out an equitable solution. I did not expect you to undermine the relationship between the services, not to mention the relationship between you and the admiral."

I jerked a thumb back toward the platoon bay, where rifles clattered. "You were just running down squids *and* jarheads!"

Ord paused, then nodded. "Fair point, sir. I'd have thought the general would understand the difference between a bit of fun and the absolute need for teamwork when the chips are down."

Ord's sergeantly idea of a bit of fun evidently extended as far as knocking out some squid's teeth in a bar fight. But I took his point.

"Learn from this, sir. The next time you and Admiral

Brace have to work together, lives may hang in the balance. Inter-service rivalry should end after the Army-Navy game."

"Understood, Sergeant Major." I said it solemnly. In fact, I believed it. But the truth was that once we got home Brace would swirl away from my ground-bound future like a gum wrapper down a flushed toilet. Ord had taught me a sound lesson, but an irrelevant one.

Other than that trial, the voyage home was what space travel really is: a boring, cramped prison sentence. Except convicts don't have to inhale sour air that somebody else just exhaled.

Excalibur returned to her birthplace, orbit around the moon, 240 days later. She settled in like she had never left. I expected that whatever changes Earth had undergone during the five years I had been away wouldn't faze me either, not after what I had been through.

I was as wrong as hogs in skirts.

TWELVE

TWO WEEKS AFTER *EXCALIBUR* RETURNED to lunar orbit, Howard and I stepped through *Excalibur*'s lock to board the V-Star Mimi Ozawa would pilot home. My troops had been first down, then Third Division, then *Excalibur*'s nonessential crew. Brace would be the last man off.

A red-haired Space Force enlisted man, using an old-fashioned bristle brush in the low-gravity, confined atmosphere, painted clear gel along the plasticine hatch seal.

"Does Admiral Brace ever get tired of making you folks paint?" I asked him.

The EM grinned. "The admiral is fond of his paint, sir. But this isn't paint. It's preservative. Once this V-Star clears this lock, we mothball the whole ship. When we go dirtside, *Excalibur*'s gonna have just enough power and brains left to park herself out here in lunar orbit."

I shot Howard a glance.

He shrugged. "It's no secret. You've been busy with division mustering-out paperwork."

He was right. A twenty-four-year-old could no more keep up with even a skeleton division's paperwork than a hamster could keep up with Yiddish. It was one more reason I looked forward to tagging dirt and getting shed of command.

We sidestepped through the umbilical companionway and over the hatch lip into the troop bay of Mimi's V-Star.

Howard continued. "What did you expect them to do? It costs billions of dollars every month to keep a ship like this operational. Luna Base is getting mothballed, too."

The fact was I had not expected one way or the other. I heaved my duffel into an overhead cargo net and shook my head. "What does it cost if the Slugs come back and we aren't ready? How much is a city full of people worth?"

"It's been almost three years since we destroyed the Pseudocephalopod presence on Ganymede. We have no evidence that anything's lurking out there to be ready for." He flopped into his seat. "Jason, you have more to get ready for back on Earth than the remote possibility of the continued existence, much less the hostile return, of the Pseudocephalopod."

Mimi slid us away from *Excalibur* with bow thrusters, then she flew one lunar orbit, lit the main engine, and slingshot us toward home.

Three days later we dropped through the stratosphere, crossed the Pacific Coast thirty miles above Oregon, and burned east.

A V-Star isn't the unmaneuverable bullet that the old space shuttles had been, but it's no personal stunter. Mimi bent a turn south so wide that we overflew Niagara Falls, then arrowed toward Washington, D.C.

The *Excalibur* Venture Stars that had landed in the preceding days had all landed at Canaveral, the only extended runway specifically designed to receive them.

Only Mimi Ozawa was pilot enough to be trusted to land a V-Star on a conventional runway like the one at Reagan.

Mimi greased us down like Pooh Hart would have. I stared at the hull and wished for a window. I was home, but the only way I knew it was because my liver and all the rest of my guts pressed down on top of one another with full Earth weight for the first time in five years.

The bulkhead viewscreen flicked to life and I pointed with a leaden finger. "Howard, it's still gray!" I knew the planet hadn't bounced back from the Projectile attacks but somehow I still expected green grass and blue skies.

Mimi rolled us to a stop on the Reagan runway and the ramp dropped with a hydraulic whine. Home at last, I unbuckled and jumped to my feet. Or tried to. My knees buckled. I sat back down and pressed my palms to my trembling thighs. "Crap!" I had worked out like a fiend, twice every day of the Jovian crossing, but still I could barely stand.

Howard just sat in his seat and grinned at me. "Wait for the medics."

Minutes later two zoomie corpsmen gathered me up, one under each armpit like I was someone's grandpa, and we trundled down the ramp.

I nearly drowned in thick air salted with smells I didn't know I'd missed. Dust. Kerosene. Asphalt. For me, that was like orchids. I wobbled along, grinning.

I half expected a brass band, or at least someone to shake my hand, but the medics just loaded Howard and me and our duffels onto an Electruk no fancier than what you'd see in any mall and we whirred off across the tarmac to a hangar.

In the hangar sat a blue bus fleet. Formed up in front of

the buses, at ease with hands clasped at the small of their backs, stood my seven hundred GEF survivors. We had left Ganymede a dirty band of Lost Boys, with me playing Peter Pan.

The seven hundred soldiers who gleamed before me stood as fully formed and disciplined as Roman legionnaires.

We hadn't worn battle-rattle aboard *Excalibur,* so the quartermasters and armorers had spent two years repairing and reconditioning our Eternad armor.

A GI in polished, crimson Eternads with visor retracted and decoration ribbons arrayed across the breastplate is truly a knight in shining armor. Seven hundred knights make a crusade.

Munchkin, being Muslim, always hated that comparison, but there she was, on the left flank, the second-smallest troop in ranks. The smallest troop, in crimson pajamas and a cut-down breastplate, sat in an Eternad-crimson Earth-bought stroller alongside her. I caught Munchkin's eye, winked, and grinned, then my grin faded.

Jude wasn't the only one seated. Slug weapons made mostly corpses, not wounded, but a dozen wheelchaired amputees sprinkled the ranks.

Earthside medtech would rebuild each man and woman among them with organic prosthetics, but for now they were reminders that these shiny recruiting posters had been to hell.

So this was our welcome home. One final formation, then dismissed. Heat rose in me from anger, sorrow, relief, and all the emotions that come with a parting. And a pang because I was here and thousands as good and as brave as I was were not.

The Electruk slid up behind Brumby, who, as division sergeant major, faced the troops, front and center.

I swung my legs over the 'truk's side to touch the hangar floor. One medic grabbed my arm and whispered, "Sir, you shouldn't—"

I shrugged off his hand and pointed at my division. "*They're* standing!"

"*They're* acclimated," the medic hissed.

It was my last moment as a general, a farewell to comrades-in-arms. Acclimated, schmaclimated. I choked back tears and thrust myself off the seat. My legs trembled. Not as bad as back aboard the V-Star, though. I caught myself and hobbled forward.

Brumby sang, "Division!"

The preparatory command echoed back through shrunken brigades, battalions, companies, and platoons and bounced off the hangar walls.

"Atten-*shun*!" At the command of execution, the division snapped to attention like statuary.

We were young and we were beat-to-crap but we were professionals.

Brumby faced about and saluted. "Sir! The division is formed!"

I returned his salute, then leaned forward. "A few words, then dismissed, hey, Brumby?"

Brumby's right eyelid fluttered as he shook his head. "Sir, the parade—"

"Huh?" For an omniscient leader, I said that a lot.

"You got the Chipmemo, sir. It's why you flew into D.C., instead of Canaveral. The division marches from the Capitol, up Constitution Avenue to the Washington

Monument. You present them to the President and the UN Secretary-General."

A division commander, even of a shrunken division, plows through four hundred Chipmemos each day. I skimmed over too many of them. One more reason I wasn't General Staff material.

"So what do I have to do, Brumby?"

He slid his eyes left, to a windowless bus. "You go in there, sir, while the division mounts the buses and heads into D.C." He looked at the windowless bus like a mallard looking down a twelve-gauge barrel.

How long had my soldiers been standing in armor? I sighed. "Okay, Brumby. Dismiss 'em, mount 'em up. Get 'em off their feet."

Amid the clatter of fourteen hundred armored legs, I shuffled to the bus, dragged myself inside, and flopped on a purple crushed-velvet sofa.

Sofa? I looked around. The bus was tricked out like a pop star's tour vehicle, with a bar, multiple holo tanks, and bolted-down furniture that must have been bought at a turn-of-the-century pimp's estate sale. I would have thought that for a Washington parade the vehicles would be brand new.

The bus lurched forward and pulled up to the tail end of our bus convoy.

Space Force ratings wearing Signals collar brass swarmed me. By the time we crossed the Potomac into the District of Columbia I had been reshaved, stripped to my underwear, and refitted into my Eternad armor, which had been patched, polished, and smelled like pine inside. It was mine, alright, down to the pale blue Medal of Honor ribbon on the breastplate.

A female in a well-cut black business suit bustled up, Chipboard in hand. Pencil-slim, Howard's age, she wore her black hair spiky. The effect was witch and broomstick wrapped up in one package. "General Wander? Ruth Tway." She shook my hand while she reached across and straightened my ribbons.

Tway read her Chipboard screen. "I'm with the White House. Today, you ride and wave. No speeches. No interviews."

Each of the three holotanks across the bus aisle from me played a different news net. Each anchorperson stood with emptied Constitution Avenue in their background, crowds lining the sidewalks.

"Fine by me, ma'am. But we're infantry. Why are we riding buses in this parade?"

Tway shook her head. "Just to the parade staging area. Your troops march. You sit in an open limousine and wave to adoring crowds."

Our bus stopped on the Mall, near the Capitol. My troops were already forming up. We would be led by a band, Marine Corps by the look of it, and followed by Third Division and then *Excalibur*'s Space Force swabbies. Behind the band parked an open Daimler limousine, with a red two-starred front plate. I turned to Tway. "You think I'm riding in that while my troops walk?"

She pressed her lips into a thin line. "Of course. It gets you up high. The holo crews are coordinated to close up on you every two hundred yards."

"No. I'll walk. Put a couple of the amputees in the limo."

"It's a global hookup holocast. It's more tightly choreographed than Worldbowl Halftime. The holos—"

"Holos are for heroes. The amputees are bigger heroes than I'll ever be."

Tway drummed a finger against her Chipboard. "General, even if we could do it that way, you're just off the ship. It took most of your soldiers days before they could walk two hundred yards, much less this parade route. What's the big deal?"

I folded my arms. "My troops walk. I walk. I command this unit."

She snapped an audiophone wafer off her belt and held it to her ear. "I'm calling the chairman of the Joint Chiefs. He commands *you*."

I swallowed while she whispered a dial code. Crap, crap, crap. I wore stars but I was a spec four at heart. I had only had my boots on dirt for twenty minutes and I was in trouble with authority just like I was back in Basic.

At the parade's head, a holo-director type wearing neon-orange gloves glanced at his 'puter, spoke into an audio wafer, then pointed an orange finger at the band. They struck up "Stars and Stripes Forever" and stepped off.

Tway turned and watched them. A gap grew between the band rear drummers' rank and the still-empty limo.

"You're losing your tight choreography, Ms. Tway."

Ruth Tway apparently had the stroke to phone the Chairman of the Joint Chiefs. But she was evidently also political enough to cut her losses.

She shook her head and let her breath hiss out between her teeth. Then she dropped her audiophone hand to her side and pointed from the corpsmen behind the wheelchairs to the limo. "Wander, were you such a butt-pain when you were a spec four?"

I grinned. "Worse."

One hundred yards later I didn't feel clever. My butt wasn't the only pain. My thighs burned and quivered, and my grin was pasted on. Tway may have been a bitch, but on this point she was a bitch who was right.

My pain went beyond my leg throbs. D.C. looked and sounded and smelt as healthy as cancer. The Slug Blitz had missed Washington and so many other cities. The familiar buildings still rose all around me. Crowds lined the street. But the sky was so gray, the air so chill, the faces in the shivering crowd so pale that it scarcely mattered. Loss and effort had sucked mankind dry.

Still, as we marched, I heard cheers, both ahead of GEF and behind us.

The crowd would rev up as the band at the parade's head marched by.

Then the limo bearing our wounded appeared and the cheers died as though a curtain had been dragged across the crowds.

I think the civilians' shock was as much from seeing how few of us remained as seeing the wounded. There were high school marching bands nearly as big as what was left of GEF. We had marched past before people even knew we were coming.

I locked eyes with an old man at the curb, a scarecrow wearing a VFW cap in the dun-camouflage pattern that had been current during the Second Afghan Conflict. In the stillness, he cupped a hand to his lips and called, "Why you? Why me?"

I blinked. He had had a lifetime to think about the question and he still couldn't answer it.

By the time my boots dragged across the Ellipse's

brown grass, my grin stretched like a death mask and my waving arm had turned as wooden as a galley slave's oar. The reviewing stand, draped in UN-blue bunting as well as red, white, and blue, loomed ahead, backstopped by the Washington Monument's white obelisk. Atop the flag-poles that ringed the monument the flags of a hundred nations snapped in the wind.

I teared up. Not with soldierly pride but because I knew I was going to have to climb a flight of stairs at the stand's side to reach the Sec-Gen and the President.

When all the troops at last stood, leg-dead and shivering, on General Washington's dead grass, the band struck up and played what seemed to be the extended, studio version of every march written since World War I.

This was a soldier's glory moment. The fact that all I wanted was to sit down tells you how much soldiers love parades.

Finally, silence returned, except for a chorus of arrhythmic clangs as those multinational flags drummed their hoist ropes against their flagpoles.

President Lewis stood—he had sat and watched us slog—and advanced to the lectern in silver-haired glory.

"Welcome home! The world salutes you for a job well done!"

The crowds behind us cheered, their voices snatched away on the wind. Lewis spoke for, by my 'puter, ten minutes. Then he said, "General Wander!"

By the time I stumbled up the stairs to the lectern, the Sec-Gen, an African who looked like mahogany wire in a Savile Row suit, had joined him.

How long we stood there and what was said I don't

recall. I recall I was tired and in pain. I've never chipped out the holocast to listen to the speeches.

It must be dull footage. The war had ended almost three years ago. Made-for-holo moments of soldiers reuniting with loved ones didn't apply for us survivors of the Ganymede Expeditionary Force, since a prerequisite to assignment had been that we had lost our entire immediate families to the Slugs. A ticker-tape parade would have left behind an expensive clean-up, so nothing to see there.

Besides, whatever novelty GEF's return might have held for the holo audience had worn off as seven hundred other troops had arrived before me over the last weeks, one transport at a time.

I can't say I minded. I had leave accumulated and five years of back pay, most of it with combat and flight supplements and much of it in officer grade. I just wanted this day to be over.

The Secretary-General looked up from his prompter— I was standing behind him, so I saw that clear glass in front of him was covered in scrolling, blue text, the way data displays on the Battlefield Awareness Monocle of an Eternad helmet. He folded his notes, and the band played "Stars and Stripes Forever," which I guess was right since we were in America, though soldiers from thirty-one nations besides the U.S. had gone and come back from Ganymede.

And that was that, I thought.

Fingers closed on my elbow. "General? A word?" The President of the United States steered me beneath the reviewing stand.

Fresh sawdust smell and light filtered through cotton-bunting walls stretched around a two-by-four frame. It was hardly the Oval Office. A Secret Service man stood at the door while another hovered, in earshot but acting like he wasn't listening.

"Jason—may I call you Jason?" He was the most powerful man on Earth. He could call me whatever he chose. Whatever else I may have thought of Lewis, the guy was disarming. He wore the whitest shirt I had ever seen, his teeth matched it, and he showed them in that famous former senatorial grin.

"Jason, you performed a wonderful service. You all did." Then his eyelids sagged like a funeral director's. "I'd like to have a word with you about your new assignment."

O boy. Here it came. Lewis was about to break the news to me that I was being busted back from general to platoon leader.

If only he knew I didn't mind. I lacked the life experience to thrust and parry with diplomats, staff officers, and members of a House Appropriations Committee. Getting busted back to lieutenant was going to be a relief.

"Of course, sir."

Wind snapped the bunting wall up and wedged it into the two-by-fours, letting the view in. The Secret Service man interposed himself between us and the view and reached to tug the cloth barrier back down.

The President waved him away and pointed up the Mall, toward the Capitol dome. The National Gallery was somewhere off on our left, the Smithsonian museums on our right. The most powerful man on Earth leaned close enough that I smelled peppermint on his breath. "Jason, have you been to Washington before?"

"Yes, sir." Class trip. On and off the bus. If it's Tuesday, that must be the rocket-ship museum.

"The Mall. It's the essence of America, isn't it?"

"If you mean a place where the National Park Service sells overpriced hamburgers, I suppose so. I'd have thought Arlington Cemetery, sir." I winced. Four hours back from outer space and I was as insubordinate as a high school dick again.

The President clapped me on the shoulder, threw his head back, and laughed, too sincerely to be real. "They said you'd have a chip on your shoulder." He sighed.

I cocked my head. He might want to break it to me gently, but how hard could it be to tell me I was going to be an infantry platoon leader?

"Jason, do you know what it cost to send a member of the Ganymede Expeditionary Force into battle?"

"One life. That's the only number that matters."

"Of course. Of course." He looked away and licked his lips. "I'm asking you to step back emotionally, see the cost of national defense, worldwide defense, objectively. Like the general you are."

"I'm no general."

"The world thinks you are. It thinks you saved it. You symbolize the shield the military provides. For all Americans. For all humanity." He stretched a smile. "When you think of America, what do you think of?"

I shrugged. Traffic jams? Infomercials?

"Prosperity!" The President punched air. "Not just for Americans. America is the engine that pulls the train of the world economy. Jason, the Slug War killed sixty million people. After subtracting defense spending, the current, combined Gross National Products of the UN's member nations today equals China's, pre-war. It will take years before Americans can think about buying a new holoset, much less about taking the kids to Virtuworld. That's why Margaret Irons got chased out of the White House."

I inclined my head. "Sir, what does this have to do—?"

"Jason, we have to return the world economy to a peacetime footing. President Irons's deficits left humanity with a bleak future."

"If she hadn't spent that money, humanity wouldn't have a future."

Lewis stopped and turned to me, hands on hips, eyes narrow as he let the mask slip. "Margaret Irons was your commander-in-chief. Now I am. Do you have a problem with that, General?"

I stiffened. One thing Sergeant Ord had drilled into my little trainee's brain was that soldiers followed orders and that, ultimately, those orders came from civilians elected by a civilian majority. Take away that discipline and America was a banana republic. "No, sir."

The President lit his grin again. "Good! Stability. Reassurance. Team play. That's what we're going to need."

"Of course, sir."

He jerked a thumb toward the parade staging area. "That business before the parade, putting the casualties front and center in the limousine? The event was carefully arranged to project a positive message. Ruth Tway reports direct to me. She's the best in her business. Why she volunteered to take you on I don't know. But pay attention to her! We needed a young, hologenic leader in those shots. Someone to demonstrate that the world was safe to shift to a peacetime economy. To encourage the world to follow our lead on defense spending. What we got was a horrifying bunch of people showing off stumps. We won't be seeing more of that counterproductive behavior from you, will we?"

I shrugged. "I'm just glad to be home, sir."

"You dodge questions like a politician. That's encouraging."

To the President, maybe.

THIRTEEN

AFTER THE PRESIDENT LEFT, Tway handed me my new orders as I climbed into a limousine. Yes, handed. The Army, being somewhere back from the cutting edge of innovation, still delivered personnel orders on paper, like it was 1995. I climbed the steps into the hospital, turning the envelope in my hands, in no hurry to open it. It was a demotion, certainly. Why else would Tway have held the news unless it was bad?

I had been assigned a hospital room at Walter Reed, rooming with Howard Hibble while we both underwent two days of welcome-home medical tests. I opened the door and found Howard sitting on his bunk, hunched over a football-sized mechanical cockroach.

The roach swiveled its head my way and bounced up and down on the blanket on six metal legs.

"Jeeb!" I said.

Howard looked up at me and smiled. "Ordnance just got him cleaned."

Like every other Tactical Observation Transport, this particular J-Series unit, unit E, Jeeb for short, was factory-wired with plastic explosive under his radar-absorbent skin. If captured, he would not only have blown his top-secret carcass into bb-shot, he would have taken some bad guys with him.

Therefore, all the way home from Ganymede, Jeeb had ridden in an ammunition bay, like the animated hand grenade he was. And I thought I had been lonely.

I sat next to him on the bunk and stroked his coat, radar-absorbent bristles like short-pile felt, while he trained round eyes, as large and flat as Oreos, on me.

It is, of course, absurd to pet a robot. But Jeeb was more than a robot. He was my robot. Maybe. "Howard, did you seal the deal?"

Howard tossed his head in the direction of the desk. "The title documents are on the table. Even as scrap, he cost you three months' pay. You realize most people would think that's an absurdly high price to pay for a worn-out bundle of nanochips."

I picked up the old-fashioned papers. Certificate of Original Commissioning. Finding of Battle Damage, Equipment Obsolescence and Surplusage. Jeeb was battle-damaged and obsolete, all right. The explosion that had won the Battle of Ganymede had fried his circuits. Five years is forever in nanoputer technology. Jeeb was decrepit. Next was a Certification of Value of Salvageable Components. Then a Bill of Retransfer from United Nations Joint Command. Finally, a Bill of Sale and Salvage Title from the United States Department of the Army to Wander, Jason.

I swallowed. That was Jeeb's life story, as far as the Army was concerned. Nowhere did the papers say that Jeeb's wrangler, the GI who had been brain-linked to Jeeb by surgical implants, had been my bunkmate until the day he died. Nowhere did the papers say that Ari Klein had asked me, as his guts leaked into the dust of Ganymede, to adopt the robot who was closer to Ari than an old K-9 Corps dog to his handler.

Howard handed me a flat palm-holo receiver. "It's not like implants. You and Jeeb will never be linked like Ari and Jeeb were. This cube's not like implants. But when you switch it on, you'll see what Jeeb sees, visible spectrum, infrared or ultraviolet, hear what Jeeb hears, audio or electromagnetic, in your earpiece. He'll translate foreign languages, teach them to you while you sleep. He'll fly at near the speed of sound or run as fast as a cheetah, anywhere you tell him to. And he'll never gripe or be too tired to do anything you ask of him."

"And what does he want from me, Howard?"

Jeeb flexed his three right-side legs and rolled onto his back. I scratched his ventral armor. Jeeb had a way of cocking his head that mimicked what Ari used to do when he heard a joke he liked.

Howard shrugged. "His creator, Lockheed, says he doesn't want anything. There are no nerve endings in that belly you're scratching. He's just a machine."

"You believe that, Howard?"

Another shrug. "Even chondrichtyian fishes recognize individual humans and display affection behaviors. He's a lot smarter than a sting ray. There's plenty of room in his thinking apparatus to imprint human behaviors and to remember. Oh, you also granted us rights to recover his survey data from his Ganymede overflights."

It measured the Slug War's irrelevance to the post-war world that data gathered about another world had been sold off as part of a war souvenir.

Jeeb, Howard, and I spent an hour that afternoon out-doors, playing fetch with a tennis ball. We might have played longer, but brain-link, even the watered-down ex-cuse for it that we shared, let Jeeb sense where I was going to throw the ball. So the old pretend to throw and hide it behind my back didn't amuse either of us.

Besides, being outdoors, even in Washington, halfway down the USA toward Florida, depressed me. Earth would need a decade to recover from the near nuclear winter the Slugs had brought down on her. Every day dawned gray and dry. Grass wasn't green and trees quivered leafless in perpetual chill. Temperate crops had relocated to the equator. That made for some strange holos of overalled Nebraskans saddling up their combines on the Brazilian plains.

Jeeb had just dropped the tennis ball at my feet and telescoped his wings for the hundredth time when I real-ized that I hadn't read my orders. But now, I had run out of other things to do.

I sighed, tugged them from my pocket, and slit the en-velope with a fingernail. Howard moved downwind and lit a cigarette.

I had read half a page before I realized what I was read-ing. I blinked, then stiffened.

Howard picked up the tennis ball, looked away from me, and chucked it for Jeeb to chase. Howard voluntarily doing anything athletic was as improbable as a tap-dancing trout.

I rolled the paper and waved it at him. "You knew about this! But you didn't tell me!"

He shrugged. "That wouldn't have changed it."

I crumpled the page and threw it at him. "You *did* know!"

Jeeb hovered, optic sensors swiveling between the tennis ball and the paper knuckle ball I bounced off Howard's chest.

Howard watched my orders hit the dirt, then turned his palms up. "Don't be such a pooby!"

I had been trying to teach Howard to swear for years. Drill sergeants spun in their graves, from Fort Benning to Fort Carson. I ground my teeth. "A *pooby*?"

He flapped a hand at me. "Don't worry. You'll love it!"

FOURTEEN

AT SIX HUNDRED HOURS the next morning, during my post-ten-K-run shave, our infirmary-room door flew open as a fist rapped the doorjamb.

"Good morning!" Tway, the White House publicity woman, stalked in like a drill sergeant into a barracks. She centered herself in the room and crossed her arms. "We're late."

I turned from the sink without shaving off my eyebrow, waved off the running water and stood barefoot and bare-chested in fatigue trousers. "Late for what?"

Jeeb perched on the sink edge, clucking like an electric chicken. Howard said it was just diagnostics. A TOT, according to Lockheed, did not, could not, imprint its wrangler's personality. But Ari had always fussed whenever I left whiskers in the sink. Not that Ari had always been critical. One night when we were both tired and scared and lonely, he had told me that greatness was my destiny.

Tway stared at Jeeb. TOTs were so rare and so expensive that people did that. But TOTs didn't look so different from the swarms of dumber utility 'bots that vacuumed everybody's carpets and pulled everybody's weeds. And

I'd have expected somebody with Tway's chutzpah had seen it all.

Howard sat up in bed and coughed a phlegmy barrage. It subsided and he swung his feet to the floor and into slippers with duct-tape-wrapped toes. Yawning, he flapped plaid-pajamaed arms above the nightstand until he found his glasses. "You the flack?"

"I'm Ruth Tway. I report directly to the President of the United States. You can call me Ms. Tway, Major Hibble."

Howard grunted, then creaked to his feet and shuffled to the latrine.

Fwop-fwop-fwop.

Howard's rubber slipper soles flapped with each step. He had only duct-taped the toes. He closed the door behind him, sparing Tway and me further sound effects.

Tway poked me above my trouser pocket with her Chipboard's corner, then frowned. "Love handles gotta go. Holocam adds ten pounds already. Heroes aren't fat."

I straightened. Maybe I sucked in my gut a little. What did she expect? I'd been cooped up in a spaceship or a cave most of the last five years. "Heroes aren't heroes because of how they look."

She squinted at my chin while she tugged something from a pocket. "Manual shaving's impractical on tour. You've gotta be as shiny-cheeked at dinner as at breakfast. And"—she wiped a finger across my chin and it came away red-streaked—"no nicks." She slapped a pressurized plasti into my palm. "Dipil cream. Lasts longer. All the holo stars use it."

I shook my head. "I look fine!"

Her lip curled. "Sure."

"My orders say I'm assigned to the joint media liaison command. Does that mean I report to you?"

She bent and rummaged on my wall locker's floor and dug out my boots. "We'll put lifts in these. No time to make you slim. But we can make you tall."

"I thought we were going to explain post-war defense spending to the taxpayers."

"Yeah. But you gotta look good doing it."

The latrine door opened and Howard returned, hair combed, hands thrust into robe pockets. He held out his hand to Ruth Tway, like an old flatscreen hero. "Hibble. Howard Hibble."

Except James Bond never *fwop-fwop*'ed when he walked.

Tway moved us out of the infirmary that afternoon, to a still-open hotel in Georgetown so fancy that a maid turned down your bed each night. Breakfast the next day was in the dining room, with tablecloths and linen napkins, each thick enough to stop shrapnel.

"You'll do a half-dozen live spots each morning, moving east to west with the time change. Local news and morning shows," Tway said.

I spread preserves, oozing hunks of fresh strawberry, on a muffin, still bakery-warm in my fingers. "How can we be—"

Tway snatched my muffin and replaced it with a brown rectangle that felt like plywood. "Protein bar. You'll lose six pounds the first week and you won't spill jelly on your uniform."

I bit the bar, then spit it into my napkin. "It tastes like dung."

"I told you you'd lose weight." She broke a piece off

my muffin and popped it in her mouth. "The morning appearances are all holo. You'll be in a studio, say in New York. The interviewer sits in a chair in Detroit and it looks like you're sitting in the chair alongside her. And to the homers, you're both sitting on their living-room rug."

I stared at my vanishing breakfast. "Why are you doing this with us?"

"Because fresh-grown food is too valuable to waste."

"I mean this PR circus. We're cutting defense spending but I'm staying in this palace?"

"America wants to give back."

"Then give back my muffin."

Tway frowned, then glanced at her 'puter. "Eat your protein bar. We've got thirty minutes to prep before your first interview."

Twenty-eight minutes later I slouched in a blue Plastine chair, in a hotel conference room converted to a holo studio. That meant an echoing, bare room, with daybrites on spider stands glaring into my eyes, a refrigerator-sized holo generator to the left of the lamp bank and a tripod-mount holocam. Black cables pythoned between them. The holo operator and the show's director stood in the cable snakepit.

Tway stood behind me, pounding my shoulder blades as she puckered my uniform jacket's back with duct tape. "Your lapels gap."

"If I turn around the tape will show."

"Don't! We'll have a tailor here before lunch. In five . . . four . . ." She brushed a protein-bar crumb off my tie and backed out of camera range.

Pop.

I'd never seen holo produced before. When the image

flickers up, the generator makes a *pop* like uncorked champagne. That's why newbies like me look wide-eyed when the viewer first sees them.

The interviewer sat in a maroon leather armchair, just like the one that now seemed to surround me. The arms on my real chair were the same height, so my elbows didn't disappear. Not only that, if I moved an elbow, the generator inserted a tiny, cloth-across-leather squeak in the delayed soundtrack.

The anchor was already speaking to the holocam, her head turned away from me. "—news for the Sox, Eddie. Next, we have someone truly special for Boston to meet. General Jason Wander, the hero of the Battle of Ganymede."

I leaned forward, nodding, like Tway had coached me, prepared and focused.

She turned to me, blond with jewel-blue eyes. *Her* pale pink lapels didn't gap. Imagining duct tape under there evaporated my focus.

"It's an honor, General."

"Uh. Yeah . . ."

Next to the holocam, Tway pointed at a cue card, held by the show's headsetted director.

I read off the card, "Tawny."

Two minutes later, Tawny had expressed to me the sorrow, pride, and gratitude of the entire Greater Boston viewing area. Then she vanished while emotional file footage of returning troops entertained the home audience.

Tway bent beside me and spoke in a strawberry-preserve-scented whisper. "Next segment coming up. The threat is over. If there were Slugs left, my command would handle them just like it handled the last bunch."

The lovely Tawny reappeared, wiping away a tear, or stray mascara. "General, is this episode behind us?"

Tway's words spewed from me like a Pavlovian poodle.

Tawny nodded thoughtfully. "Then the Lewis budget makes sense?"

"Excuse me?"

"Drastic defense cuts make sense?"

Alongside the holocam's red light, Tway nodded like an antique bobblehead doll.

I swallowed a snort. "If the Slugs are gone."

Tawny's smile fluttered, then dropped, like a table-bred turkey chucked from a plane. Behind her tinted, lased lenses welled dark terror. "They're not?"

"They are. I mean, as far as we know."

Tway leaned toward the director and whispered. Tawny fingered her earpiece. We went to commercial and she vanished.

Tway pounced. "What the hell was that?" She glanced at the holo producer and twirled a wrap-up motion with one hand while she guided me out to the hall with the other.

Glancing up and down the empty corridor, she said, "Jason—General Wander—you're on holo to soothe people, not scare the pee out of them!"

"I just said 'if.' "

"Except for Major Hibble, you're the biggest expert alive on Slugs. The last five years were the most horrific in human history and you just told people they might come back. You have to watch what you say. The public believes you when you belch."

"They should believe the truth! Even Howard thinks

the Slugs may still be out there. Let *him* be your spokes-person."

"You know Hibble. The public doesn't want a hero with duct tape on his bedroom slippers. We may use him for hard news. But nobody under eighty watches hard news. It went out with paper newspapers."

It was an old expression, and since the war, an inaccu-rate one. Paper newspapers had come back after the war cut commercial holo transmissibility.

She crossed her arms and sighed. "You needed more prep. I should have seen it coming. I thought the President told you in person that the world needed reconstruction, not panic."

"President Lewis told me America needed reassurance. I'm not so sure I'm reassured, myself. What are we re-constructing?"

She sighed. "Okay. Rule number one. If you don't want to see it on the *Washington Post* frontscreen, don't say it." Tway tugged her lip. "You know, you're not stupid."

"Thank you very much."

"The underlying problem is you haven't seen the world you came back to. We'll educate you."

"Will I like being educated?"

"You like the protein bars, don't you?"

FIFTEEN

TWAY SCRUBBED THE REST of the morning talk shows. Forty-five minutes later, an Air Force executive jet rolled up to Tway and me on the tarmac at Reagan, shut down one engine while we boarded, then swung back out and shot south toward Florida.

I stared down at dead ochre hills, my forehead on the jet window's cold, ancient plastic. Caterpillar-yellow specks of reconstruction equipment scurried like ants as we overflew the crater that had been Richmond. A real general knew how to deal with the media. A real general understood the interface between his civilian superiors and the electorate. I hadn't even lived long enough to vote for President.

Tway, facing me in an oversized leather recliner, leaned forward and pressed the steward call button on her seat arm. Posh. The business of government was booming. In American-style democracy, government feeds on misery. People who don't need help don't need government, or so they think. People in trouble do, or so they think.

Need a crater the size of Richmond cleared? Call Washington. Or, at least, call a consortium of contractors hired by Washington. Want to invent cold-and-drought-resistant wheat? Apply for a federal grant!

Even so, fuel was scarce so Washington traffic during the ride in from Reagan had been sparce. Bureaucrat pedestrians shuffled home from jobs where they allocated scarcity, bundled in long coats in the dead of D.C. summer. Buildings hunkered in the chill, as gray as the sky, unrelieved by a green leaf or a yellow dandelion. Depressing as that ride had been, beyond the Beltway there was only the very scarcity the D.C. bureaucrats were allocating.

President Lewis was trying to revive a flat world. Maybe his work was noble.

But my heart thumped. After all the death and destruction I had been through, what did he and the world want from me now?

Tway cleared her throat. "We need to understand each other."

"We can't. I'm no politician."

"That's why we need to talk."

"We already did."

The flight steward appeared and Tway held up two fingers. "At the least, General, I owe you a drink."

My stomach growled. "And a sandwich?"

She shook her head. "Protein bar."

The steward walked aft to the galley.

"Ms. Tway, who are you?"

She nodded. "Fair question. I'm media advisor to the National Security Council. For this assignment I report directly to the President of the United States. I have a master's in media science from Stanford. In the last twelve years, I've remade congressmen, colonels, and captains of industry and saved them from PR disaster. Some of *them* sulked like thirteen-year-olds, too. I'll save you, anyway. Because it's the right thing to do for the world." She paused. "But you think I'm a duplicitous bitch."

I shook my head. "Not duplicitous."

She smiled. "Infantry is an unforgiving business, isn't it?"

I shrugged. "I can't say. It's the only business I know."

"Well, my business, even though I do it in marble conference rooms and cozy bars, is unforgiving, too."

"Sure. Raping the truth is a full-time job."

She sighed as the steward pulled out a side table and set out martinis between us, frosted glasses and little crystal pitchers of gin set in individual silver ice buckets.

Tway waved him off, reached across the table, and poured one pitcher into my glass, then filled her own and raised it. "To the truth, then. Long may it wave, General."

I held my glass up, crystal sang as we touched rims and we sipped.

"Generals have responsibilities. All I have are protein bars and stars on my collar."

"We know you'd be content as a lieutenant, but the public wants you to be a general, so a general you stay. For the moment. You're a hero. You and the others like you saved the human race." She uncurled her index finger from the stem of her glass and pointed at me. "That's the God's truth."

"And this road show is the administration's way of thanking me?"

She stared at the ceiling and blinked. "Your chip says you earned a correspondence master's in military history."

I nodded.

"During what half century of peace did America spend the greatest percentage of its gross national product on national defense?"

"I don't think anybody knew what GNP was until the 1940s. So I'd say the last half of the 1900s."

Tway nodded. "You *are* smart. In 1945, we won the most destructive war in history. But we were so paranoid about making sure it never happened again, we squandered our capacity to rebuild a better world to fight a 'Cold War.'"

"I don't buy that. They accomplished a lot in those years."

She steepled her fingers. "But what *could* they have accomplished? The western democracies hung humanity from a cross of iron."

I recognized the quote. Dwight Eisenhower, a Cold War President, said it in a speech in 1953 about balancing guns and butter.

But I thought of Eisenhower as a general. Everything that I, as a general, wasn't. Eisenhower orchestrated the resources of pre-environmental society to invade Europe. He juggled egos, obscure today but monumental at the time, like de Gaulle and Montgomery. I don't think Ike ever fired a shot himself. Eisenhower and I had as much in common as a puppy had in common with Einstein.

Tway continued. "Jason, we stand today upon the threshold mankind stood upon in 1945. Defense industries and those who serve them want to keep spending on space-capable ground forces. To protect against a threat you and the GEF obliterated over two years ago. We don't need to invade Mars."

How many times had I read that generals prepared to

fight the last war? I couldn't disagree with Tway. As a post-war infantryman, I already felt like a 180-pound dinosaur. The monthly cost of maintaining one space-capable infantryman would probably pay the prescription drug bill for sub-Saharan Africa for a decade.

Tway swirled her martini. "Sensible people want to redirect those defense resources to rebuild the world. The stakes are more than important."

"And a little truth-stretching never hurt anybody?"

"Politics are a bitch, Jason. You've commanded in combat. How much did you have to stretch to win the war?"

"We won the battle. I'm not sure we won the war."

"Even Hibble thinks we did. The Slugs have been absent without leave for almost three years."

"The absence of proof isn't proof of absence."

"Jason, your caution is understandable. I'm not asking you to dishonor the truth. I'm asking you to honor the data." She tapped her finger on the table with each word, hard enough that her martini shimmered. "There . . . is . . . no . . . evidence . . . that . . . Slugs . . . still . . . exist!"

I stared at her. Accepting the obvious has never been Infantry's strong suit. There's a reason the Army mascot is a mule.

Tway grunted. "Okay. Assume, against all rational thought, that you're right. We're maintaining necessary defense assets."

"What does that mean? Tell me in terms somebody from outside the Beltway can understand."

"I'm doing better than telling you. I'm showing you. That's why we're going to Canaveral. I owe you that."

She drained her glass, set it on the table, and stared into

it, like she could find something in its emptiness. Tway could be two people in one body. Hard as flint one minute, then sentiment fought its way to the surface.

A silent hour later we landed at Canaveral. A limo hauled us from the plane to the headquarters building, past gantries set with Interceptors, noses to the clouds. Tway pointed. "Space Force remains generously funded. We've built a new generation of Interceptors. And they're on alert twenty-four/seven."

The Interceptors weren't the ancient, airplane-on-fuel-tank space shuttles from the days of the Slug Blitz. These were big, single-stage UN-taupe wedges. Venture Stars.

Tway said, "We've got four times as many Interceptors operational as we had of the old, space shuttle–based crates at the height of the Blitz. These are faster, more maneuverable, better armed, and better coordinated. It's an impenetrable defense."

I sighed. "So was the Maginot Line. The Germans bypassed it twice. Impenetrable. Says who?"

"Says COIC. Commanding Officer, Interceptor Command. He's retiring. We're sitting in on his replacement's briefing."

The limo dropped us outside headquarters and Tway led me through security.

The Ops room stretched around us in a semicircle, ballroom-sized and ranked with data displays that were state-of-the-art holotanks. I stopped counting personnel bustling around when the number reached fifty. Space Force had progressed. During the Blitz, they had dusted off cathode-ray-tube boxes and flatscreens.

The COIC sat in a swivel chair on a podium in the

semicircle's center. He was a gray-headed Air Force major general.

The gray-hair's replacement stood alongside him. Brace. I groaned to myself.

"Welcome to United Nations Space Force Base Canaveral. Canaveral is the consolidated Space Defense and Research and Development Facility of UNSF." The COIC grinned at Tway, me, and Brace. Brace and I grinned at no one, least of all each other.

Tway turned to me. "Counting civilian contractors plus military personnel contributed from forty member nations, that's eighty thousand solid jobs. Always work in facts like that."

With Projectile strikes on Miami and Tampa, Florida was one of the hardest-hit states. No wonder it was getting military-spending dollars.

We three clattered after the outgoing COIC, up catwalk stairs, outside onto the building roof. Salt breeze off the Atlantic chilled us and the general raised his voice to be heard. He swung his arm at an arc of four dozen gantries, half with V-Stars poised, half empty. "At any time, twenty-four V-Stars are on-station in orbit. We can put up another squadron within hours. We've completed a runway long enough to recover the newer V-Stars. Lop Nor will finish theirs next year. Scramjets also operate from the Long Strip. They don't need it, but every pilot likes extra space."

Brace asked, "You launch from Earth every time?"

I whistled. "That must cost The Brick!"

Tway and the COIC looked at me and frowned, for no apparent reason.

COIC paused, then continued. "That's why we're

minimizing recovery-runway spending." He turned and pointed to other, more distant gantries. "That's the heavy-lift complex. Space Base One will be launched to orbit from there, in sections. Interceptors should be operating from permanent orbit within a year. Not V-Stars but true space-capable fighters. The V-Star's a sound ship, but she's a design that was discarded four decades ago. We're also putting up an unmanned tracker and hunter-killer satellite umbrella, too. Those launch out of Vandenberg."

It sounded impressive. And expensive. And a hell of a responsible job for Brace. Me, my responsibility was to not spill jelly on my uniform.

I turned to Tway, as the Atlantic breeze snapped at her coat, and said, "Why do you need me to shill for this?"

She ran a hand through her hair. "Expenditures for this project would fund a couple of brand-new cities, domestically. So half of the country thinks it's a defense pork barrel."

"Is it?"

Tway looked away and continued. "And the jobs and factories and this base are in the U.S. The rest of the world thinks this project is just America rebuilding itself with the rest of the world's money, while the rest of the world starves."

"Is that true?"

Tway crossed her arms.

Brace asked the outgoing COIC, "Research and Development's based here, too?"

COIC nodded. "Conventional *and* PTR."

PTR was Pseudocephalopod Technology Recovery. I asked the old general, "What about PCBR?" That was

Howard's baby, Pseudocephalopod Cryptozoology and Behavioral Research.

COIC wrinkled his nose and pointed at a small building that seemed set apart, out on the horizon. "The Spook House is over there."

I smiled. The military recognized that Howard Hibble's intuitive genius was critical to its success. I always believed that if we dissected Howard's brain, we'd find the definitive history of the galaxy already written in there somewhere. The military also recognized that professorial Howard's wrinkled uniforms and freak-show sidekicks—yours truly excluded—didn't fit its paradigm.

So Howard and his merry band of loons functioned in a parallel military universe. The generals and politicians set him off to the side, disconnected his leash, and let him run. Then they allowed themselves to be pleasantly surprised at the bones he brought back.

The Department of Defense had finally set, in isolated bricks and mortar, the unspoken organizational chart that Howard barely fit into.

Tway spent the rest of the afternoon with Brace, presumably educating him on the fine points of media relations.

I hitched a ride to the Spook House. The building was two stories tall and brand-new. Hacking up green worms was Howard's idea of an all-day frolic, so I expected to find him there. I didn't expect to find Munchkin and Jude.

SIXTEEN

HOWARD HAD TOURED ME THROUGH LABS, collection rooms where catalogued Projectile fragments were stored, and data-processing facilities. I didn't expect our last stop to be a playroom. The place was classroom-size, the walls painted with pandas and smiling purple lizards. In the room's center, Jude caught bean bags, chucked underhand by a lab-coated woman in a clown wig, which was actually her hair, while a lab-coated guy who wore a separate goatee on each cheek holo-cammed each toss.

Munchkin sat in a room corner in civvies, arms crossed.

I tiptoed alongside her. "Home movies?"

She spun her head toward me. "Jason!" She smiled, then jerked her head at Jude. "Howard wants to measure his reaction times. The Army gave me alternatives. Bring Jude down here or they would."

I raised my eyebrows. "Howard strong-armed you?"

She shook her head. "Howard wouldn't strong-arm a goldfish. It was Space Force. Anyway, it's warm down here." She hugged herself. "Well, not like home."

Even Munchkin's home, Egypt, wasn't warm since the

war. I pointed at the catch game. "What're they trying to prove?"

She glowered. "That he's different because he wasn't born here."

Howard stepped alongside us. "You make it sound like Apartheid."

"It is." Munchkin pouted. If Munchkin ever got U.S. citizenship, which her son had because his father was born here, I doubted she would register Republican.

I changed the subject. "Howard, when do you want to download Jeeb's data?"

He shrugged. "You brought him to Florida? Well, bring him by when it's convenient."

I turned to Munchkin. "See? I'm letting them examine *my* baby with no fuss."

She rolled her eyes and muttered in Arabic.

I asked Howard, "Speaking of examining strange machinery. Where's The Football from Ganymede?"

He said, "Space Force R and D still has it." He frowned. "They've been studying it like they were going to cut the Hope Diamond. They start intrusive testing in a week." He circled his finger at us. "We're all invited. Ceremony to demonstrate spin-off technology gains from the war."

I snorted. "Space Force will be lucky if they don't blow themselves into rutabagas." In the Projectile days, Howard always used to complain that the biggest fragments he recovered for study were the size of rutabagas. Whatever they were.

Munchkin thrust Jude at me. "Here. Your robot doesn't need changing. Your godson does."

I never made *that* comparison again.

Howard took us all to dinner and spent most of the night watching Jude eat.

My eyes were gritty from a long day when I drifted, alone, through the lobby of the Ritz-Orlando.

The night concierge called across lavender carpet, "General Wander? Holo!"

He pointed across the silent room at a holo booth with a light flashing above the door.

I cocked my head at him and called back, "Who is it, Rudy? Holo calls cost The Brick."

He motioned me over, then leaned across his curlicue-legged desk. "General, nobody uses that expression in polite society anymore. Today, it refers to"—he dropped his voice—"constipation."

Every day I learned again that five years in space and training had left me out-of-touch.

I nodded.

He nodded back, toward the booth. "Sir, the gentleman has been a guest here. You'll recognize him." Ritz guests paid for privacy and discretion and got it.

The man in the booth wore a flowered shirt, untucked over shorts, and sandals. He held a stemmed glass in one hand and I recognized him from someplace, too.

"Jason?" He smiled through a salt-and-pepper full beard that covered a fleshy face. "Aaron Grodt."

Ah! I nodded. It might seem strange that anybody wouldn't recognize Aaron Grodt, but I hadn't seen the Oscars for six years. Also, he had grown a beard since I had met him. "How's the producing business been, sir?"

He shrugged. Blue liquid slopped over the lip of his glass. I wondered whether it was really blue. The booth was so old that Grodt was fuzzy around the edges. "Would have been better if you had taken that job I offered you."

In the war's early days, Grodt had offered to weasel me out of the Army. I would have been a consultant for the military-story holos he planned to make. Really, I would have been a glorified Holo-wood go-fer, I suppose. Somebody else would have gone to Ganymede. I doubted that would have changed history. I was an accidental hero.

"Well, you look *simplement* fabuloso!"

After two years in space I looked as flabby and pasty as unbaked bread.

Grodt was sixty pounds overweight with an artificial tan and teeth. Greased hair curled fashionably over his collar. "Thank you, sir. You, too." I had learned during our one prior meeting that, in Holo-wood, everyone and everything was *simplement* fabuloso.

"I'm having a few friends over to my little place in Orlando tomorrow night. Would you join us?"

My last visit to Grodt's little place, all twenty thousand gilded square feet of it, nearly got me laid. "That would be great, sir."

He grinned. "I'll send a car."

He didn't know that my last visit ended with me hungover, hauled off by MPs, shot to the moon in an antique rocket, and attacked by monsters. "I hope it's as great as last time, sir."

The Daimler limo that purred up under the Ritz portico the following twilight was polished to its last square inch, but ten years old. The black-suited driver scurried around to open the rear passenger door for me. "Been away long, sir?"

I nodded while I eyed my uniformed reflection in a Plasteel fender. "Long enough to save the price of a Daimler. Could we detour by a dealership on the way to Mr. Grodt's?"

I'd never owned a car. Mom had driven a family Electra with synwood sides. In the passenger seat, I used to bend down and tie my shoes when we drove past anyone I knew.

He wrinkled his brow.

"I didn't mean stop. Just, you know, drive by the new ones on the lot."

He grinned and nodded. "Good one, sir."

He held the door for me and I ducked in. "If it won't make us late."

He peered in as I settled into worn suede upholstery. "You really have been away a long time, sir."

"Huh?"

"There hasn't been Plasteel for new cars in five years. War Procurement Act. Even Mr. Grodt couldn't buy a new Daimler, today."

The Daimler hushed away from the curb as I watched my openmouthed reflection in the partition rearview. *Hope* had been a mile long. *Excalibur* the same. The transport fleets and support infrastructure to build them in lunar orbit and launch them, with their cargo of high-priced mudfoots like me, to Jupiter's orbit on a panic schedule must have drained the world economy. Especially since the Slugs had permanently reduced the workforce by tens of millions.

A chilled Dom Perignon bottle sweated in the console ice bucket at my elbow. Not everybody seemed to have been drained. My first real look at post-Slug War America came through a pre-war limousine window, needlessly tinted today. What I noticed was what was missing more than what had changed. Few cars roamed the streets and fewer pedestrians. Straw-drab trees and lawns bored the eye. War had sucked the life from America and, I supposed, everywhere else on Earth. Yet here I was in a limo bound for a bomber, or whatever the current slang was these days for a rippin' big party.

A half hour later, my remorse at disproportionate sacrifice had dissolved in a half bottle of champagne sloshing in an empty stomach. At the gate in the wall that isolated Grodt's mansion, a tuxedoed guard waved the Daimler through. His green laserflash spun bored corkscrews in perpetual twilight. I waved back, invisible to him behind dark glass. My ticker-tape parade for saving the human race.

At first, Grodt's driveway curved through brown lawns and dormant palm groves. But when we crossed a ringing perimeter of guest bungalows and headed up to the main house, the lawns rolled by the acre, green and jeweled with sprinkler spray, beneath sun lamps hidden in overarching palm fronds. Grodt's monthly energy EFT had to cost enough to heat Toledo for a week.

At the mansion entrance, a valet opened my passenger door and I stepped out into seventy-degrees Fahrenheit, squinting against phony sunshine. The valet flicked me a civilian excuse for a salute, and I returned it, grinning.

The main entry hall seemed smaller than my last visit, maybe because the walls were darker. I touched one. It had been repapered in emerald silk. The foyer remained big enough to host basketball playoffs.

Tanned, tuxedoed, gowned, and beautiful, Grodt's guests

clattered across marble tile and swirled up the curve of the grand staircase. Scents of perfume and passed hors d'oeuvres filled the air along with live music.

Evidently, Plasteel wasn't the only material rationed by the War Procurement Act. Unlike the dresses I had left behind five years ago, the average female hem hovered two inches below paradise. Historically, hemlines rose during wartime. Material conservation, the chips said. But the Slug War had shrunk skirts to an endangered species. One more year of war and dresses would have gone the way of the trilobite. Perhaps war wasn't completely hell.

I hadn't seen an available woman out of uniform in five years. Across the room, a stunning brunette tugged her tiny skirt down as she prepared to settle onto a low sofa, a futile wave at modesty. I held my breath. In moments, I would learn whether fashion had also changed in women's underwear.

A hand clapped my shoulder. "Jason!"

I exhaled and tore my eyes away from the tableau about to unfold on the sofa. "Mr. Grodt."

He spun me toward him and clapped his other hand on my other shoulder, holding me at arm's length. "Jason!"

"Mr. Grodt."

This had all the earmarks of a boring conversation.

His grin melted and he brushed a curl off one ear. "My boy, I prayed to God each day for your safe return."

A female server slithered up to us in the uniform of the day, four-inch heels and chrome-studded leather straps that covered only erectile tissue. She offered Prozac wafers and pills I didn't recognize, mounded on a silver tray. I smiled and shook my head. Grodt dismissed her with a pat on her bare bottom.

I watched her slink into the crowd. Maybe she helped Grodt with his daily prayers.

"Was it terrible, Jason?" Grodt asked.

It was worse than that.

I sighed. How could I explain to someone like Grodt? Someone had written about it. Isolation. Self-doubt. Boredom punctuated by terror. The random chaos of battle. The bond between people who have no more in common than absolute responsibility for one another's lives. I opened my mouth, "Well—"

He pressed the back of his hand to his forehead. "My God, say no more. I can imagine." Staring over my shoulder, he raised his glass to someone.

"Jason, we need to talk." He wrapped his arm around my neck and steered me through the crowd.

My heart sank. The brunette had folded herself demurely into sofa cushions and smiled up at some bald civilian in a raspberry-colored jumpsuit.

Grodt led me down a carpeted hallway that stretched so far that the band and crowd dwindled to a murmur. He stopped and pushed open twelve-foot-high double doors, grinning. "My library."

His library actually contained one shelf of paper books, sealed under glass. All the remaining wall space, except for French doors that led to outdoor gardens, was hung with flat film posters, also behind glass, and theater-front holos of Grodt features.

Grodt International had made its share of tripe, period-piece musicals featuring women in turn-of-the-century thong swimsuits and men with tattoos. But Grodt International had also remade some highbrow stuff, Graphnov classics like *Crusades of the LaserLeague*.

Stepping to a sideboard, he poured an inch of amber liquid each into cut-crystal snifters as big as pineapples. He handed me one, then raised his in a toast. "To your return. Hell, to your future!"

I raised my snifter to my nose. Even a few days in hotel bars with Tway picking up the tab had educated me. It was cognac strong enough to clear my sinuses. "Sir?"

He motioned me to sit in one of a pair of wing chairs, then sat in the other. "Your story needs to be told."

Exactly what I had tried to do when he had cut me off a few minutes ago.

He crossed his legs. "An autobiography, then a holo based on it. Ten-thousand-theater multinational release."

I frowned. "I'm no author." I leaned forward. "But I kept a diary! If you want to read it."

He raised his palm. "Read it?" He fluttered his hand. "No, no. We hired a freelancer. He's already writing your autobiography chip. Then my team adapts it to a holo-play."

"But how do you know—?"

He waved me off, then held his hands at arm's length and made a frame with thumbs and forefingers. He squinted through it and said, "Your face is going to be too familiar to the public. So we can't get away with having you played by a hunk."

"Thanks a lot, Mr. Grodt."

The table phone glowed and he waved it on and whispered into it.

I looked out the window at a gardener. The man frowned as he trimmed Grodt's roses with a laser wand. I shook my head. Nine thousand soldiers forever on Ganymede would have smilingly traded places with that gardener. "It seems too soon for a holo."

"You'll make a fortune."

I already had enough to buy a car, if they ever started making them again. Bachelor officers' quarters cost less than fertilizer for Grodt's roses. "I don't need a fortune. And I don't want to make one off my dead buddies."

Grodt sighed. "I expected something like this. You'll get over it. I'll keep the offer open. Until I find a more commercial project. Don't agonize too long."

I returned to Grodt's party and ate everything that didn't taste like a Tway protein bar. I washed it all down with *beaucoup* cognac. I didn't find a woman to, uh, liaise with. Much later I learned that the only person I had screwed that night was me.

The morning after my last Grodt party, I got rocketed into space and landed on the moon.

This time, the morning after was calmer. I just got shot into the stratosphere at seven thousand miles per hour and landed in the Sahara Desert.

SEVENTEEN

My Ritz suite was big enough for me, my hangover, and Jeeb. Most important, it had an old-fashioned security chain on the door, so Tway couldn't barge in. But she could call, and then badger the hotel to activate the room phone's emergency shriek when I ignored normal ringing.

On shriek twelve, I unwrapped the pillow from around my ears, waved the phone on, audio only, and croaked, "General Wander."

"Are you packed?" Tway.

"Huh?"

"We leave this lobby for the Long Strip at Canaveral in twenty minutes."

"I thought the Long Strip was just for Interceptor landings. And international Scramjets."

The phone hissed.

One thing Ord and the Army had taught me was to never go to sleep unpacked, drunk or sober. I shaved, showered, and slid into a limo alongside Tway with two minutes to spare, bent under my overstuffed duffel, and a throbbing head just as swollen.

We rolled out into the smattering of cars that constituted post-war traffic and Tway turned to me. "You were at Aaron Grodt's."

My pale face and red eyes stared back at me as I gazed out the tinted window. "It shows, huh?"

"We just tracked your dogtag. I see you got zogged. Did you get laid?"

I shook my head. Slowly. "If it's your business, no. Just propositioned by a fat man."

She nodded. "Book deal?"

"How did you know? Chipbugging's illegal, even on military personnel."

"Curb your paranoia. Grodt called us and cleared an autobiography proposal before he talked to you. It's good exposure and you get to keep the money."

"I turned him down."

Tway rolled her eyes. "Okay, give the money away. Altruism sells."

"It's still exploiting dead soldiers. No." I faced the window, watching the 'burbs roll silently by until we cleared Canaveral's gate.

Then my jaw dropped. We rolled up alongside wheeled stairs that climbed to the door of an unmarked passenger Supersonic Combustion Ramjet liner. Shaped like a surfboard with tail fins, it had mammoth air intakes that gaped at me.

Scram travel cost The Brick. It made sense only for over-water flights where the passengers thought they needed to get to another continent faster than they got to the airport. But my traveling companions, waiting on the tarmac, were a bigger surprise.

Jude clapped when he saw me climb out of the limo. "Dason!"

Munchkin smiled and hugged me. "Are you ready?"

My intestines gurgled. Everything I had overeaten last night picked this moment to make a break for it. "Huh?"

"Jude's going home! My home, anyway!"

I struggled up the stairs to the Scram. "Egypt?"

"Jude's half Egyptian!"

"Sure." I clenched my teeth and climbed aboard. To reach the Scramjet's bathroom, I would have agreed Jude was half Martian.

Ten minutes later, I sank, relieved, into a window seat alongside squirming Jude, with Munchkin and Tway across the aisle.

Few people besides diplomats, tycoons, and hopstars have been inside a Scram. The cabin ceiling's so low a guy like me has to bend a little. The seats are butter-soft leather, deep-padded, but narrower than coach-class airliner seats. They don't need to be big, because a Scram can reach any place on Earth in under two hours. They do need to be well padded because those short flight times mean heavy takeoff Gees to reach seven thousand miles per hour. And the seat-belt system includes padded shoulder straps, because deceleration is multi-Gee, too.

I looked around. We had the Scram cabin to ourselves. A steward offered pre-takeoff coffee. And, better, Tylenol powder pax.

The plane shook as the takeoff engines lit. I winced at the roar that pounded my pounding head.

Munchkin frowned. "You won't barf on us?"

I shook my head. "Nothing to barf. Why Egypt?"

Tway said, "Cairo was the cultural capital of the Pan-Islamic world. What's left of it still is. We persuade Egypt about our plans, we persuade the Third World."

Munchkin's Class-A tunic buttoned at the throat, any-way. But she wore uniform trousers, not a skirt, and her beret covered her hair.

I said to Munchkin while I pointed at Tway, "She's been helping with your image?"

"Lieutenant Munshara-Metzger doesn't need my help." Tway leaned across and brushed spilled Tylenol powder off my lapel.

Lieutenant? I squinted at Munchkin's collar. The change would have been obvious but for my hangover. "You got your lieutenant's bar back!"

Munchkin had been a commissioned officer in the Egyptian Army. All of us volunteers had given up rank and accepted redesignation as a condition of Ganymede Expeditionary Force assignment.

Munchkin pushed her collar brass out with her thumb and smiled.

Tway said, "Democratized or not, Egypt is still Muslim."

At least Tway wasn't making Munchkin wear a sack with eyeholes.

Tway said, "She needs to be nearly equal. But if she outranks her male counterpart, we kiss off the fundamen-talist demographic."

I looked at Tway while she arranged a black scarf over her own hair. "Why don't *you* do the talking? You excel at that."

Tway wrinkled her nose. "The Muslim world's still not ready to hear from a nice Jewish girl."

I raised my eyebrows. It never occurred to me that dark-eyed Ruth Tway was Jewish. I'd bunked with Ari Klein for two years and never cared about his Jewishness, either. One more reason I didn't belong in politics.

I was getting to keep my stars for PR, not because I was making a military difference. I was supporting another Tway political ploy so Machiavellian that I didn't even know what it was. However, the fact that I still outranked my shrimpy, de facto little sister soothed me. Maybe there's a little Muslim fundamentalist in most guys.

The intercom sang. "Steward, please prepare the cabin for takeoff."

Engine vibration and roar shook the cabin. Jude looked up at me, wide-eyed, lip quivering.

I smiled down at him. "It's alright."

Jude frowned.

I stroked his hair. "We're all safe."

He smiled back, then we lurched into takeoff roll.

I turned to the window and watched central Florida blur. Beside me, Jude imitated engine roar, his cheeks puffed, as I hugged him against me. If I told someone we were safe, that someone believed me. That was a good thing. Wasn't it?

Acceleration pushed me back into the seat cushions and Jude gripped my arm as the rocket disposables beneath the Scram's fuselage pushed us higher, and farther out over the Atlantic.

The rocket bottles accelerated the Scram toward supersonic flight, where speed would ram enough air into the now-lifeless main engines to light them up.

The Scram jumped, like a bus hitting a speed bump. Jude squeezed my arm harder.

The pilot's voice crackled from the ceiling. "That jolt was us dropping our rocket bottles. You'll feel another in a minute, when we climb up on the air wave we're piling in front of us. Once we're surfing the wave you'll be free to move about the cabin. Speaking of surf, we are now two hundred nautical miles east of the Florida coastal surfline."

I glanced at my 'puter and whistled. We had only been up a couple minutes. And we weren't near cruising speed yet.

I rolled my head, now heavy from acceleration as well as from prior debauchery, toward the window. Below us, through the lingering haze of atmospheric Slug impact dust, the horizon curved in the distance and the sky was indigo. I wasn't back in space, but I was close.

The steward made a quick pass with a snack tray. Tway wagged her finger and held out a protein bar. She needn't have bothered. Between the bumpy ride, the Gees, and last night's excess, I planned not to eat. Ever again.

Just after the steward retrieved Jude's fruit wrapper, deceleration pressed me forward against my shoulder harness. By the time my Tylenol kicked in, the Sahara spread beneath us like a dune-wrinkled Persian carpet, but monochromatically ochre.

Munchkin leaned across and pointed to a distant silver ribbon that snaked across the lifeless sand carpet. "The Nile. For five thousand years, everybody lived along the Nile."

And that had been the death of them.

I had done my reading. The Nile floodplain was desert that bloomed each spring when the river faithfully overflowed. For millennia, the Nile nurtured agrarian millions who lived along its low banks and welcomed fertility brought by the encroaching waters.

No one knew how many the Cairo Projectile vaporized in the impact instant. Cairo's census had been acknowledged to understate the population by millions for, an Egyptian proverb said, as long as the Nile had flowed. People with a five-thousand-year history seemed to like time-related proverbs.

But the Nile, giver of life, ran through Cairo's heart. The impact crater's south wall dammed the river, already in annual flood upstream, instantly at two A.M. For the first time since before the Pharaohs, the Nile did not flow. The government and media in Cairo, which might have spread warnings, vanished in an eyeblink.

So, upstream, flooding claimed millions more lives. Children died disproportionately, their smaller, sleeping bodies swept away.

I hugged Jude closer.

We landed at the strip outside the suburban sprawl that now was Cairo. I had to carry Jude down the departure stairs. Munchkin's tears flowed. Jude's maternal grandparents and his six aunts had disappeared in the heartbeat of impact.

The strip had been bulldozed across desert, and I squinted against sand on the wind.

Ahead of me, Tway hung her hands on her hips and whistled.

My jaw dropped. To our front, the Pyramids rose.

Munchkin stood beside me and wiped her eyes. "Visitors don't expect them to be so close to Cairo."

To what had been Cairo. Yet here they stood, and so did we, still and silent.

"Egyptians say, 'All the world fears time, but time fears the Pyramids.' Welcome to Egypt! I am Haji." Our tour guide, a mustached Egyptian whose smile showed off a gold incisor, motioned us to our tour vehicle, a UN-blue, diesel-powered relic he called a Humvee. Only a few ancient people have ever driven a diesel-powered vehicle. My head snapped back as the Humvee lurched away, then forward as he jerked the automatic transmission. Haji was plainly not among the ancient few.

The time the Pyramids themselves should fear is time spent riding in a Humvee. Humvees ride like ox carts. I know that because Haji stuck our Hummer in a mud pit and we finished our tour riding in an ox cart. Tway's tour did teach me that most of the rest of the world lacked the tech to build spaceships.

Our first stop was the impact crater's west rim. Munchkin kept Jude in the Humvee. Somewhere in that vast hole rested the remains of the family Jude would never know.

I stared three miles across, to the opposite rim, a shallow Grand Canyon. Like the Grand Canyon, a river ran through it.

Haji pointed at the wide Nile, and at the smaller crater that overlapped the impact crater's south side. "Thanks be to God, United States reopened the Nile, or many more would have died in the floods."

A U.S. nuclear missile had broken open the crater-rim dam and released the Nile to flow north to the Mediterranean. But there had likely been innocent Egyptians alive at ground zero when President Irons ordered the button pushed. Who could say that Margaret Irons had not killed Munchkin's family? But who could say that Irons's decision to save millions of Egyptians by nuking Cairo was wrong? The word was that Margaret Irons got forced to resign. But with a job like that, maybe she just quit. A lump grew in my throat. Command was a bitch. The stars on my shoulders weighed tons. I wanted to be a grunt again.

Tway shook her head. "Forty years ago, no one would have believed that Muslims would thank the U.S. for nuking the largest city in Islam."

We spent an hour lobbying the mayor of New Cairo, in a Quonset-hut city hall. He greeted me Arab style, with a kiss on each cheek. He also seemed to me to be hitting on Munchkin, whether she was bundled up or not. The whole thing conjured visions of quasi-incestuous ménage à trois that I didn't need with a queasy stomach. Then the Egyptian foreign minister showed us around the Pyramids while Munchkin chatted him up in Arabic.

Tway was smiling. We were winning over Muslim demographic groups like Grant took Richmond.

Later, Haji buried our Humvee axle-deep at a muddy clean-up and reconstruction site in the Nile floodplain, south of Cairo. I rolled up my trouser legs and climbed out, barefoot, in my American uniform, to see whether a push would free us. A turbaned man, ankle-deep in muck and digging with a wood-handled adze, looked up. He scooped mud with the adze blade, then flung it at me. Evidently, not all Muslims thanked us.

I asked Tway, as she leaned out the Humvee's window, "What demographic is he?"

"Get used to it. Politics is no popularity contest."

"I thought that's exactly what it was."

She sighed. "Wander, what made you so difficult?"

I tore one foot free from the mud with a sucking pop. "Difficulty."

We outran the sun back to North America, but the Scram was returning us to Washington, not Canaveral.

While Munchkin and Jude dozed, I asked Tway, "Doesn't it strike you as ridiculous that Blitz survivors in Egypt are rebuilding with ox carts while we're hunting publicity in a Scramjet with a fuel bill that would feed them all for a year?"

Tway smiled. "See? You're beginning to understand why the world can't afford soldiers as expensive as you are. But no, I don't think the Scram is extravagant. Or, at least, it's a necessary extravagance. You and Lieutenant Munshara-Metzger have another appearance in Washington in the morning. Only a Scram could get you to Egypt and back in a day."

In the limo to our hotel, Munchkin bounced Jude on one knee and asked me, "What do you think?"

"I think the world's in the toilet. I think we need to spend every penny on reconstruction. I also think we need to spend every penny on defense. I think politics is an impossible balancing act and I hate it. I think this job fits me like bicycle shorts fit hippos."

She sighed. "Maybe the thing tomorrow will change your mind."

"What thing?"

EIGHTEEN

THE NEXT MORNING Tway stood on the gravel path that split the Capitol Mall in front of the Smithsonian's Air and Space Museum while she read from a Chipboard. She shouted at me, "Well, not even you can screw up today!" An early-morning jogger stream parted and flowed, panting, around us.

Tway had to shout because, behind us, hydraulics whined as winches mounted on two diesel trailers big enough to move houses inched Mimi Ozawa's V-Star, floodlit in dawn half-flight, onto the Mall's dead grass. Alongside the V-Star rose a bunting-draped stage, UN blue and American-flag-striped, ringed by spindly temporary bleachers.

Tway adjusted her glasses and pointed at the stage. "You sit up there with the other veterans. The assistant to the Secretary-General hands over the title papers to the director of the Smithsonian—"

"She's already an American ship!"

"Technically, she's UN Space Force property. Look, it's a chance for the world to thank America. Most of the

Ganymede Expeditionary Force were American. It's a friggin' symbol. Like you."

A friggin' symbol. The V-Star, still painted Ganymede-tan camo, would squat on its landing gear as a static display, on the Mall in front of the museum, for a year. Then more flatbeds would haul it off to be gutted of its avionics and engines. Then the V-Star would be tucked into some aircraft nursing home of a hangar, alongside other winged relics of other wars. That's what happened to symbols. I blinked back a tear.

Tway looked in my eyes. "It's just a hunk of titanium."

I pretended to scratch my nose so I could wipe it.

"Hibble will be up on the stage, too. And Sharia with her little boy. And your Senior NCO, Brumby." She drew a finger across the blank bottom of the Chipboard screen. "You've got the next two days off. After the ceremony, make the reception a reunion. Relax. Stay out of trouble."

I straightened and smiled.

The ceremonies went off hitch-free. I had no responsibilities while the politicians spoke, so I sat onstage next to Howard and divided my attention between making eye contact with a business-suited brunette in the bleachers and watching three-year-old Jude Munshara-Metzger squirm on his mother's lap. Brumby sat beside Munchkin. He squirmed, too, looking like he was searching for something to blow up.

Afterward, the Smithsonian hosted a buffet in the Air and Space Museum for ceremony participants.

Brumby, Munchkin with Jude, Howard, and I shared a table. At another table, the brunette in the business suit sat facing me in a group and smiled. Celebrity had its good points.

Brumby chewed a National Park Service cheeseburger. "They should have let President Irons accept the ship."

Muchkin read nutrition labels on a chicken sandwich while she cut it into small pieces for Jude. "The crowd would've booed her off the stage. They think she wrecked the economy."

Brumby waved his cheeseburger. "The crowd wouldn't be here if she hadn't! And the Slugs had just a little bit to do with it."

I asked, "So, Brumby, what's your new assignment?" Tway had me so conditioned that now I changed the subject away from controversy even when talking to friends.

He blinked. "You didn't hear? Next month I'm gone. Medical."

My mouth hung open. I had let myself get so wrapped up in fancy hotels and flirting brunettes that I had lost touch with a man who had become my brother. "Why?"

"Punched a guy. Like on *Excalibur*. They checked me into Bethesda and 'observed' me. PTSD."

"They think a civilian with Post-Traumatic Stress Disorder is better than a soldier with it?"

"Civilians don't usually carry guns." His hands shook until he pressed his palms flat on the table. "It's okay. I mean, where would I be in twenty years if I stayed in? Sergeant Major Ord's got a cleaner record than I'll ever have and I hear he's pushing papers at the Pentagon since we got back. I can take a Gratitude Act pension, if I opt in by tomorrow."

Congress had accelerated pension eligibility for Ganymede Expeditionary Force veterans who wanted to retire. Brumby could collect his pension based on his acting rank. In the long haul, it was cheaper for the country to get rid of us than to pay us and train us and maintain us. There were only seven hundred survivors to pay off, anyway.

I had been thinking about it, myself. A major general's pension was The Brick. Time for another subject change, before I thought too closely about it. "Howard, what's new with you?"

He tapped an unlit cigarette against his palm. "We transcribed the Ganymede survey data we downloaded from Jeeb. You should have let me keep hunting artifacts. The Football? It wasn't unique. They were tucked away all over Ganymede, like eggs on Easter morning."

I looked over at Jude. "Easter eggs get hidden just enough so they get found. What were the Slugs up to?"

Howard shrugged. "Could be a message. We're waiting for Brace's people to carve up The Football. It'll be another flea circus like this. You'll see for yourself."

"Can't wait."

As youngest among the three juveniles, Jude got restless before Brumby or Howard. I walked Munchkin and my godson down the Mall to her rental car. If new cars were scarce, rental cars were scarcer. But Uncle Sam was generous with her per diem because Munchkin had mothered the only extraterrestrial-gestated child in human history. Her disembarkation physical was being conducted at Walter Reed Hospital. That was a short drive.

We might have been a family, Jude my three-year-old son, instead of my godson. But he had Metzger's strawberry-blond hair and Munchkin's café au lait skin, and I was as honky-white as five sunless years can drain a cauc. I tossed a styrofoam glider—a V-Star in UNSF blue I had bought at the Smithsonian. Jude chased it like any three-year-old.

Munchkin caught my elbow with gloved fingers and whispered, "Watch!"

The glider arced up into chill, dry air, then stalled and swooped back to the ground. Jude ran twenty feet to it, giggling.

Grinning, he ran back to us, waving the tiny blue wedge like a flag. "Frow! Frow again!"

Munchkin had paled beneath her café au lait. She hugged herself against the Washington chill.

"What's wrong?" Was she afraid he would become a pilot? And die like his father had?

She shook her head. "They think he's a freak. Something about reaction times. They can't measure the differences, yet."

Jude sat cross-legged in the grass, hand-flying the glider and making roaring noises punctuated by drool sprays.

"He's a kid, Munchkin. A cute, smart, healthy kid."

She frowned. "Gamma rays. Low gravity. Who knows what about him is different?"

I rolled my eyes. "It's not like he has a third eye."

She turned to me, hands on hips. "It isn't that. I'd love him if he was as ugly as you. It's them."

"Who them?"

"The doctors. The cognitive scientists. The Intel weenies. They think the only extraterrestrially born and conceived human is their lab rat. I think he's my son."

"You're exaggerating."

"Am I? Look behind us."

I didn't have to. Twenty yards behind us sauntered a male-female plainclothes MP team, playing tourist. "You're a celebrity. So's Jude. Lots of nuts are still mad at

Jude's father for wiping out the only other intelligent species in the universe."

She poked her hands into her parka pockets and hissed. "Right."

I smiled. "Your trusting and jolly demeanor is one reason I'm glad you're staying in the service. I need the example of someone more paranoid than I am."

She scuffed grass bristles with her shoe.

Finally she looked up at me. "I've been wondering how to tell you. I'm leaving tomorrow."

"Leaving where?"

"Washington. The Army."

She might as well have slapped me. "But—"

She glanced back at the MPs. "Jason, even if I trusted the government, why stay in?"

"But you're leaving me alone."

"I'll be close. There's a place I'm looking to buy. In Colorado."

"You're not going back to Egypt?"

"It isn't home. Cairo's gone. My family with it. Besides, America is the free-est society on the planet."

I jerked a thumb at our guards. "You think?"

"In America, secret police are a joke. In the Middle East, they still are a fact. Real democracy is still new to Egypt. In the U.S., I can buy my own forty acres and raise my son in peace. With a couple good guns." I had seen Munchkin shoot. Any would-be Jude kidnappers had better strap on their Eternad armor. "If I opt in to the Gratitude Act by tomorrow, we collect my pension plus Metzger's. What about you, Jason?"

Jude stretched his arms and she picked him up as we walked.

I raised my eyes to the Capitol, far up the Mall. I shrugged. "I dunno." I told her about Grodt, about the book.

She frowned.

"Should I do the book?"

She shrugged while Jude tugged her hair. "If you give the proceeds to charity, I guess so. But that's not a life. This whole circus tour they have you doing. It's not you."

We arrived back at her rental car and I slid the door up so she could fit Jude into his seat and pump up the bolsters. I turned away.

"Jason? You're coming back to our place for dinner, aren't you?"

A nearly visible sunset was beginning beyond the Washington Monument. I shook my head. "I've gotta think."

She reached out from behind the wheel and touched my sleeve. "Take care."

I pressed her door down. Through the windome Jude saluted. I returned it and the car purred out into sparse traffic. The incognito Olsen Twins followed behind her in a Ford four-door so plain it had to be government.

I thrust my hands in my pockets and walked back down the Mall, toward the Washington Monument. The wind off the Potomac picked up and I bowed my head against it. I had thought it was cold earlier in the day. Now it seemed as cold here as out by Jupiter.

I was an orphan. My surrogate family, the Army, had become as irrelevant as it had been before the war. The woman I loved was buried three hundred million miles away. And now I had to face my next crisis, whatever it was going to be, without the person who had grown to be my sister.

I drifted down the brown lawns of Washington and wondered what I was going to do with the rest of my life.

In a quarter of an hour I reached the White House fence and paused to stare through the wrought iron across the south lawn.

The house lurked as pale as a ghost in the gloom. External floodlights would have sent the wrong, unfrugal signal to a nation and a world bowed beneath war spending. Jude Metzger's grandchildren would still be paying off the Slug War's budget deficits.

But had there been a choice? Evidently a lot of people thought so, in hindsight. Margaret Irons, the first African-American, not to mention the first woman, to inhabit the White House as President, hadn't agreed with those people. While I was away, winning that war in spite of my own incompetence, Irons was forced from office. I never even got old enough to vote for her.

I shrugged my collar up around my ears again, turned away from the fence, and walked farther into the darkness.

I hiked alongside the wind-wrinkled Reflecting Pool, unfrozen since this was July. People stayed indoors after dark since the war. Impact dust blotted out moonlight and starlight, and evenings were meat-locker cold even in July.

I passed by the World War II Veterans Memorial, the Korean War Veterans Memorial, and finally the Vietnam Veterans Memorial, a flat reminder of a historical blind alley.

Someday, I supposed, Slug War veterans would have their memorial. Washington still had empty lawns. But America seemed in no hurry. Ours had been a different war. In a world of billions, only ten thousand of us had fought. And we had been handpicked war orphans. We left no one behind to tie on yellow ribbons. And the mission had been so secret that the billions who didn't know us hadn't even known we had gone to battle until the war was over. Seven hundred of us lived through it.

What the world remembered about this war was sixty million civilians dead. And the diversion of the world economy to beat plowshares back into swords so completely that the evening lights of Washington were still out, three years after the war was won.

No wonder we hadn't rated much of a welcome-home celebration.

A car, just an urban electric, whispered up along the curb and the passenger side window dropped. "Come in out of the cold, soldier?"

The brunette in the business suit leaned across her center console.

My heart skipped. Ogling women was one thing. Actually becoming involved with one was another. Pooh had been gone nearly three years now. We had only 616 days together from the day I first spoke to her until the day I laid the last stone on her grave. My parents had been married eight years when Mom lost Dad. Had Mom ever gotten over it?

My head shook slowly. "I'm flattered. You're very attractive, but—"

Her head shook, too. "I'm not hitting on you. I'm very married. I recognized you in my headlights. It's cold outside. You just seem like you could use someone to talk to."

That I could.

A gust cut at my cheek and I climbed in the passenger door.

"Lynn Dey." We shook hands.

"What were you doing at the reception?"

She shrugged. "I write. Tech stuff free-lance. I thought there might be an article in the V-Star thing."

"And is there?"

She laughed. "Article, sure. Sale, no. The technology's too old."

"But the National Park Service makes a mean cheese-burger."

We both laughed at that.

We sat and talked while the wind rocked her little car as it sat at the curb.

She and her husband had moved from Minneapolis. Technical ghost-writing was a good living in the District. Most bureaucrats couldn't spell "declarative sentence."

She looked across at me. "The travel sounds exciting. People love you. Why so gloomy?"

I shrugged. "I'm telling the world that the Slugs are all gone so we don't have to spend money defending against them."

"That's not true?"

"That's not knowable. Between you and me, Lynn, I'd rather be safe than sorry."

We talked another hour. About the last Worldbowl, Broncos against Vikings. About her kids. About what makes a good cheeseburger. We laughed a lot.

She offered me a lift to my hotel. I smiled, out in the wind, as I closed her car door. "Nah. It's an infantry thing. We walk."

I was still smiling a half hour later, gone midnight, as I lapped the Mall again. People like Lynn Dey renewed my faith in humanity.

"General Wander?" The voice shouted, battling the wind. I jumped and turned my head.

The speaker wore a civilian overcoat, neck-tied collar peeking from between the lapels. But his eyes scanned me, and everything around me, like a soldier's eyes when walking point.

"If you're offering therapy, I already had mine for tonight."

He knit his brows. "No, sir. Nothing like that. Agent Carr. United States Secret Service, sir."

He wore an earpiece. Protection Service, not a counterfeit-money chaser. I cocked my head. "You want me?"

"I don't, sir." He turned his head and nodded. At the curb thirty yards away, limousine headlights shivered as it idled. "Someone would like to meet you."

I tugged up my collar. The limo would be out of the wind. This was my night to seek shelter in mysterious automobiles.

The protection-detail agent opened the rear door and swept his palm at the darkness within.

I ducked my head inside and let my eyes adjust for four heartbeats, before I could make out the silhouette pressed against the opposite door.

I barely recognized her.

NINETEEN

"JASON, CAN YOU SPARE A MOMENT?"

I had to lean farther into the limo to understand her. The 'zines had always carped that she was too soft-spoken to be President. Tonight, a rejected ex-President, Margaret Irons barely whispered.

Arms clasped across her chest, legs crossed, she coiled as thin as a doll twisted from pipe cleaners, and shivered in the wind that swirled through the open door. The Secret Service agent nudged the door against my butt, I climbed in and he shut it behind me.

"Jason."

Head bowed beneath the velour headliner, I shook her extended right pipe cleaner. "How . . . ?" I paused. No need asking how the Secret Service had found me. I fingered my chest. Implanted beneath every soldier's breastbone was a GPS tracking and Graves Registration dogtag chip. Government satellite tracking of natural persons was unconstitutional, but "soldier's civil rights" was an oxymoron. "How can I help you, Madame President?"

The smile that launched a hundred million ballots warmed that mahogany face as she shook her head. "You already have, Jason. All of you. I wanted to thank you for what you did."

The partition separating us from the driver's seat hushed open and the agent glanced back and asked, "Ma'am? Usual stop?"

President Irons nodded, the partition closed, and acceleration pushed me back into the seat cushions.

She sat back and eyed me. "You look older than I expected, Jason."

"They say it's not the years, ma'am, it's the mileage."

She smiled and fingered a parchment cheek. If six hundred million miles and one war had aged me, her White House days had robbed her of a lifetime. "You're glad to be home, Jason?"

"It doesn't feel like home, ma'am."

The limo slowed and stopped. We had only traveled a few hundred yards.

"I know the feeling. I grew up in Washington. My daddy was a janitor at the National Gallery. I worked here all my life in one job or another."

She said it like she had waited tables, not been a senator, secretary of state, and vice president.

Her shoulders sagged. "Now, I have to go out at night, so I don't run into someone who lost a husband in Pittsburgh or a child in New Orleans and thinks I should have prevented it."

"Madame President, nobody could have prevented it."

She shrugged. "Or I'd run into somebody who thought we paid too high a price to end it."

"That's stupid. We had to fight."

She shrugged again as the Secret Service agent rounded the car and opened the curbside door for us.

We stepped out into the cold darkness as she said, "They say the only thing worse than fighting a just war is not fighting it."

She turned to the protection-detail agent and touched his elbow. "Tom, Sarah packed sandwiches and coffee in the console. There'd be enough for an infantry squad even if Jason, here, eats for three. You get in out of this wind and help yourself."

The agent's lips tightened. I knew the look from my own personal security detail days. You didn't leave your subject. Unless ordered.

He nodded. "Yes, ma'am. Thank you."

She leaned into the wind, quivering but unbreakable as steel cable. Ahead of us stretched the steps of the Lincoln Memorial.

We made it halfway up the stairs before her knees quivered and I had to catch her by the elbow and boost her. Finally, we stood side by side in the dim lighting, at Lincoln's feet. We stood for three minutes until her ragged breathing smoothed. "I come here every night."

"Ma'am?"

She gazed up at Lincoln's unyielding marble face. "If there had been Instapolling in 1863, Lincoln's numbers would have been worse than mine were at the end. Sometimes I think Abe's the only person in this town I can still talk to. Politicians are a strange breed, aren't they, Jason?"

"I couldn't say. I'm no politician, Madame President."

She swiveled her head and looked up at me. "The best soldiers aren't."

I looked around at the marble walls, carved in gold with the Gettysburg Address and Lincoln's Second Inaugural. "Then why me, ma'am?"

She stepped to the wall and ran her fingers along the marble. "Do you understand what your baby-kissing is about, Jason?"

"Yes, ma'am. The public needs reassurance."

She shook her head. "The war's over. The public's already reassured about that. We won. We paid a terrible price. The issue is where America and the world go now. The military is expensive, Jason."

The image of the crater that had been Cairo flicked across my mind. Mankind needed every nickel to rebuild the world. "Civilian spending's good, ma'am."

She nodded. "But in politics it isn't enough to be good. Something else has to be bad."

"Ma'am? I'm new here, but that seems stupid."

"It is. But if things turn sour, they need an unsympathetic target. They also need one who hasn't learned to shoot back. And one who has skeletons in his closet."

I smiled. "Ma'am, I'm no target. I've made mistakes but I'm not ashamed of them. And I figure if I tell the truth I can never get in trouble."

She stared down at the marble floor, shook her head, and sighed. "You *are* new here."

We left the Lincoln Memorial after that. The ex-President of the United States gave me the twenty-five-cent driving tour of the city she knew better than anyone else in the world, while we ate ham sandwiches. Then her limo dropped me at my hotel.

She leaned across the seat as I stepped out. "One last tip, Jason. In this town, if you don't want to see it on the *Washington Post* frontscreen, don't say it!"

TWENTY

THE NEXT MORNING I LAY IN BED while pale light filtered through my bedroom's curtains. Jeeb hovered at the door, opened it with one forelimb, then swooped into the hall and returned with our complimentary *Washington Post*.

He dropped it on the floor next to the bed, settled in front of it, and trained his optics on the front page. Next to the masthead, the weather forecast called for cold, gray, and dry. Like every other day since the war started. "No. Not now. I need to think."

He folded all six limbs beneath himself, drew in his antennae, and shut down with a sigh. I laced my fingers behind my head and stared at the chandelier.

Over the last two days, Tway had educated me, alright. Infantry had no place in the post-war world. People like Brace, and the zoomie projects he managed, were all the military the world needed now. In fact, me vegetating under linen sheets like I was doing at the moment, while drawing major general pay, was taking bread from the mouths of Egyptians and Iowans and Panamanians for no reason.

Today was the last day to opt out of the Army under the

Gratitude Act. If I did, Tway could no longer drag me around like a show dog. I'd collect a pension big enough that I could sit around and write a proper autobiography. If I didn't want to lend my name to an Aaron Grodt holo, I wouldn't have to. If I wanted to say Slugs might still be around, I could. I shuddered even at that thought. Maybe I wouldn't go so far as to say that.

The smart thing was to join Munchkin and Brumby as a civilian. I nodded to myself. Command experience had made me decisive.

Opt-out was simple. Any GEF veteran just talked up the Website, confirmed ID, then checked Box Number One, orally. You were prospectively discharged officially as of that moment, even if out-processing took longer.

I smiled. That could wait. My last soldierly act would be to order whatever I wanted for breakfast. I waved up room service on the phone.

"How may we help you, General?"

I felt a pang. There was a certain cachet to the title. I'd miss that.

"You have any protein bars?"

"We used to carry them, sir. But the guests complained they tasted, well, like dung."

I grinned at the ceiling and stretched. "Perfect. What do you recommend, then?"

The phone whined. Emergency override. I frowned up at the crown molding and said, "Hello?"

"Put me on visual." It was Tway.

I waved her up, then raised my hand and shaded her image against the window light, because her complexion looked purple.

It *was* purple. She seemed to be stalking down a hallway.

"I'm on my way to your room. Have you seen this morning's *Washington Post*?"

TWENTY-ONE

I SAT UP, swung my pajamaed legs over the bedside, nudged Jeeb off the morning paper, and picked it up. Below the weather forecast and masthead I read:

Ganymede's Hero Claims Slugs Still a Threat
Wander Calls Defense Cuts Bogus

"What the hell? I never said—"

Jeeb shot to the door and opened it. Tway stepped through and stood in front of me, arms crossed. Jeeb hovered, then dropped a probe against my carotid artery. He did that if my breathing elevated.

The article's byline read "Lynn Dey, Special to the *Washington Post*."

"Fuck!" I slapped the page.

"Then you did say it?" Tway's eyes burned me.

I pointed at the sub-headline. "Well, I never used the word 'bogus.' I didn't know she was a reporter!"

Tway leaned forward. "She lied to you?"

"Well, she said she was a writer. I didn't think—"

Tway's breath hissed between her teeth. "Jason, how many times have we had this talk?"

I slumped. "Too many, Ruth."

This was the end of nightly mints on my pillow. Which was fine by me. "Politics is impossible. You have to balance things when neither way is right. I'm tired of hotel sheets. I'm tired of eating dung bars to look prettier. I'm tired of being told what I shouldn't say. I was going to tell you. I'm opting out."

Ruth shook her head. "Too late for that."

"Huh?"

"This administration has sweated bullets. It has called in every favor from every legislator with a defense contractor in his or her state or district. It has finagled around every possible filibuster. It has set in stone for next week a vote on an appropriately lean defense budget."

"It'll be leaner with one less general to pay."

Tway said, "Lieutenant."

"Huh?"

"Read the fine print. You can't opt out under the Gratitude Act if you're the subject of pending disciplinary proceedings."

"I'm not under discipline."

"You are now. Your demotion to lieutenant was filed two hours ago. You're in the Army until your demotion's final."

"And when will that be?"

"When the Army says so."

Now there was the military circularity I had come to know. "But if I'm such a screw-up, why do you still want me in? Me opting out is exactly what you should want."

"Because we don't have a replacement, yet. We've

invested in you as our poster child. If you stay in and do what you're told from now on, your years of service will still be adjusted by the Gratitude Act formula. You'll still be allowed to retire with an honorable-discharge General's pension."

Jeeb buzzed. My blood pressure had hit pre-stroke levels.

"And if I don't? I could talk to Grodt. My autobiography would sell better with a chapter about how the Hero of Ganymede got railroaded."

Tway smiled and shook her head. "We can add lots of chapters to your bio, if that's how you want to play it."

"Huh?"

What had President Irons told me last night, a million years ago? In Washington, it's not enough to be good. Something else has to be bad.

"Ruth, you know I never did anything bad."

"That won't matter to the media. Let's pretend you go public. Here's how it will play out." She pulled a silver saucer from her pocket. "I'm stenobotting this."

She cleared her throat. "Lieutenant Wander, you've had your share of disciplinary problems in the service, haven't you?"

Crap. "I'm not proud of everything I've done. But I'm a better person and a better soldier for it now." That sounded pretty good.

Ruth ran down my Basic training record. Brawling; insubordination; half-ass drug abuse, just some ill-timed Prozac II, and a horrible training accident that resulted in the death of a soldier I called my friend.

I rebutted. "Those incidents were resolved. There's

no double jeopardy under the Uniform Code of Military Justice."

Ruth nodded. "Lieutenant Wander, let's turn from your early history in the service to more recent events."

I breathed easier. As an eighteen-year-old wiseass, Basic training had been my soldierly low point. What happened since I shaped up would be better.

"You were the first soldier to actually encounter a Pseudocephalopod Warrior."

"Yeah. On the moon. We recovered the Slug's body." I straightened up. I'd nearly gotten killed, but the intelligence we gained helped us win the war.

She frowned. "When you returned to Luna Base, an investigation was convened into the circumstances of the prisoner's death."

My heart thumped. "He was never a prisoner. We fought. He died."

"Hmmm. So the Army's official investigation concluded." Ruth paused the stenobot. It sounded like I had abused a prisoner!

"Lieutenant, regulations strictly prohibit confraternization among combat troops?"

"Absolutely." Crap. I knew where this was going. "However a commander in the field has broad discretion—"

She cut me off, again. "Regulations weren't followed during the Ganymede campaign, were they?"

"General Cobb decided you couldn't coop up five thousand men with five thousand women in a spaceship for six hundred days and expect—"

"Regulations weren't followed during the Ganymede campaign, true?"

I nodded. "True. But it didn't affect the soldiers' performance."

"Not even the pregnant ones?"

I felt myself redden as adrenaline tingled through me. "There was only one pregnancy. A soldier married to another member of the Joint Force." I had given Munchkin away at the shipboard wedding, myself.

"One you know of. Since more than ninety percent of those soldiers were killed and buried on Ganymede, you don't know how many were pregnant, do you?"

"Uh, no."

"Or whether their condition got them killed?"

I had chewed Munchkin out, myself, for letting herself get pregnant when After-Pills had been nonprescription for decades.

I drew a breath. "That's unfair—"

"Let's move to another topic. Substance abuse got a friend of yours killed in Basic."

"We've been through that."

She nodded. "So you of all people know how strictly the armed services regulate substance abuse."

I nodded. Now what?

"During your tenure as commander of GEF, did your troops manufacture and consume alcohol?"

She was talking about the still that my guys had maintained on Ganymede.

"I—"

"And you knew it?"

We had nothing else to do on Ganymede during seven months stranded following the war's end. My survivors had been through hell. Of course I had looked the other way.

"Not officially."

"Ah." An imperial nod.

Did Ruth think anyone cared whether GIs cranked out a little bootleg moonshine? Aboard *Excalibur,* Brace, the ship's master, no less, had served rum at Captain's Breakfast, himself!

Ruth reached into her pocket and dropped papers on the mattress beside me. "Recognize these?"

They were just the salvage-title paperwork that declared Jeeb scrap and transferred ownership of him to me. "Sure. I bought a battle-damaged Tactical Observation Transport. Its Wrangler was—"

Beside my ear, Jeeb's circuits whined. I swear the noise was "Uh-oh."

"How much does a TOT cost taxpayers?"

"Lots. That's why even a division-size unit's Table of Organization and Equipment allows for only one." A Manhattan skyscraper cost less than Jeeb. Even allowing for government-procurement overengineering, that was serious money for a mechanical cockroach no bigger than a watermelon.

She nodded. "And what did you pay for this unit?"

I shuffled papers. Howard had said a couple months' pay. Of course, that amount was a few seconds interest on Jeeb's original sticker price.

Ruth switched her Chipad to hand calculate, punched it, then showed me the display. There were seven more zeroes tacked on the original price compared to what I had bought Jeeb for. "That discount's correct, isn't it?"

I shrugged. "I guess."

"Quite a bargain, wouldn't you say?"

"It wasn't a question of a bargain." It was a question

of loyalty and friendship and duty and of adopting an orphan.

"Of course not. Any citizen could have made the same deal. If he or she had the inside information you did."

I stood up. "I don't have to take this. Maybe I'll take Aaron Grodt up on his book deal. I'll tell the world what a hypocritical, screwed-up mess—"

She dropped another packet facedown in front of me.

I peeled it off the bed linens and turned it over. A Grodt International book contract. The advance number was filled in and it was obscenely large.

"If you sign Grodt's book contract you'll look like—"

A cheap opportunist. Besides, the producer who *Variety* called "The Sultan of Slapstick Sex" wasn't likely to let me publish a sociologically responsible exposé.

Ruth's eyes softened. "You see? You can't play Zorro even if you want to."

I sat back down on the bed, elbows on knees. Jeeb perched on my shoulder. "You just showed me how you can get rid of me. You think I'm a hopeless fuckup. But you're still helping me. Why?"

She shrugged. "Maybe I believe that greatness is your destiny."

I snorted. "One other person said that. But he's . . ." Ari Klein had looked at me with dark, deep-set eyes when he had said it. Ruth had Ari's eyes. My heart skipped. "Tway. That's not your maiden name."

"Ari was my brother." She stroked Jeeb.

"He lost his parents but he couldn't have gotten into GEF if he had a live sister."

"Would you have lied to get a ticket to Ganymede?"

In a heartbeat.

"You spend enough time in Washington, you learn how to tweak government records."

I pointed at the 'bot on my shoulder. "You put up with me to be close to what's left of your brother."

She shook her head and blinked, but a tear escaped onto her cheek. "I put up with you because my brother said you and I were the only family he had left. Jason, if you and I aren't together, we're orphans."

My throat swelled and I blinked back my own tear.

"Okay. What next?"

"First, nobody knows there's a demotion pending. The President insisted on it, to keep a sword over your head."

"He doesn't need it."

"That's what I told him, but there it is. And this record-ing. We keep it as a road map to court-martial if you do try to play Zorro. Stay the course and I can undo all of it." She clapped her hands. "Okay. We'll spin the story from our side. You were misquoted. For now, you go on like noth-ing happened, attend the big Ganymede Egg Cutting to-morrow down at Canaveral and smile a lot. And stop talking nonsense about Slugs coming back."

I stepped to the window and pulled back the drape. The Potomac almost sparkled in half sunshine. I took a deep breath. "Fair enough. It's just print on a page. Not the end of the world as we know it."

That was still twenty-four hours away.

TWENTY-TWO

THE PSEUDOCEPHALOPOD TECHNOLOGY RECOVERY CENTER
at Canaveral employed six thousand scientists, engineers,
cafeteria cooks, and janitors.

The morning after my impolitic headline ran, every
one of those employees who wasn't pushing a spectro-
scope, a spatula, or a broom had squeezed into the auditorium that occupied the Center's sub-basement. The
auditorium seating was upholstered blood red, what
could be seen of it beneath the crowd. Ceiling fixtures
gleamed in sleek glass and chrome.

Three holo crews occupied the front seat row. Onstage, Brace sat with the governor of Florida while the
lab-coated research director stood at a podium, thanked
everybody for coming, and explained that from the ashes
of war might come better things for better living through
chemistry.

Also onstage, Howard represented the Spook House;
me, the veterans of Ganymede; and Munchkin, in civvies
with Jude in tow, the rest of the United Nations and their
forces. We were relegated to a corner where an earphoned
technician sat at a console. Ruth sat behind us, just off-

stage. She didn't have me on a short leash, but I suspected she carried one in her purse, just in case.

I leaned toward the console-minder and lifted one earflap. "Are you the sound man?"

He shook his head. "I monitor signals."

"What signals?"

"Exactly." He shrugged. "But it's a living."

That was what this ceremony was truly about. Nobody really thought The Football was the gift that would lead us to cure cancer or create calorie-free cheeseburgers. But the project sure spread paychecks across eastern Florida.

All eyes focused on the spotlighted table to the podium's right. In a titanium cradle nested The Football, a featureless egg, shimmering dull Slug-metal blue.

Brace spoke about duty, technology, and the wonderfulness of the Navy, then stepped out into the audience, so as not to upstage the governor of Florida.

The governor wore an orange-and-blue tie adorned with some crocodile. When he stepped to the podium, the holo recorders fired up with a popping chorus like New Year's Eve in a champagne factory. The governor extolled the virtues of Floridian labor and—I am not making this up—orange juice.

The research director stepped alongside The Football.

Between gleaming rails above the blue egg hung an automated diamond saw assembly, its start lever tied with a blue ribbon.

Jude squirmed on Munchkin's lap.

I whispered, "He's a handful today."

She said, "I don't know why. He isn't running a fever."

Howard leaned toward me. "I've been thinking about The Football."

"Me, too. I've been thinking you should have left it behind on Ganymede. This is a circus."

"What you said yesterday about how we were supposed to find it. There's a mythological parallel."

I smiled. Howard had found a mythological parallel to a political pork barrel. He whispered, "I just had a thought. We need to stop this."

I glanced over my shoulder at Ruth. She frowned at us the way my first-grade teacher used to do before she asked whether us boys had something we wanted to share with the rest of the class. "Howard, there are three thousand people and the governor of thirty-four percent of the world's citrus fruit production in this auditorium. We're on live international holo. You can't stop this show because you had a thought!"

"Brace can!" Howard slid from his seat, stepped backstage around Ruth, and emerged headed into the audience, hurrying toward Brace.

The research director reached for the start lever to scattered applause.

He rotated the lever and the saw's whine echoed across the suddenly still auditorium.

Jude shrieked and thrashed in Munchkin's arms.

The vibrating saw blade inched down toward The Football's blue skin.

Munchkin stood and carried Jude offstage.

The saw's edge bit into The Football.

"Aaah!" The console-minder next to me tore off his headset.

I leaned toward him. "What?"

The console-minder rubbed his ears and whispered, "I dunno. Microburst transmission."

In the audience, Howard waved his arms, his face dark.

The racked spotlights above the stage flickered.

Then they fell on us, along with the ceiling.

TWENTY-THREE

I LAY ON SOMETHING SHARP, stabbing the small of my back. Red-light bursts, crackling in air fogged with dust that stank of sulfur and ozone, tore the darkness around me. Men wailed. I moved one hand, tried to move the other, and screamed as shock shot up my arm.

I had died and gone to hell.

The pops, cracks, and smells sparked from severed electrical wiring. The red light pulsing from a sputtering EMERGENCY EXIT ONLY sign hung crooked at my vision's limit.

I turned my head. The console-minder lay beside me, his chest crushed under a jagged concrete block as large as an urban runabout. From the block's opposite end protruded trousered legs, a lab-coat hem, and the overturned saw, its blade gleaming like a crimson saber in the sparks' light. The research director.

I rolled my head in the opposite direction. The governor of Florida lay on his side, weeping. Two steel reinforcing bars thrust through him, splitting his crocodile tie, now crimson instead of orange. Blood pulsed from the wound, enlarging a pool on the floor as large as a throw rug. He wouldn't weep much longer.

A small figure crept across jumbled concrete and furniture. "Jason?" It was Munchkin. Blood streaked her cheek, her right sleeve was missing, and her hose were torn, but she was ambulatory. She waved a flashlight, probably from the kit by the EMERGENCY EXIT sign.

"What happened, Munchkin?"

"My baby. I can't find my baby!"

She reached me, saw the governor, and sucked in her breath.

She trembled, flung herself across a concrete boulder as big as an old-fashioned television box, and threw up her guts.

The governor stopped weeping. Electricity sparked and sputtered. Something dripped. From a distance echoed muffled screams.

Munchkin pulled herself to her knees, then turned to examine me. Drool and puke strings dangled from her chin and her eyes watered. She muttered to Allah.

"Munchkin, I can't see what's pinning my left arm. I can't help you find Jude if I can't move."

She shone the light down my left uniform sleeve and I gasped. The same concrete slab that had crushed the console-minder and the research director pinned my little and third fingers as flat as Kleenex. My shock must have been severe or I would have felt it more.

Someone moaned. Munchkin swung the light. Ruth lay pinned by a tabletop that had collapsed across her thighs. Her face was pale, powdered with concrete dust. "Help me."

Munchkin looked down at my crushed hand.

I nodded toward Ruth. "See about her."

"But Jude—"

"He'll turn up."

We had been through enough together that Munchkin nodded, then crawled toward Ruth. The tabletop weighed easily eight hundred pounds. Munchkin weighed a soft 102 dripping wet. I said, "Find a lever."

She jerked her light around the room, the beam lancing through roiling concrete dust. It flashed across metal.

"There!"

She swung the light back. A pipe as big around as a garden hose ran from floor to ceiling. Munchkin took it in two fingers and tugged. "It won't budge!"

"Goddammit! *Pull* the son of a bitch!"

She stood, grasped the pipe in both hands, and threw herself backward.

Metal popped and a six-foot pipe segment popped free from its upper and lower joints. Munchkin staggered backward, holding the segment like a tightrope walker.

Something hissed. Mercaptan-sulfur smell pricked my nose.

"Crap."

She turned to me. "What?"

"We snapped a gas line."

Electric sparks crackled.

Munchkin played the flashlight around the space we were in. The ceiling's collapse had split the auditorium in two. It seemed half the building had fallen on the holo crews, isolating us from the rest of the auditorium. My bright idea was now filling our little pocket of hell with methane gas. The screams of the audience's survivors leaked through to us across a concrete-and-steel wall formed by the building's collapse. It might be bad over there, but to stay here meant quick and certain death by asphyxiation or immolation. The screams seemed strongest at a dark spot forty feet from us.

I pointed with my free hand. "That place over there. It's a gap you should be able to crawl through, to the other side. Get out of here!"

"But the baby. And you—"

"Tway first. Then me. Then we find Jude. Everything's gonna be fine." There wouldn't even be time for me. But if I could damp her panic over the baby, I might persuade her to save herself and Ruth.

She scurried across rubble, wedged the gas pipe under a tabletop corner, and leaned her weight on the pipe. It bent like a Tootsie Roll and the tabletop didn't budge.

She knelt alongside the table and heaved her shoulder against it like a blocking lineman. Nothing.

She drew back and plunged against the tabletop again, screaming like a karate champ. Maybe the tabletop twitched.

The gas smelled stronger. The room was becoming a bomb. I looked up at the sparking wiring. It was everywhere, and out of reach, besides.

If I could push, too, we might spring Tway. I tugged at my pinioned hand. Pain flashed purple spots before my eyes but I remained stuck fast.

"Munchkin! The saw!" I pointed my free hand at the saw assembly that lay alongside the research director's legs.

She turned her palms up. "What?"

"Bring me the saw blade."

"Why?" She coughed into her fist as the gas hissed louder.

"Now!"

She crept to the machine and tugged at the blade. "Aaagh!"

"Loosen the chuck first."

She freed the blade, then knelt alongside me, turning it in her hands like a jagged knife and eyeing the tabletop. "This is stronger than the pipe, but it's too short, Jason."

I breathed through clenched teeth. "Not a lever."

She looked down at my hand, the concrete's edge just below my knuckles. Her eyes widened and she shook her head. "I can't!"

"I'm gonna lose the fingers either way."

"The blade's not sterile."

The gas choked me.

Ruth pounded her fists against the tabletop that imprisoned her.

"Munchkin! Come on."

She held the blade in two hands, poised above my knuckles, her eyes closed. The blade quivered. Munchkin sobbed, her face red in the EMERGENCY sign's glow.

Ruth yelled, "It's too late!"

Munchkin didn't move, didn't open her eyes.

I balled the fist of my free hand and raised it over the saw blade.

Sparks crackled.

I squeezed my own eyes shut and pounded my fist down. Daylight brightness sparked beyond the lids.

TWENTY-FOUR

I SCREAMED AND CLUTCHED MY FREED HAND in the other, eyes still squeezed shut. I couldn't look at the place where the rest of me was, couldn't look at the stumps. I tugged out a handkerchief and pressed it to my self-inflicted wound, then opened my eyes. My handkerchief was already red and as sodden as a dishrag.

I pushed Munchkin with my clasped hands until we both knelt beside the tabletop. "On three."

She nodded, vacantly.

I counted. We heaved. Nothing.

"Again, Munchkin."

Something creaked.

"Third time's the charm, Munch."

This time, my shoulder hit the tabletop so hard that I saw stars and forgot about the screaming throb in my ruined hand.

The tabletop raised six inches and I wedged myself underneath it.

Munchkin seemed to wake up and dragged Ruth free. I started to shrink back, then saw a tiny shoe. I grabbed with

my good hand and yanked. Jude popped free, I dragged
him out, and the top fell, exploding a cement dust cloud.

"Go, Munchkin!" Gas so thickened the air that I could
scarcely catch my breath. No time to decide whether Jude
or Ruth should be moved.

Munchkin grabbed Ruth by one of her arms. I grasped
the other with one hand, tucked Jude under my other arm
like a flour sack, and we scuttled toward the opening.

Ruth screamed.

Munchkin paused.

"No. Go!"

Munchkin dove under the gap and disappeared. I followed. Ruth's shoe caught on rebar as I low-crawled
under a hundred tons of concrete. Something creaked, six
inches above my head. I pushed Jude's body through the
opening. Arms reached from the other side and pulled
Jude through to safety. Gold admiral's stripes shone on
one torn sleeve, field-grade officer's stripes on the other.
Brace and Howard.

As I tugged Ruth loose and pushed her under the gap,
I saw yellow flame bloom along an electrical cord behind
me, across the stage space.

I rolled under the gap, free on the other side. Brace was
already hammering debris with a stanchion.

The stage chamber exploded in an orange burst.

The debris Brace pounded gave way, crashed down,
and sealed the auditorium off from the blast that shook the
floor.

I lay motionless on the auditorium floor. On this side of
the barrier wounded sobbed. On the other side, flames
rumbled and cremated the bodies we had left behind the
debris wall.

Brace knelt beside me and opened a white metal first-aid kit. He bandaged my stumps, handed me a morphtab, and fed two to Ruth.

Her abdomen had been perforated by a table leg as big around as a Louisville Slugger. I was no medic but her pelvis appeared to have been crushed. Our efforts had likely just altered Ruth's final resting place by thirty feet.

Munchkin looked up at the sagging ceiling. Jude conscious and squirming in her arms. A hundred feet of pork-barrel concrete separated us from daylight. "What do you think happened?" she asked.

I shook my head. "Howard seemed to know."

Ruth moaned.

Whatever had happened up above, us survivors were unlikely to learn.

I stared at what was left of my hand as darkness shrunk my field of vision like I was entering a tunnel. Light and consciousness disappeared.

The next thing I heard was birds chirping.

TWENTY-FIVE

Watery sunlight bathed me.

Thok-thok-thok.

Above me drifted orange emergency helicopters, and, silently, Jeeb.

"How you doing, sir?" An upside-down face peered at me through the face shield of Eternad infantry armor, but this armor was yellow-and-orange-striped, emergency gear. Eternads heat, cool, insulate, and absorb shock as well as they stop bullets.

"What happened?"

Chirp-chirp-chirp.

The gurney on which I lay had a wheel that squeaked as the armored medic pushed it. The smell and crackle of fires pressed around me.

"Nobody knows, sir." He waved a gauntleted hand. "We hear Canaveral's the only place that got hit."

I levered myself up on one elbow. The Canaveral main gate parking lot flickered with the lights of jumbled emergency vehicles and sizzled with the static of firefighter-net radios. Beyond the lot, though, the whole complex was gone. A smoking, black crater a hundred feet deep, littered with bursts of fire, remained.

"We got out of that?"

"Ms. Tway's GPS beeper showed her still alive. She's Cabinet-level. They get priority in emergencies, sir. So she was the first target we went after. Rappelled down an elevator shaft and there you all were. You were in the right place at the right time."

In the distance, a woman wept. He paused. "Sorry. I guess that's not true."

"There was a lady with a baby?"

"Cuts, contusions. They're around here someplace."

"Tway?"

The medic shook his head. "Not gonna make it. Internal injuries. Blood loss. But she's in the same ambulance we're headed for."

The medic jacked my gurney into the ambulance, next to Ruth's. They had sawed off the table leg but the stub made a tent out of the bloodstained sheet that covered her belly.

The medic asked Ruth, "Ma'am, hate to bother you, but we found this down in the sub-basement, near where we found you. It's got a locator beacon on it, with your ID code. So we figured it must be important. The data's still retrievable."

The medic held up the stenobot that had recorded my demotion and all my transgressions. It was smoke-blackened and bent. "What should we do with it, ma'am?"

The medic held my future in his hands.

Ruth lolled her head toward me, her eyes glazed. "That? It's nothing. Back a truck over it, then pitch it back in the crater."

She paused, squeezed her eyes shut, then opened them. "And get General Wander, here, to a plane. The world will figure out that it needs him. Somewhere."

"Yes, ma'am." The medic fingered his audiophone.

An Electruk squealed to a stop behind us and firebots unfolded their legs and dropped from its flanks to the asphalt, like waking crimson spiders.

Ruth shivered. I pushed myself up on an elbow, reached across with my good hand, and covered her bare shoulder with a sheet.

Jeeb climbed Ruth's gurney and perched on the silver rail at her feet, backlit by fires. His circuits whined.

Ruth smiled at Jeeb, then pointed past him at the firebots, her hand scarcely raised above her chest. "It's their destiny to put out this fire, Jason. Yours, too."

Braap. Braap.

A firebot test-fired its water cannon. A gust blew droplets from the pulses back through the ambulance's open doors, across Jeeb.

Ruth said, "Thanks. Jason, remember how I told you that if you don't—"

"Don't talk. Relax."

She set her jaw. "If you don't want to see it in the *Post,* don't say it?"

"I'll remember."

"No. Forget that. Always say it." She coughed again and a blood thread trickled from her nostril. I wiped it away.

"Rest. You're tired."

"Jason, don't ever get tired of being right." She closed her eyes.

The medic checked the read on her vitals, then disconnected the monitor and pulled the sheet over Ruth Klein-Tway's head.

Jeeb's whine rose to a wail. Firebot overspray trickled from his optic sensors and ran down his ventral plating. Or he wept. That was impossible, of course.

Behind Jeeb, firebots marched into the flames, turrets swiveling. They were doing what they were destined for, hunting the roots of this hell, digging for some way to make it stop.

I squeezed my gurney's rail until it shook. I didn't know yet what had just happened. But I was going to find out.

TWENTY-SIX

THE NEXT MORNING I was one of forty senior officers who climbed down from a bus, duffels in hand, like a trainee platoon, at the rusty-doored mouth to a tunnel mouth dug into old Cheyenne Mountain, above Colorado Springs.

The Alternate National Military Command Center had officially been at Offut Air Force Base in Nebraska for years. But ALNMICC was now a target. A target like the Pentagon or the Kremlin, obvious and indefensible against whatever had destroyed Canaveral. So Cheyenne Mountain had become the alternate to the alternate.

To give you an idea how old the Cheyenne Mountain complex was, it was built to command American air defenses against Communist nuclear bomber fleets screaming in on America over the North Pole.

Since the Geneva Anti-Terrorism Compact, Cheyenne Mountain had deteriorated. A civilian led us into the mountain. He wore jeans, a T-shirt, and scuffed lace-ups. A janitor, really. He led us through an open blast door as thick as a tail-standing bus, hung on barrel-sized hinges that had not budged in years, based on their dust coating. Not, I supposed, since the Russians figured out that after a half century of communism in the world's biggest country, Denmark had a bigger gross national product than they did.

We double-timed four hundred yards into the mountain, descending a rock-walled tunnel, our steps echoing in chill, dead air. Theater-grade officers hustling like trainees. It looked like the Fun Run at a West Point reunion.

My hand throbbed and the loss of even the few ounces that two fingers weighed unbalanced me. There was something mentally unbalancing about amputation, too. It would have been more traumatizing if they hadn't shot me up. The medics had implanted a Loc-Anest dispenser in my hand subcutaneously and in a duffel pocket I carried a bottle of pills that hit like bombs and were about as big.

I was lucid enough to have absorbed the bare bones of what we knew. It took no crystal ball to guess that just as Earth was starting to get back to normal, the slimy little animated zucchinis had sucker-punched us again.

Initial briefing was in an auditorium swollen with the flat smell of mildew and the nose-prick of disinfectant. Like the rest of Cheyenne Mountain, the old barn got demothballed when the Slug War had started. Then, in the finest military tradition of digging holes, then filling them up again, Cheyenne Mountain got remothballed when we won. Now we were scurrying to spruce the place up again.

Brace briefed from a podium on a low stage. Howard sat to Brace's right, a Chipboard on his lap.

Brace's eyes had sunk into a pale face. The impregnable defense of the planet, *his* impregnable defense, had failed. His command had been wiped out after having failed to fire a return shot. But he had no ship left to go down with.

His podium sat left of a flatscreen that filled the wall behind the stage. He cleared his throat, the lights dimmed like in an old film theater, and shuffling and coughing died as fast as a swatted fly.

Brace began, "Yesterday, at 1605 hours Zulu, UNSF remote-sensing pickets deployed in geosynchronous orbit detected an incursion into intra-lunar space by a presumed-hostile object."

The wall lit with a still image of space. Stars salted blackness. At the screen's center glowed a slim red streak. Brace turned toward the screen and stirred a circle around the streak with his green laser pointer.

"How many hits beside Canaveral?" I asked.

Brace faced back toward us. "Just the one."

"Interceptor Command couldn't stop just *one* Projectile?" The general who spoke rolled his eyes. His lapel brass was Air Defense Artillery. They spent their careers in air-conditioned bunkers, following manuals to the letter.

Brace's head snapped back like he'd been slapped. "This wasn't a Projectile. Not as we know them. It was too fast to catch and too small to hit."

"Nuclear?"

Brace shook his head. "Usual Pseudocephalopod methodology. Solid object moving at high speed to destroy by application of kinetic energy."

The ADA general said, "Projectiles during the Blitz came in at thirty thousand miles per hour. That was plenty fast. But by the end of the Blitz we were knocking them down. The Slugs are still just throwing rocks at us and you can't stop them?"

Howard stepped to the podium and leaned in to the mike. "The Projectiles that hit us during the Blitz moved at the speed they did so they could maneuver, hit their targets. This one appears to have homed in on a microburst signal."

The Football. All those Footballs, scattered across Ganymede so we couldn't miss them. "A goddamn Trojan Horse?" I spit it out into the silence.

Howard nodded. "We only brought back one, by fortuitous coincidence."

Coincidence my ass. Howard would have filled up *Excalibur* with Footballs like it was an Easter basket if I'd let him wander around Ganymede picking them up. The Slugs seemed to know human traits like curiosity like the backs of their hands. Except Slugs had no hands.

Howard continued. "As the general said, Blitz Projectiles moved at thirty thousand miles per hour. That's eight miles per second. Four times faster than a Scramjet cruises."

Somebody whistled.

Howard ran his laser pointer along the red track of whatever had smeared Canaveral. "Our best estimate is that when this object began to leave this visible track, due to atmospheric friction, it was moving at *one hundred thousand* miles per second. Too fast for our technology to record a visible image, much less intercept it."

The Air Defense general shook his head. "That has to be wrong. That's more than half the speed of light. The Rocket Equation—"

"We believe the Pseudocephalopod has bypassed the Rocket Equation."

I raised my hand. "Howard, in English?"

He nodded. "Any reaction-based propulsion system, a rocket for practical purposes, can ultimately reach a speed no greater than twice its nozzle-exhaust velocity. You'll recall that Tsilkovsky postulated this in 1903."

"Who could ever forget?"

"A chemical-fuel rocket like the old space shuttle blew out at less than three miles per second. The fastest it could ever have gone would have been six miles per second. Worse, top speed is proportional to the natural logarithm of the percentage of mass left after the fuel's gone."

I rolled my eyes.

Howard scowled. "For heaven's sake, Jason! It's only rocket science!"

He tapped his pointer on his palm and stared at the ceiling. "In other words, according to the Rocket Equation, a rocket that's 99.9 percent fuel—you could strap a fuel tank as big as the moon to the space shuttle—would take a thousand years to travel one light-year. The fastest propulsion systems we've conceived, even theoretically, are antimatter-fueled rockets and nuclear-fusion Scramjets. They could perhaps, if they accelerated long enough, attain half the velocity this object did. So, inferentially, this was no rocket. Besides, the configuration of current Pseudocephalopod vessels shows no trace of conventional rocket exhausts."

"How do you know? You said you couldn't see this object. That it moved too fast."

Howard nodded. "That's true. We couldn't. But the rest of the fleet's moving slower."

Somebody whispered, "Fleet?"

TWENTY-SEVEN

THE SCREEN BESIDE HOWARD DISSOLVED into a new picture. Howard said, "Visible-light optical image from the early days of the Blitz. The Shanghai Projectile, as photographed from Palomar Observatory."

The object was too familiar, an iridescent-blue egg, whorled like a snail shell. A Projectile, the Slug War's primary strategic weapon. As huge as flying football stadiums, Projectiles had vaporized Earth cities like extinction-event meteors and the impact dust they exploded into the stratosphere plunged us toward a new ice age within months. Projectiles had killed my mother and sixty million more human beings. I shuddered at the sight.

Howard said, "Destructive power is a function of kinetic energy. At thirty thousand miles per hour, objects this huge obliterated whole cities. But kinetic energy is one-half its mass times the square of its velocity."

I looked around. Brace was nodding. Equations were tidy. They always gave the same answer if you plugged in the same values. They never left you scrambling around in the dark. Brace, I guessed, loved equations.

Howard continued. "If you plug in half the speed of light

for velocity, give or take, then, depending on the density of yesterday's object, yesterday's object may have been no bigger than a refrigerator. A thrown medicine ball may knock you down. But a bullet will kill you."

Brace asked, "You're saying the Slugs expected us to pick up this lure? Like dumb animals?"

Howard nodded. "We expect mice to take cheese in traps."

"We're smarter than mice!"

"So we thought."

At the turn of the century, we thought we were too smart to let nineteen fanatics with box cutters bring down the biggest buildings in New York. Hindsight was perfect. However we got there, we were in a war, now. This debate was pointless. I raised my hand. "You said there were Slug ships?"

Howard pressed his remote. A second object's picture faded in as he said, "Scales are equalized."

Alongside the Shanghai Projectile, and about the same size, floated another Slug-blue vessel. Howard said, "This image was gathered by telescopic sensors aboard a picket satellite."

My hand throbbed beneath its dressing. I bit back nausea.

The new Slug vessel was as enormous as the old Projectile, but different. Humans are used to balance in our machines. Our machines echo the bilateral and radial symmetry of animal life on Earth. This blue-black monstrosity bulged unevenly, covered in overlapping plates, like a tumorous cockroach. From one tapered end—I thought of it as the front end—protruded six armlike crescents, from the rear and from one side pointed two cones, like thorns or stingers.

A similar vessel was visible behind the first one, tiny in the distance. An odd thing about the new photo was that, unlike the older, no stars were visible in the background.

Howard's pointer slashed across the objects like a fencer's foil. "We believe these to be war-fighting vessels for space combat. Fighters, if you will. Albeit enormous ones. The forward six-arm array we don't understand. The United Nations universal phonetic designator for this model is 'Firewitch.' We identify variants Alpha and Bravo, distinguished by the number of forward arms. This six-arm model is the Alpha. A Firewitch Bravo deploys eight arms."

I sighed. If the military got rid of the people who did nothing but think up acronyms and abbreviations for stuff, the Pentagon could have been cut down to the Quadragon. UN phonetic designation just continued last century's NATO system. Fighters got two-syllable names starting with "F."

I asked Howard, "Where are these ships now?"

"Between Earth and Mars."

Someone let out a breath.

"How many?"

"There seem to be two escorts deployed forward at any one time. But we estimate the total is one hundred twenty-one Firewitches."

"Escorts? Escorting what?"

Howard ran his pointer tip around the screen's edge. "This."

The Shanghai Projectile faded offscreen and a new image replaced it. Howard said, "This is a pullback image taken at the same time as the close-up."

Another bulbous Slug ship floated on the screen like a blue-black watermelon grown by the Mad Hatter. Two watermelon seeds drifted in front of it. I squinted at the seeds, which had tiny whiskers growing from their front ends. They were the two gigantic Firewitches. The Slug ship behind them was so gargantuan that it had blocked out space in the prior picture.

Some officer muttered, "It's not a big ship. It's a small planet!"

Howard said, "We believe the Firewitches escort this big bertha. A transport. United Nations phonetic designator 'Troll.'"

"What does this Troll transport?"

Howard tapped the pointer against his palm and cocked his head. "My hunch is troops."

No one spoke.

"It's an invasion fleet. At present inbound speed and course, and presuming the ability to decelerate at G-forces commensurate with those observed as these Firewitches altered their course, the invasion fleet will reach Earth in twenty-two days."

More silence.

I raised my hand. "Why invade us? The Slugs haven't come within three hundred million miles of us before."

Howard shrugged. "Best reason in the universe. Their last plan failed. Time for a change."

The ADA general asked, "How did the fast-mover that hit Canaveral affect our defense capability?"

Brace stepped to the podium and Howard sat back down. "Space Force is developing launch points at Vandenburg in California and at Lop Nor in China. We were moving to deploy an orbital operations platform and a hunter-killer satellite umbrella." Brace paused to clear his throat, then blinked. "However, at the moment, and for the next twenty-two days or longer, every war fighting vehicle on Earth capable of reaching low Earth orbit is scrap metal at the bottom of the Canaveral crater. Our defense capability is zero."

This wasn't the time to lecture these old men. But as far as I could see, somebody's failure to disperse our defense capability was about to end the human race.

Someone said, "That's wrong. There are twenty-four V-Star Interceptors in orbit right now."

Brace nodded. "I said 'every vehicle on Earth.' Not one of those twenty-four can stay up more than ten additional days. We have no present capacity to relieve or refuel them. The only strip that could land them intact was at Canaveral. A few of the pilots may make walk-away landings on shorter strips somewhere on Earth, if we get good weather. But the ships won't be launchable again for weeks."

"We're finished."

It seemed no one in the room breathed.

Howard said, "There's one substantial ship left. And twenty fighters."

Brace swiveled his head toward Howard. "The major's right. *Excalibur*'s stored in lunar orbit. Twenty extra-orbital-variant Venture Stars are moored to her."

Howard said, "We know *Excalibur*'s up there. But we don't have ships to get to her. Even if we had ships down here, we wouldn't have a facility to launch them from."

A barrel-chested lieutenant general stood. He wore Infantry's crossed rifles. "If interdicting the invasion fleet in space isn't an option, we need to mobilize the population."

He wasn't wrong. Mankind had no options. Fight or die. But in just days it was going to be villagers with pitchforks against swarming, black-armored Slug legions, armed, armored, disciplined, and coordinated like a slimy Bolshoi Ballet. None of these military men had faced Pseudo-cephalopod Combat Infantry. I had.

Shooting the Slugs down with ground-based missiles as they tried to land on Earth seemed like a good idea. An invasion force is most vulnerable during landing. Especially coming down from the sky. A century ago, Rommel had fortified the European coast to throw the Allies back into the sea and nearly succeeded.

Then I thought about the present situation. There were, I supposed, antiaircraft and antimissile systems in place around high-value targets around the world. If the Slugs tried to land on top of the White House or the Kremlin, we would probably ruin their whole day.

But Earth is a big place to defend. If the Slugs were smart enough to land in the middle of Saskatchewan or the south side of Borneo, there wouldn't be much we could do to stop them.

We broke for twenty minutes. I cornered Brace before he left the auditorium stage. "Admiral?"

Brace turned to me and frowned.

I said, "Thanks. I owe you."

"For what?"

"For pulling us through that hole before the building blew. You saved my life. And my godson's."

He smiled as tightly as a walking cadaver. "Saved you for what? General, you'll go down swinging. We all will. But any chance we had to keep that invasion fleet off this planet vanished when my command did. Do you know how many died at Canaveral?"

A balloon seemed to swell in my chest. On Ganymede,

I had felt like Brace felt. Now we both knew the emptiness of losing our troops in combat. I suppose if Ord hadn't taught me better, I would have rubbed it in. I suppose I could have smirked. Could have asked Brace how smart his Annapolis education made him now.

I said, "We do the best we can. We screw up. We come back and do the best we can again."

He smiled once more. "Infantry can do that. Infantry can fight with fixed bayonets, or throw rocks. But I don't have anything to come back with."

He sighed as the sound of our footsteps rattled off granite tunnel walls. "If we had just one space-capable ship, we could get a skeleton crew aboard *Excalibur*. A few people could take her out and fight her V-Stars against that fleet," he said.

"One hundred twenty against twenty. Those are bad odds."

"They're the only odds we have."

I had experienced those odds with Slugs before. I could still see them, black armor glistening, rear ranks swarming over fallen front ranks by the thousands.

At the tunnel mouth, Howard stood, smoking. No one who hadn't been on Ganymede really could visualize a Slug river surging up the national Mall, parting around the Washington Monument. I locked eyes with Howard.

He saw that river as clearly as I did. The Slugs would land. As a species, we would fight. But as a species, we would die.

And then it hit me. I turned back to Brace. "I said I owed you. If I could get you aboard *Excalibur,* would we be square?"

TWENTY-EIGHT

WE REASSEMBLED AFTER OUR BREAK. Earth's military brain trust hid and plotted in a mildewed auditorium beneath a rock pile. I leaned toward Howard and whispered, "Could Brace fight the Slugs in space? If we could get him there?"

He shrugged. "Better than trying to fight them here. If the Firewitch fights as poorly relative to our V-Stars as Pseudocephalopod warriors fight relative to human infantry, Brace might make a contest of it. One hundred twenty to one are quantitatively long odds. Not impossible. But even if we defeated 121 Firewitches, the Troll seems too massive to be destroyed by conventional missiles. Anyway, with no spacecraft, the odds are moot."

I shook my head. "No they aren't. There's a fully operational V-Star parked on the Mall, outside the Smithsonian. You saw it yourself."

Howard shook his head. "It's a static museum display."

A colonel next to us frowned at me for whispering. I tugged Howard up from his seat and we bumped a few knee pairs sidestepping down the row.

In the dank granite passageway, my voice echoed. "They

wouldn't have yanked that V-Star's guts yet. That would have cost money. You want odds? I bet you a year's pay that ship's still flyable. It can jack itself up vertical and take off with no gantry. I saw it do that on Ganymede."

"That was in one-sixth Earth gravity. It would take some hot pilot to fly a Venture Star from the national Mall to lunar orbit."

"Mimi Ozawa's some hot pilot."

"Then we'd have one ship."

"The V-Star could carry pilots to the moon. It already docked with *Excalibur* once. Then we'd have twenty-one fighters plus a big ship to support them."

"That V-Star could only carry fifty people, if we dope 'em up and then pack 'em in like sardines. Twenty of those would have to be pilots. That leaves thirty billets to fly *Excalibur*. Normal crew's five hundred."

"*Excalibur*'s all run by 'puters. A skeleton crew could fly her for a while. She'd just be an aircraft carrier for the V-Stars, anyway."

Howard rolled his eyes to the ceiling and pursed his lips. "V-Stars were designed to reach low Earth orbit, not the moon. They can't carry enough fuel to continue to the moon."

"Brace said we couldn't get more fuel to the ships up in orbit now. Could we change that?"

"Possibly we could refuel one V-Star in orbit by docking with an unmanned satellite launcher with a fuel tank for a payload. Possibly we could demothball *Excalibur* and her own V-Stars in time. Possibly we could devise a space-fighting strategy. Possibly—"

"Possibly we'll all die if you don't stop saying possibly!"

*　　*　　*

A plane ride later, I followed Howard around the Capitol Mall as he walked around the last operable manned spacecraft on Earth, his hands clasped behind his back.

He pointed up at the hydraulic struts of the V-Star's undercarriage. "It's designed as a single-stage vehicle. And the Ganymede variant can lever itself vertical and take off with no gantry. But . . ." He shook his head.

"But?"

He said, "Refueling in orbit would be total improvisation. Assuming we can adapt a commercial satellite lifter as a tanker, rendezvous with it, refuel, then continue."

"Can we do that?"

Howard shrugged. "We can't, if you ask Brace. But Mimi Ozawa can."

Over the next twenty-four hours, the United Nations pulled together twenty astronauts and former pilots, including Mimi Ozawa, who had enrolled to finish a doctorate, and called them a squadron.

Brace and a tiny crew would try to fire up *Excalibur,* while the pilots did the same with the V-Stars.

It was all very straightforward. It was all very desperate. It was all going to happen without me.

I assigned myself to compile a militia handbook for the ground campaign. We'd send it online to the public. They'd have to learn from it and organize themselves to fight.

Improvised explosive devices were an obvious chapter. And I knew just the guy to write it, Brumby.

The following day, Howard sat in my Washington office in the zoology lab of the Smithsonian.

He tapped a cigarette out of a pack.

I stared at his lighter.

"My office. My rules. For once!"

"How's the Space Force mission going?"

He blew smoke at the ceiling. "Well, Admiral Brace has a plan. *Excalibur* will assume a blocking position between Earth and the Pseudocephalopod fleet. She will deploy, recover, refuel, and rearm Interceptors."

I shook my head. "Midway!"

Excalibur was going to function as a naked aircraft carrier in space, deployed to block a vastly superior invasion fleet. After Pearl Harbor, American planes, operating from aircraft carriers stripped of proper escorts by the attack on Pearl, intercepted the Japanese fleet and sank four Japanese carriers. Brace planned to replicate the naval battle that had won the greatest maritime victory in American history.

I cocked my head. "What if the Slugs don't come in on the moon's orbital plane?" I asked. "Brace is planning for a two-dimensional surface-naval battle. But space is three-dimensional. The Slugs could just loop around *Excalibur*. That's not just a plan for the last war, it's eight wars behind!" Footsoldiers had learned the value of small, dispersed units the hard way, from the American Revolution to Vietnam to the Tibetan Insurrection of 2020.

But Swabbie officers still saw combat in terms of set-piece battles, as though Admiral Mahan was still in charge.

Howard shook his head and lit another cigarette. "On Ganymede, the Pseudocephalopod could have evaded us or waited us out. Instead it attacked. Frontally, in waves, with no regard for its losses. The Pseudocephalopod will seek out and engage *Excalibur* to destroy it, not because *Excalibur* forces the issue."

"So, no matter what Brace and the UN think, as far as you're concerned, *Excalibur* is just bait?"

Howard stood and looked around his office. "I need an ashtray. I'll be back." He left and pulled the door shut behind him.

It didn't occur to me to ask Howard what he hoped to catch using a mile-long spaceship for bait.

My mistake.

TWENTY-NINE

I STARED AT THE CLOSED DOOR for twenty seconds, trying to figure out what Howard meant. That was typically futile.

I sighed and turned back to the business at hand, compiling a primer on homemade bombs. On the off-chance that Brace and his space cowboys failed to destroy a force ten times their size and eons more technically advanced. In which case Earth would have to kill Slugs on our mud.

I talked up a desktop screen. Drugs or no drugs, my hand throbbed and I was glad I didn't have to keyboard.

Finding Brumby would be cake. The Domestic Defense Command was a vestige of the War on Terror, exempt from the Bill of Rights. DDC was prohibited by constitutional amendment from satellite tracking of natural persons but that didn't mean DDC *couldn't* track anyone if the law could be, um, neutralized.

Brumby had mustered out under the Gratitude Act and was for practical purposes a civilian. Nobody could track a civilian, legally. But he was at the moment still on the rolls as active-duty Army. The tracking chip implanted behind every soldier's breastbone at induction was still in Brumby.

I patched through on my 'puter to Department of Defense Central Records. A 'puter spoke, throaty and feminine. "Coordinates or place name, please?"

"Um. Place."

"Level of detail, please?"

"I dunno. City. And an audio phone number."

Pause. The 'puter purred. "Your subject may be found in, in"—pause—"Falls Church, Virginia. Connecting your audio phone link now. Please remain close by."

I leaned on my elbows. Where else did my silicon-chip friend think I would remain? But the news was great. I glanced at my 'puter. I could be with Brumby in an hour or less.

I thought as I waited to learn his location. Brumby, blinky and jittery as he was, was now a civilian. Had he found his destiny? A reason to live out the rest of the life with which fate had gifted him?

A 'puter voice answered, this one male and priggish. "You have reached"—click, pause—"the Falls Church Municipal Jail. Please select from the following options—"

I straightened in my chair. Before I got to option one, Howard stuck his head and torso back in my door. In one hand, he held an ashtray. "I have a plan. But it's fly by the seat of the pants. The military won't like it. Somebody like Brace would say it's insane."

"Did you ever have a plan the military liked?"

Howard knit his brows. "It will present you with Hobson's choice. Would you rather die an infantryman or a mutineer? Of course, it could save the world."

I disconnected from the jail. "Talk to me, Howard."

THIRTY

THE FIRST THING HOWARD'S PLAN REQUIRED was that I assemble a combat team. Well, an assistant. Three people was the most we could swing. We needed demolitions expertise and I needed a noncommissioned officer who functioned like an extension of myself, someone whose combat reactions I knew and who knew mine just as well.

That meant I had to spring Brumby.

The police officer at the Falls Church jail visitors' desk wore his hair GI-short, but his eyelids drooped. I supposed catching bad guys was more invigorating than watching them pace in their cells.

He sat behind a gray metal desk while, on a tabletop holo in the corner, daytime news showed endless images of destroyed Canaveral and civilians fleeing presumably targeted cities. I figured the holo also had a channel to monitor the prisoners' cells, but it looked like nobody bothered. The cop flicked his eyes up from my visit request form to the ribbons on my uniform blouse. Then he looked at my face and his eyes widened. "You're Jason Wander!" He stood and stuck out his hand. He jerked a thumb at a locked, reinforced door. "You? You're here to visit that guy, Brumby?"

In the corner, commercials hummed.

I nodded. "That guy and I served together."

The cop nodded, smiled, and reached for his belt key card. His belly hung over his belt. Another downside of not chasing bad guys, I supposed. But the nightstick and holstered stunner on his belt announced he could make springing Brumby difficult if he had to.

Brumby sat on a cell bunk, engrossed in a book titled *A Brief History of Explosives*.

The Army had made Brumby fit to be a soldier.

But when it discarded him, it left him fit to be little else.

He leapt to attention when he saw me through his cell bars, civilian or not. I looked around. Currently, Brumby was the Falls Church jail's sole guest. He looked healthy so I figured the vomit smell was the gift of a prior tenant.

I waved him to "At ease."

"Sir!" Unconsciously, Brumby reached to his waist and straightened his gig line, though his orange "detainee" smock didn't even have a belt buckle. He twitched. "Good to see you, sir. But why—?"

"You're the one in the slammer, Brumby. I ask 'why' first." I raised my eyebrows at the cop.

The cop flipped on a Chipboard display attached to the cell door and read aloud, his finger tracing print on the screen. "'Detainee is charged with five counts of assault, malicious property damage, resisting arrest, and reckless endangerment.' And that's just in one saloon!"

Brumby winced.

I fingered the credit chip in my pocket. I had back pay

to burn and I didn't figure to be spending it once the Slugs landed. "What's his bail?"

The cop pointed at the display, again. " 'RMD.' RMD means Recidivist, Mandatory Detention. He evidently had a record of violent episodes in the service. No bail. That saloon was the third place he busted up in one night."

Brumby hung his head.

I tugged out my credit chip. "I know it's gonna be steep—"

The cop raised his palm. "Read my lips. No. Bail."

I straightened. "But the Army needs him."

"Maybe so, General. From the holos, it looks like the Army needs everybody. But it's not up to me. You can schedule a hearing." The cop shrugged. "The magistrate calendars a motions day every Wednesday. Next one's in six days."

"In six days, it'll be too late!"

The cop hooked a thumb in his belt, alongside his stunner holster, as he turned away. "You're a soldier, sir. You know we gotta go by the book, just like you all do. There's a Department of the Army release form you could get, I think. They process through in a couple of weeks."

"In a couple of weeks the Department of the Army will be hip-deep in Slugs! Cops aren't so different from soldiers. You never went around the book?"

He paused and looked from me to Brumby. Then he sighed and walked backward toward the cell-block door. "Your visit limit's ten minutes, sir."

The slammed door echoed while Brumby grasped the bars and rested his forehead on them. "Sir, I'm sorry. I don't sleep good. When I sleep, I see it. I see it all. Then

I'm tired." He looked up and grinned. "You know how I am when I'm tired."

I nodded. "You go to the VA?"

"Since I got back. They made me take Prozac II. So I quit going."

Drugs were wonderful things, I supposed. At the moment I was functioning after a traumatic amputation only because of them. But I had done 'Zac when the Slugs killed my mother. It made me stupid. Stupid enough that I had cost a friend his life. Should have been my life. The memory made me squeeze my eyes shut.

I opened them and touched my hand to Brumby's. "I don't blame you." I kept pressing his fingers until he looked up, then I leaned forward. "Brumby, I need you to reenlist."

He shook his head and squinted. "Huh? But, sir, I'm locked up. No bail. You heard. It's not so bad. I get to read a lot." He pointed at his do-it-yourself bomb book. "You know, sir, you can make a bomb out of almost anything."

I gazed at the peeling ceiling and sighed. Wednesday was too long from now. And that was just a hearing. Go to the Judge Advocate General Corps? Those bureaucrats couldn't spring a private from a stockade. In civilian court they would be worthless. My old benefactor, Judge March? If I could find him, maybe he could get Brumby sprung. Unlikely. The White House? President Lewis had ordered Ruth Tway to keep a sword over my head. If I could reach anyone in authority at the White House, they might be in no mood to help me. And Howard's plan depended on us coming in under the bureaucratic radar. A general lobbying to get a former enlisted man out of a local pokey would pique curiosity. High-level scrutiny was the last thing we could stand.

The judge had told me long ago, "If the truth won't set you free, lie your ass off." But springing Brumby would take more than lies.

Brace blamed himself for leaving Earth defenseless. But *he* was getting a second chance, an opportunity to redeem himself. Around the world, soldiers scrambled, preparing for the worst with too little time and material to prepare.

Brumby and I dangled. If I couldn't get Brumby out of here *right now,* his destiny and mine would be to make no difference in the coming battle. That was all we had left. The slim chance that we could make a difference.

I leaned close and whispered, "Brumby, there's no time to argue with judges and lawyers. I'm busting you out."

He drew his head back as his eyes widened. "Sir? If you get caught you'll be in here with me. That would be a real career-bender for you."

Brumby didn't realize that I had no career. But it was because he thought about me, first, that I needed him. And that he deserved the chance to go down swinging, not in a cell.

I stabbed my hand through the bars and covered his mouth. "You coming or not, Brumby?"

The cop was the only other person in the building. My GI pool car sat curbside, fifty feet from the building entrance.

Beneath my uniform I wore my Eternad underblouse. It was nonconductive. If the cop could draw and fire his stunner before I could drop him, a torso shot would sting me like sticking a finger in a wall socket, but I would still be able to function. Like every other infantryman, I'd been hit with stunner shots during training, to build my confidence in my armor.

If I could get Brumby back onto any military reservation before the cops tracked us and pulled us over, red tape would protect him. Bureaucratic delay worked both ways. Possession was nine-tenths of the law. Or something. While Brumby was behind bars, the system allowed him to languish there. But if I could get him out, no matter how, it would take days for the system to reverse the process. In a few days, it wouldn't matter, one way or the other.

I was pretty sure I could drop the cop with a sucker-punch chop to his windpipe, without killing him. However, in training only instructors like Ord had been authorized to demonstrate the blow because trainees routinely killed one another when they tried it. Murder was a problem I didn't think red tape could make go away.

I ground my teeth while I self-debated.

Upholding the Rule of Law, as established by the Constitution I was sworn to uphold and defend, depended, at this moment, on my breaking the law. Brace would never do it.

I looked at Brumby and pressed a finger to my lips.

He nodded.

I pointed at the corridor across from Brumby's cell door. "I'll be out of the guard's sight. When he walks back in, you hold his attention. Do something, anything. Just make him come to you."

Brumby nodded, but his brow wrinkled. "Sir, are you sure this is a good idea?"

Masterminding a failed jailbreak would land me next to

Brumby, behind the bars. And a violent felony conviction doesn't build the ole résumé. But in days, nobody's résumé would count for flea snot. The reason Brumby and I survived Ganymede, it now came clear, was to defend this planet to our deaths. We could only do that if he got out of the slammer.

I pressed my back against the opposite corridor's cool wall. My breathing shallowed and I flexed my right hand. The instructors called it the killing hand.

Brumby yelled, "Hey! Help! I have to go to the bathroom!"

I looked into the cell and winced. An ivory commode was built into the far wall. Brumby was a born soldier but not a born liar.

Silence from the next room.

Brumby stuck his fingers in his mouth and whistled 'til saliva sprayed. He snatched up a Plasteel chair and rattled it against his cell bars.

My right hand hung heavy alongside my body. Pulling a trigger with a Pseudocephalopod in my sights was one thing. Killing—no, I reminded myself, I wasn't trying to kill him—an innocent police officer in cold blood was another. If I killed him, my life could end. If I didn't, the world could end.

I peeked around the corner, my heart pounding.

At the corridor's end, the doorknob rotated.

THIRTY-ONE

I WATCHED THE COP, or rather his dull reflection, in the polished-metal mirror above the sink in Brumby's cell.

Rubber cop soles squeaked on the floor tile. I tensed my arm.

Then I relaxed it. I couldn't kill an innocent cop in cold blood. Some soldier I was. The mission should come first. Killing was my job.

I slumped against the wall. We were beaten.

"Mr. Brumby, after we have the conversation we're about to have, just forget it."

Huh? The cop stepped past me, waved his pass-card across Brumby's cell's lock and the door hissed open.

The cop turned to me and shook his head. "General, I don't know why you think this guy can make a difference. I do know that we're all in trouble. You wouldn't be here if it wasn't important. I figure I gotta exercise my discretion."

My mouth hung open. I blinked, then said, "He's free?"

"If he was anybody else, you could bail him out after a bar fight no problem. I put real bums back on the street every week. Doesn't seem right Mr. Brumby should stay in jail just because he went to war for the rest of us."

Brumby gathered up his clothes and kit and scurried into the corridor.

The cop pointed at the table holo. An anchorwoman stood in front of a holo showing Earth, the moon, and a distant, pulsing red dot that moved visibly closer to Earth as she spoke. The cop said, "I can draw up forms that say the 'puters misidentified Mr. Brumby. We automatically release the subject if that happens. You saw how this place works. We go by the book."

The officer unlocked a wall locker, rummaged, then handed Brumby a personal effects envelope. "But sometimes you gotta go around the book."

I could have kissed the cop for springing Brumby. But if he knew how far around the book Howard planned to go, the cop might have slapped me.

THIRTY-TWO

AT ELEVEN P.M. TWO WEEKS LATER, I buttoned up my gear, including Jeeb, and punched "checkout" on the bedroom screen in my Ritz suite.

A British-accented 'puter assured me that the Ritz looked forward to welcoming me back soon.

I snorted. "Fat chance!"

Two beats later the 'puter apologized and offered me a complimentary suite upgrade.

I said, "No. It's just a scheduling problem." A big one. Well, if one had to spend a last night on Earth, I supposed the Ritz was as good a place as any. Space Force's latest estimate was that eight days from now the Slug invasion fleet would cross inside the orbit of the moon.

I detoured to the holo booths off the lobby, talked up contact info, and spent money I would never need on a Max-Qual link.

Munchkin faded in as clear as spring water. A fire crackled in the hearth behind her, real down to a spray of wood smoke smell. She wore a robe and juggled Jude, tousle-headed, on her hip. She draped a towel over his hair. "He was in the tub. What's wrong?"

"You mean besides the Slugs? Nothing." I hated lying to her but she was a civilian, now. "We'll be in the field a couple days so I thought I'd, y'know, check in with you."

Mom or not, Munchkin was soldier enough to know this was the last call.

She stared while Jude squirmed. "Sure."

I almost wished I hadn't paid for the Max-Qual, because I could see the tears swell in her eyes. Jude touched a finger to her eyelid. "Mommy, you're wet." A heartbeat later Munchkin's tears streamed down.

She stepped toward me and made a kiss on my forehead that I couldn't really feel. The soap and water I smelled wasn't really her but Max-Qual meant scent and by gosh AT&H delivered.

I broke the link before she saw *my* tears.

Under the hotel's dimmed portico lights, the anonymous pickup car rolled up and its driver stepped out. I sucked in the chill, damp breeze off the Potomac, smiled, and closed my eyes. Simple pleasures delight when you're living them for the last time.

The driver's hand brushed mine as he reached for my duffel. "In the back, sir?"

For a driver, the voice was too old, too commanding. Too familiar. I opened my eyes and my heart skipped. "Sergeant Ord!" He saluted and I returned it. "What—?"

"I'm over at the Pentagon, temporary duty, just now, sir. Happened to see you were scheduled to need a driver."

Happened to use a command sergeant major's security clearance to 'puter-dig through a couple million top-secret records until he matched my name with an assignment. I smiled. "Fortunate coincidence you came across me, Sergeant Major."

"Indeed, sir."

I climbed in the passenger side of the Pentagon pool car and looked around. Ord slid behind the wheel. "Car's bug-swept and surveillance-insulated, sir. And we have a few minutes. If you want to talk."

"How much do you know?"

"I know that orders and planning documents show that Major Hibble is supposed to be assembling a scientific exploration team to board any Slug vessel that may be captured in the battle."

"What battle?" I smiled.

"Yes, sir. There can be no battle because we have no ships. I watch holo news like everyone else." In the dimness I swear Ord smiled.

"However, sir, I also noted that Major Hibble's command had recently requisitioned and taken delivery on six thousand pounds of Semtex-51. Why a lab would need the most powerful conventional explosive in history, in quantity great enough to blow up a small city, seemed problematic, sir. The lab also requisitioned a wheeled, tubular delivery canister that would be just large enough to hold three tons of S-51. Also enough Thermite to burn holes through several battleships. It seems a very unusual group of requisitions for a laboratory. Equally strange Table of Organization and Equipment for a post-battle inspection mission."

I swallowed and squeezed my eyes shut. Howard was Military Intelligence Branch. He was supposed to be a *spy,* for crying out loud. But Ord, who was older than the Internet, had already hacked into Howard's plot. We were going to be denied our lunatic chance to save the world because I hadn't checked up on Howard's cheating skills.

My heart thumped. Ord, by-the-book Ord, was onto our little mutiny. He would never let us get away with it.

Ord reached inside his uniform jacket. His hand came out holding an automatic.

I felt my eyes widen and I pushed my hands out, palms up. "Sergeant Major—?"

Ord shook his head. "Normally, sir, Pentagon Internal Security procedures would have picked up those aberrant requisitions during the normal forty-eight-hour scan."

My heart sank. Ord had found them even sooner.

"However, Pentagon security procedures also require that individual personnel test the encryption technology of their workstations on file groups daily. I chose, purely at random, to move those files and backups to my workstation and encrypt that group."

"So, Internal Security—?"

Ord nodded. "Will find them, eventually. But for the next seven days, as far as Internal Security or anyone else can tell, those requisitions and deliveries don't exist. Fortuitous coincidence, sir."

I realized my hand had been strangling the door handle. I released it. Fortuitous coincidence if some lunatic bunch was trying to conceal its plan to save the world. Ord had been saving my ass and calling it fortuitous coincidence for years, now.

"Thank you, Sergeant Major." I furrowed my brow and pointed at the gun. "Then why the hand cannon?"

Ord turned in the driver's seat, faced me, and held up the pistol. The slide was back. It was the blue-steel Service .45 I had seen him practice with two years before, aboard *Excalibur,* during our voyage home.

"This .45 is strictly nonstandard. Some might call it

obsolete. But I carried it in combat and it always served me well." He pointed at a scratch along the receiver. "I carried it in a shoulder holster. In the days before Eternad armor, this pistol earned that scratch deflecting a 7.62-millimeter round from my chest. So some might also call it lucky."

He handed it across and I hefted it. "Doesn't feel obsolete."

"Neither do I, sir." He smiled and pointed. "But they keep me behind a desk, now. Loaded with flechette, that old girl could be very effective in close-quarters battle in a confined space. Like aboard a Slug warship. If such a close-quarters battle were about to take place, which, we both know, it is not."

I swallowed.

Ord's voice dropped and he went hoarse. "If the general would consider doing me the honor of carrying the pistol? For luck?"

Swelling nearly closed my throat. Ord wanted to do something to protect me. An automatic pistol seems an odd good-luck totem to civilians. But steel makes a combat soldier's luck. Ord wanted something of himself to take part in the battle to save the human race, though duty buried him pushing Pentagon paper.

I looked down, so he couldn't see the tear sheen in my eyes, and slipped the pistol and holster into my duffel. I sucked a breath. "The honor is mine, Sergeant Major. Anything else I should know?"

He cocked his head. "You and Admiral Brace seem to understand one another better now. Combat makes us family. But when the chips are down, the admiral will fall back on the book. And in combat there often is no book."

Ord dropped me off at midnight. Howard, Brumby, and

I, all dressed in old civilian jackets and stocking caps, meandered in the dark down the Capitol Mall, pushing rattling wire shopping carts filled with plastic trash bags. To a casual observer, three homeless derelicts. Which wasn't so far from true.

If the area hadn't been sealed to vehicular traffic, a casual drive-by observer might also have noticed that there were more delivery vans and tractor-trailers than usual parked overnight along the Mall, each humming and plugged into a recharge post, but each far enough from the dark Venture Star displayed outside the Smithsonian that launch backwash wouldn't damage it. And the dead grass for hundreds of yards around stunk of something acrid that the observer might recognize as fire retardant.

As for the glazing trucks parked at the base of the Washington Monument, a story in tomorrow's *Washington Post* would detail a vandalism spree that shattered windows all along the Mall, and another would reveal a gas main explosion in central Washington that explained the enormous fireball visible as far away as Bethesda.

It was typical military operational security—overdone and scarcely credible. But, like most Opsec, it only had to fool any Slugs listening for a couple of days.

One by one, Howard, Brumby, and I came alongside, then darted into a grocery-delivery truck trailer parked in front of the National Air and Space Museum.

Inside, everything smelled of overripe bananas, because it really was just a grocery trailer, except that its single naked ceiling lightbulb had been replaced with a night-vision-friendly red one.

Howard and Brumby were already stripping down, then slipping on infantry-crimson Eternad armor, their weapons and equipment rucksacks, freed from their plastic bags, at their feet.

Suiting up took longer with three fingers, more because I babied the stumps than anything. Jeeb popped his head out of my rucksack, wriggled free, then perched on my shoulder. There he hummed cyclically, like a gnat was flying laps inside my helmet, as his diagnostics cycled, then recycled and ran again.

By the time I buttoned up, I could barely move in the trailer. Forty-seven other bums, night watchmen, and street sweeps had joined our costume party and had also changed, now wearing V-Star pilot flight suits or Space Force orbital-transit uniforms.

I whispered to Howard, "Is Ozawa on board?"

"She's been pre-flighting the V-Star for hours."

"I meant—"

"That too. I spoke with her ten days ago."

One figure in orbital-transit uniform moved our way, others shrinking back to make him a hole.

Brace wrinkled his brow at the three of us. "Hibble, I do not understand why the Pentagon wants you three and that gear taking up lift tonnage on this mission."

Howard retracted his faceplate and Battlefield Awareness Monocle, so he could focus both eyes on Brace. "You've seen the orders. If your force disables a Pseudocephalopod warship, we're to board it and gather intelligence. That gear of ours may be worth its weight in gold."

Like most good Spook lies, it had enough basis in truth to persuade someone who thought as linearly as Brace. It would seem like a logical extension of the Pseudocephalopod Technology Recovery Program. Like the Opsec explosion story, the lie only had to hold for a couple of days. We were maybe the three biggest Slug experts on Earth. Who else would be sent? Obviously, the story had won over the rest of the chain of command. "Won over" was too strong. Howard had lied his ass off to them. In a few days, it wouldn't matter.

A Space Force tech sergeant poked his head in the trailer's door. "Embarkation, one minute!"

For sixty seconds the only sound in the trailer was the clatter of gear buckles being checked, breathing, and, somewhere, the Lord's Prayer.

The tech sergeant swung open the trailer doors. "Showtime, ladies and gentlemen."

THIRTY-THREE

MY HEART THUMPED as the fifty of us walked across the Mall to the V-Star's now-descending loading ramp. A pale red light wedge flooded from the V-Star's interior across us. The thumping was partly because our puny human scraggle was all that stood between mankind and the end of the world as we knew it. Also, I was lugging 125 pounds of gear through Earth-normal gravity.

As each of us stepped onto the V-Star's cleated up-ramp, we opened our mouths and a medic popped in a lima-bean-sized pill. My last trip to the moon had been under sedation, too. It wasn't just to keep us from jostling the fellow travelers with whom we would be stacked nose to nose and toes to toes. It would keep us from overloading V-Star life-support systems designed for half as many passengers and for shorter trips than from the Earth to the moon.

Mimi Ozawa and her copilot would be the only ones aboard who stayed awake for the trip. If they couldn't get us to orbit or couldn't refuel us or screwed up some other way, I just wouldn't wake up. Since my trips with Ozawa usually ended with her scolding me, sleeping through this one sounded fine.

A Space Force rating wedged me into my travel tube, then wriggled his hand down the tube, alongside my breastplate, and connected the com and med-monitor leads.

I yawned.

"Sweet dreams, General."

Fat chance.

THIRTY-FOUR

THREE DAYS LATER Howard, Brumby, and I sat in *Excalibur*'s officers' mess sipping wake-up therm cup coffee and shivering in stale air that had been scarcely heated and unbreathed for months. We had the mess hall to ourselves. Each V-Star pilot had his or her own ship to check out and Brace and his twenty-five crew members had to get a ship bigger than Yankee Stadium under way.

Unsurprisingly, despite this being the most important mission in human history, the three of us—four, counting Jeeb who perched on my shoulder—had nothing to do at the moment except conspire to wage our own private war.

Brumby leaned back in his chair and nearly floated off it. Until *Excalibur*'s rotation fully spooled up, he weighed about eleven pounds. "What are the rest of them going to do?"

Howard, who had never gotten the hang of movement in reduced gravity, nor of infantry equipment, wrestled his helmet off and set it on the table, its BAM blinking in the visor like a question mark. I reached across, inside, and fingered the chinplate off switch.

Brumby and I knew Howard's public version of our

plans as well as his private one. If the Space Force pulled off its mission, though, we could return home sassy without executing either of our plans. I asked, "Howard, how can V-Stars hurt a Firewitch? V-Stars are hardly even fighters."

"The V-Star modifications were designed years ago. The parts are still stored here aboard *Excalibur*. Prefabricated. Installation doesn't take long." He pulled out a Chipboard and tapped its screen. The V-Star I saw there was hung with external plumbing, its sleek shape crusted with pipes, tanks, and nozzles.

"Maneuvering thrusters. Those fins and that sleek shape are useless in space. And"—Howard pointed at a rack piggybacked on the V-Star's middle—"they added weapons systems."

I squinted at white, finned arrow shapes. "Air-to-air missiles?"

He nodded. "Their fins are useless to maneuver in vacuum. But they work fine as rockets. The pilot points the V-Star on-target and shoots. They're unguided explosive bullets. Simple."

We'd learned years ago, within days of the start of the Blitz, that the Slugs had some way of neutralizing our nukes. Even an antiship missile's thousand-pound warhead seemed puny against the Slug behemoths.

"So's throwing rocks, Howard. But it doesn't accomplish much. And the Slugs can shoot those light-speed refrigerators at us."

A klaxon sounded and *Excalibur*'s main engines throbbed.

The viewscreen on the bulkhead broadcast the view from a drone orbiting the mother ship. At that moment,

Excalibur caught up with the lunar sunrise. A silver flash on the horizon spread into a crescent of fire. I squeezed my eyes shut against the dazzle. I opened them and saw *Excalibur,* afloat in full sunlight, hung majestic and silver against space and above the moon's whiteness.

Howard shook his head. "I'll bet my pension that Projectile was one-of-a-kind."

"You've only been in the Army six years. You have no pension."

Howard frowned at me. "The fast-mover was linked to The Football, which was its homing beacon. The fast-mover probably loitered along behind *Excalibur* all the way from Jupiter, then accelerated to ramming speed as soon as it got a signal from the beacon that the beacon might be destroyed."

"Destroyed when the PTR technocrats started to saw it open at Canaveral." I settled into my chair as my weight grew to fifty pounds. "You think the Slugs are that tricky?"

He shook his head again. "I don't think the Pseudocephalopod is tricky at all where the human race is concerned. I think It sees the subjugation of mankind as no more than a vermin hunt. For the Pseudocephalopod, the fast-mover was just a smart-mine system. We just made the mine look even smarter because we put the homing beacon where it could do us the most harm. I think the Firewitches will defend the Troll with weapons firing conventional objects at conventional speeds."

"Because the fast-movers are too scarce?"

"Because the Pseudocephalopod thinks it doesn't need to do anything more to defeat us. Why swat us flies with a sledgehammer?"

Brumby shook his head and blinked. "Admiral Brace

has some pretty mean flies, Major." In the drone's-eyeview on the bulkhead, V-Stars dangled at *Excalibur*'s docking bays. Twenty bays, twenty fighters.

Mean flies or not, the pickets' telescopes had counted 120 Slug Firewitch escorts protecting the Troll troopship. We were outnumbered six to one. And each Firewitch was to a V-Star as a grizzly was to a hummingbird.

Excalibur's docking bays ringed her midsection. Forward of that encircling belt stretched another, of hemispheres that roughened her massive skin like metallic goose bumps.

Howard pointed. "Mercury Mark Twenty. Each turret houses an auto-directed rapid-fire cannon system."

"Eight thousand rounds per minute."

"You think the Slugs will let *Excalibur* get within cannon range of them?"

He shook his head. "It's a defensive weapons system. More designed to disable whatever they fire at us. Adapted from wet-Navy ship-defense systems. But there's no reason we couldn't hit a target thousands of miles away, if we led it properly. The rounds just keep on flying through vacuum until they hit something."

I shrugged. That seemed like throwing salt at a charging rhino. But the defensive possibilities encouraged me.

We each picked a cabin, stowed our gear, and then, as the embarked contingent, headed to the bridge to pay compliments to the commanding officer, like old-fashioned Royal Marines.

We actually found Brace in Fire Control, not on the bridge. Red-lit like *Excalibur*'s bridge, Fire Control was a long, tubular room that housed along its edges fifty controller stations, one for each Mercury battery. Only one station was manned, the gunner hanging in a fighting chair within a gimballed cage like a gyroscope. The other cages would be slaved to whatever the gunner did in the occupied cage. If *Excalibur* had a normal crew aboard, each cage would be manned by gunners who could override the system's computer direction.

The main battle-management holotank ran the length and breadth of the room's middle. *Excalibur*'s image floated centered in the holo field's pale green representation of surrounding space, as small as a silver pencil. Flies orbited the pencil at a distance. Patrolling V-Stars.

Brace returned our salutes, his eyes tired.

The deck plates shook beneath my feet. When a Hope-class fires her main engines, you feel it a mile away. But you experience no sense of going forward. She doesn't accelerate even like an old city bus, at first. After all, it's like setting a small village in motion.

From what Howard had said, Slug ships seemed to be able to maneuver in ways that defied our ideas of physics. However, if *Excalibur* couldn't turn faster than an iceberg, I couldn't visualize that Troll transport, as big as Terre Haute, zigging and zagging.

Brace nodded as he conversed with an invisible someone at the other end of his earpiece. "Very well. Take her out, First Officer."

Brace turned to the fire-control officer, seated inside the cage of the Mercury fighting chair. "Underway stations, Mr. Dent."

"Aye, sir." The gunner strapped in.

I watched him grasp the gun controls and my heart rate sped a beat. I had found a certain sport in laying my cheek against an M-60 model 2017's receiver, then arcing rounds into a distant target while the gun bucked against my shoulder. The old girl was a throwback design. The Army could have chosen instead any one of a dozen more modern automatic weapons designs. But it chose to redo the M-60 in Plasteel. I was no gun nut, but I'd come to like her.

The thought of a Mercury on manual, rumbling out eight thousand rounds a minute under my hand, made my fingers tingle.

"—but my primary mission remains to close with and destroy the enemy."

Brace was speaking, Howard was nodding and frowning.

"Capture and examination of a Pseudocephalopod vessel—and live crew if we get lucky—is our best hope of turning this war. Or ending it."

Brace nodded at Howard. Howard barely knew how to engage the safety on his M-20. But he was the right person to carry this debate.

Brace snapped, "You get one of the reserve Venture Stars, one pilot, billets and training space for the boarding party. Beyond that, I need every resource on this ship." He stared at me and Brumby for the first time while he said it.

Brace didn't like the plan he had just debated with Howard, a plan that only kicked in if and when Brace's zoomies had won the battle. If he knew the truth, he would have thought our real plan was insane.

Which it was.

THIRTY-FIVE

LATER THAT DAY Howard, Brumby, Mimi Ozawa, and I huddled around a holotank in a conference room aft of bulkhead ninety — embarked-division country — where the swabbies, who were busy anyway, wouldn't disturb our plotting. Disturb us? There were only twenty-five of them and the space we had to ourselves had been designed to house a ten-thousand-soldier division. They probably couldn't have even found us.

We all stared into a green, translucent, three-dimensional image of the Slug Troll that was as big as a beachball.

Up here in space we were back in no-smoking land, so Howard pointed a licorice whip at the display. "This represents our best estimate of the interior layout."

Ozawa tapped her chin. I wasn't sure how much of Howard's plot she had been told to lure her in. She asked, "Based on what?"

I had asked Howard the same thing. She wore a baggy flight jacket over her flight suit, for me the day's initial disappointment.

"We extrapolated the layout of the Projectile Jason

explored on the moon five years ago, plus Jeeb's experience inside the Pseudocephalopod base on Ganymede."

George Washington said that the need for procuring good intelligence is apparent. That had been easy for George to say.

But intel errors had screwed up more war plans over the centuries than all the swords and bullets in history. I swallowed and crossed the fingers on my good hand.

Howard waved his palm at what looked like a belt of raisins stuck around the Troll's belly. "The Troll carries its Firewitch escorts tethered, like *Excalibur* carries the V-Stars. We count one hundred twenty-one Firewitches moored to the transport. That suggests It counts on a base-eleven system, by the way. Our base ten likely arose from our appendages, ten fingers and ten toes. Since It has no fixed appendages, that invites fascinating speculation—"

I shot Howard a glance.

He cleared his throat. "Anyway, we assume the escorts will attack when *Excalibur* approaches." He looked up at Brumby and pointed at a ridge near the Troll's tail. "We want to make entry here."

Brumby shook his head, slowly. "I can burn our way in any place you tell me, Major. Thermite will melt Slug metal. But there will be three of us and that thing's the size of a mountain range."

Howard shrugged. "Exactly why we should be too small to notice or care about. An amoeba on an elephant. A pilot of Mimi's ability should be able to slip us through the confusion of the initial dogfight to that point of entry. We believe that's where the propulsion system is. That should be a flammable or explosive location. If we can locate a vulnerable point to set the charge, we should be able to blow the whole thing up."

"What about the Firewitches? Maybe we do blow up the Troll, and a few Firewitches held close to it in reserve. That will still leave over a hundred warships."

"Here, we take a leaf from Admiral Brace's naval history book. If we board the Troll in the early stages of battle, then neutralize Pseudocephalopod resistance aboard for a time, the Firewitches should be returning to the Troll to refuel and rearm. At the Battle of Midway, the U.S. caught the Japanese planes on deck when they returned. We'll get the Firewitches, too, when you blow the big ship."

"Where are we when the Troll blows?" Brumby asked.

"Mimi should have us clear by hundreds of miles by then. It's an elegant plan."

Brumby frowned. "Neutralize the Slugs inside. How many warriors you figure that thing carries?"

Howard glanced at me. It was another question I'd asked. "The Troll is mainly a replication platform, an incubator if you will. The number of warriors actually combat-ready at the time of entry we estimate will be relatively small."

Brumby leaned forward. "How small, sir?"

"Give or take, maybe one hundred thousand."

Mimi and Brumby rocked back in their chairs.

Howard waved his palms. "No, it's fine! We won't have to deal with them all."

It wasn't fine, but Howard needed support here or half our team would bolt. I leaned forward. "A Projectile's like a spaghetti bowl inside. Narrow passages. We can isolate ourselves by you blowing some choke points, Brumby.

That should give us time enough to figure where to plant the Bomb. If they even notice us."

I winced internally at that fantasy. Notice us? Based on my experience, the Slugs would be on us like rottweilers on pot roast.

Silence hung in the cabin air.

Brumby turned to me. "Sir, you think this is worth the risk?"

I nodded.

"Then I'm in."

Three pairs of eyes focused on Ozawa.

Finally, she spoke. "Howard, you told me the plan was to board the Troll to steal technology. This plan is stupid. No, it's worse than stupid. It's suicidal. And it's criminal. Brace and the command structure don't know what you really plan, do they?"

Howard's gaze drifted to a corner of the cabin. "Its success probability computed rather low. The war planners preferred not to divert even your one ship from conventional combat."

"So you're asking me to mutiny, desert, and commit treason. All in one convenient package."

"You knew when we talked before that the plan I outlined was not exactly the plan I was asking you to join in."

Ozawa snorted. "I didn't think it would turn out to be such a dumb-ass plan."

I asked her, "You're a pilot. How dumb-ass is it for twenty V-Stars to attack six times their number, and a hundred times their weight, in Firewitches?"

Ozawa's answer to that had to be "pretty damn dumb-ass." But Ozawa's frown told me I needed a little more to nudge her over to our side.

If it had been Pooh Hart sitting there, she would already have been thinking about how to fly the mission. What was in Ozawa's head?

I said, "Your problem isn't with disobeying orders. You're just afraid you can't outfly the Slugs."

Ozawa stiffened. Then her eyes narrowed. She pointed at the green Troll holo. "If—when—I get you in there, you better make this work!"

A man rarely manipulates a woman successfully, especially this man. But the mindset that drove women combat pilots made them behave like men. I smiled, reached across the table, through the green holo, and shook her hand. "Done."

We spent the rest of the day brainstorming.

Howard's holo generator projected a Slug-ship passageway. Well, it was a purple-lit tunnel that looked enough like a Slug ship's gut to make my skin crawl beneath my armor.

Howard said, "The Pseudocephalopod reacts slowly to significant threats. We believe a ship-sized ganglion lacks much independence to react to unexpected situations."

"So, if we break down the door, the word has to go to Planet Zircon and back before they react?"

Howard nodded. "Crudely stated."

"They reacted pretty good on Ganymede."

"I didn't say It lacked reflexes. I think we'll have three minutes after we breach the ship before we encounter organized resistance."

My own excursion through a Slug Projectile flooded back over me. Claustrophobic passages lit in dim purple corkscrewed and swirled in no pattern obvious to men. At intervals, slots no wider than a man's palm cut the passage walls. The slots were doorways, from which amorphous Slugs could pounce on a man and suffocate him. Or they could kill him human-style, with a round from one of those twisted mag-rail rifles they carried, wrapped in a tentacular pseudopod. And somehow the slimy little bastards, clumsy as they were at close quarters, always seemed a jump ahead.

Brumby asked, "We won't know what's inside 'til we get there?"

"Not for sure," I said.

Brumby said, "Wish we had a Siegebot."

Human SWAT teams had stopped taking down urban criminal hideouts decades ago. 'Bots had saved many a cop.

"We do, sort of." I pointed at Jeeb. "Tactical Observation Transports are smarter than Siegebots. He'll walk point for us. His sensors make a Siegebot look like a deaf, blind pile of scrap pile."

Brumby and I cleaned weapons while Mimi and Howard went to inspect her V-Star's modifications.

Brumby snapped the charging handle on his M-20 for the fourth time. "Sir, what if Admiral Brace figures out what we're doing?"

"He won't. He's too busy."

"Our ship's supposed to be held in reserve. When he sees us move out early, he might shoot us down."

I smiled and shook my head. "Brace is inflexible. But he's learned a lot lately. He won't do something that stupid."

THIRTY-SIX

TWO HOURS LATER I lay in the dark on my bunk when Howard rapped on my cabin's hatch door. "We've got It onscreen."

I rolled off my bunk and tugged underarmor over my feet. "How far?"

"I would have said hours. But they're decelerating. A day to intercept at present rate of close."

"Why decelerating?"

"To engage us. I think It knows we're here. It's going to neutralize *Excalibur* rather than leave a capitol ship loose behind It."

"Neutralize. You mean destroy."

"Well, the reason we came out here was to engage It."

One hundred twenty-one to twenty odds are bad. They seem even worse when the 121 are spoiling for a fight.

We ran to the bridge, Howard leading while I hopped from foot to foot, tugging up my underarmor trousers.

The dim-lit bridge bustled with light and sound, but unlike my first bridge visit while in orbit above Ganymede, Brace was the only human there. The forward screen image had split into three. The left screen showed a pale blue light point against the stars—the Troll. The right screen flickered with *Excalibur*'s vital signs. In the center of the center, magnified, a Firewitch pointed head-on at us. Its six forward booms or horns or whatever they were rotated as the fighter whirled coldly toward us. Its surface winked with navigation lights—or what looked like navigation lights, though the Slugs couldn't see them because they were visible-spectrum lights. It was an escort or scout headed our way.

A small shadow slid past me in the dull red light.

Mimi Ozawa, in flight suit, stood alongside Howard and whispered, "We're fueled and your gear is loaded. The bridging unit's checked."

Mimi's job was not only to fight and dodge us to the Troll's skin. She had to deliver us close enough and delicately enough that Brumby could force a hull breach with Thermite charges.

But she couldn't do her job and we couldn't do ours until and unless *Excalibur* and the other fighter jocks did theirs. They had to win enough of the battle to create a melee Mimi could slip through.

Brace leaned over, peering at a display that showed fifty Mercury turrets ready. He spoke into the cherry-stem mike that curved around his cheek, to the Mercury-systems controller. "All systems on automatic. Switch to manual on my command. Only on my command."

The response echoed through the speakers. "Aye-aye, sir."

Mercury's 'puters sensed incoming targets, locked on them, traversed and elevated each turret gun, and fired on target in nanoseconds, before a human operator could blink. They were even programmed to recognize the transponder signals from our own fighters, then abort firing. There should be no friendly-fire disasters. With just twenty V-Stars against over a hundred Firewitches, we couldn't afford to shoot ourselves down.

Brace straightened, turned, saw us, and grunted.

Mimi said, "Mind if I disengage the docking boom from my ship, At?"

Former NASA astronauts, having served together as civilians, called each other by first names. Rank differences between them, like the one between Admiral Atwater Brace and Major Mimi Ozawa, were ignored. It was one of those jaunty pilot rituals.

Brace frowned. "Your ship's in reserve. I don't want it colliding with a deploying fighter."

"That boom keeps me tethered to *Excalibur* ninety seconds longer at go-time. Ninety seconds is a lifetime in combat, At. I'll be at the controls. You know I'm a good enough pilot to keep my ship out of other people's way."

Brace's jaw muscles twitched. "Strap in at the controls if you want. But the boom stays connected. Your ship's mine unless we identify a Pseudocephalopod derelict. Until then, you follow orders."

Brace did have ultimate authority if he needed another fighter to defend *Excalibur*. She was the biggest movable object ever constructed by mankind. She was home to twenty-six human beings, even if they were squids like Brace. With the exception of our little secret mutiny, *Excalibur* was humanity's sole, faint hope to hold hordes of invading monsters at arm's length. So I couldn't fault Brace for protecting her.

But Howard believed our mission would win or lose the war. Howard Hibble may have been a geek's geek, but he would fight for what he believed. Nobody else on the bridge seemed to notice that his right hand had clenched into a fist.

The fight fan in me longed to let this one go the distance. Brace's stateroom plaques announced that he had been an Annapolis boxing champion. He outweighed Howard, but the little guy had him on reach. Howard never wore the Silver Star he won at the Battle of Ganymede, but he won it for defending our command post against fifty Slugs. He had pounded the last two with his rifle butt, until the stock finally shattered.

I sighed and grabbed Howard's arm. "Aye-aye, Admiral."

We turned away from Brace. Mimi on one side and I on the other steered Howard off the bridge. Beneath my fingers, the twine-thin muscles of Howard's forearm quivered.

So did his voice. "Dammit, Jason! The man's a fool! Our only hope—"

"Howard, in twenty-four hours, Brace'll be fighting an armada, every ship in it the size of Mount Rushmore. You think he'll notice whether our boom's connected or not? Stick with the plan. We'll take off to try and board that Troll and he'll let us go."

The trouble with professors is they don't understand people like us line commanders.

I knew what I was doing.

THIRTY-SEVEN

WE SLIPPED OUR GEAR ABOARD Mimi's V-Star, then I went back to my cabin to sleep. A day from now, I was either going to be awake for a long time or asleep forever.

In my cabin I lay atop the blanket on my bunk—a soldier doesn't mess up a made bunk unnecessarily, even if it's never going to be inspected—fingers laced behind my head. Awake a long time? Who was I kidding? We were going to be dead. I should have popped a stay-awake and savored every last minute, and talked a chip diary, then sealed it in a canister, launched it toward Earth, and hoped someone would be there to read it.

Jeeb's microhydraulics sighed as he preened, perched on a chairback.

"Did it matter, Jeeb? My life? Any of it?"

"I am not programmed to respond to that inquiry. Please restructure." Jeeb didn't *say* that, of course. It just popped into my earpiece, a standardized, prerecorded soundbite.

Ruth Klein-Tway, and I as well, may have deluded ourselves otherwise out of sentimentality, but Jeep was just a 'bot.

I didn't even have a priest to hear my confession. Not that I was religious.

If there was a God I'd know soon enough. I figured he wouldn't be pissed at me for doubting his existence or for not going to church. I mean, God was supposed to be forgiving of human frailty. I smiled at the ceiling. If I had to spend eternity reporting to somebody like Brace I'd transfer to hell.

On the chance that God was listening, I covered my bet by praying. Nothing personal, just that *Excalibur* would survive long enough to let us get inside the Troll and go down fighting.

At some point I drifted off. I was lying on my bunk, then *Excalibur* exploded and I was tumbling through vacuum with bits of bulkhead and a synwool bunk blanket tumbling alongside me. I was very upset that the blanket was flopping around, unmade, in space. I waited to feel cold sear my bones, to feel the pain of explosive decompression, but I just kept tumbling.

"Jason?"

Howard peered into my face, his hand on my shoulder. "It's time, Jason."

I sat up and rubbed my face.

"The Pseudocephalopod picket ships are close. They're firing ranging rounds."

"Conventional weapons?"

We had wondered whether the Slug ships would be armed with death rays or lightning bolts or just explosives and cannonballs.

Howard nodded while I strapped on armor. He was already armored up, helmet beneath one arm. In rust-red

Eternads, Howard resembled an anorexic orangutan in glasses.

I, on the other hand, resembled a Roman gladiator, I thought.

Howard nodded at my question. "Most of their shots went wide a thousand miles. The Mercurys picked off the on-target rounds."

By the time Howard and I arrived in the passage at the air lock to our V-Star, Brumby sat there cross-legged, rewinding det cord.

Mimi arrived last, not because she was putting on makeup or something but because the pilots bunked forward, in Space Force country. In her flight suit she seemed as soft as a child in pajamas, but as she walked closer her eyes were as old and as hard as diamond. She tugged on her helmet and dropped the orange visor over her face. "We good to go, General?"

I nodded.

She stepped past me toward the open air lock that led out to her ship, past the attention-stiffened Space Force rating tending the 'lock deck.

Ten minutes later the light above the air lock flashed green and a buzzer's rasp made me jump. The Space Force man on the lock was the same redhead who had mothballed *Excalibur* when we had left her a few weeks before. He said, "Systems' checks done, General. All aboard, sir."

Weapons clattered against armor, Jeeb fluttered off my shoulder and assumed his programmed point position just ahead of me.

We stepped off, Jeeb's six footpads clicking on the deck plates.

The 'lock tender snapped off a salute, fingertips just

below the carrot-tone fuzz that showed beneath his cap. "Go get 'em, mudfeet!"

Jeeb twisted his head toward the 'lock tender and, as he scurried past the man, touched his right front forelimb to his forward antennae, returning the salute.

The red-haired 'lock tender leaned toward me as I drew even with him. "Sir, you're just boarding in case, right? I heard this ship's in reserve."

I lied but he didn't recognize it. "Yep."

The 'lock tender furrowed his brow, then brightened. "Well, good hunting, sir!"

"We'll see you soon." I looked away. That was a lie that we both recognized.

I stepped across the hatch lip and it clanged, then hissed as the 'lock tender dogged the hatch behind us.

The V-Star's cabin air carried the metallic tang of ozone to the back of my throat as we wormed around jury-rigged thruster piping and into the V-Star's troop bay.

Modified for the V-Star's deep-space-fighter role, the bay squeezed us even more than it had when it was configured for troop transport.

The canister packed with three tons of S-51 plastique was lashed to the bay's left side.

Neoplast containers filled with Brumby's fusing and detonators and Thermite were packed against the bay's right wall.

The retracted, tubular docking bridge that Mimi would extend, to let us swarm aboard the Troll like weightless buccaneers, filled the bay's front third. The docking bridge would poke out through the hull space where the other V-Star fighters sported missile racks.

I snorted to myself. One more reason Brace's insistence

on holding this V-Star close for fighter duty made no sense. With the missile rack removed, our ship was barely armed.

Our only armament was defensive. We carried a single Mercury system, its turret and operator blister swelling from the V-Star's back amidships, like a tumor. The six-foot-diameter cylinder housing the Mercury system's turret and ammunition pods, festooned with hydraulic hoses, grew through the troop bay's center from deck to ceiling, like Jack's beanstalk. It left room for two jump seats, one for Howard and one for Brumby. That meant my seat was in the Mercury system's fighting chair. This was an accident of limited space, not a functional assignment, since computers aimed and fired Mercury unless something broke. But there was a fringe benefit. Even Mimi, in her cockpit, had only a virtual windscreen, images projected by optical sensors that were located on the V-Star's nose, tail, and flanks. But the spherical gyroscope of the fighting chair's cage rotated inside a four-inch-thick quartz dome, like the gun turret of an ancient propeller-driven bomber.

Brumby helped me strap in, then settled back in his seat facing me. "Better you than me, sir."

"Huh?"

Brumby shook his head as he blinked. "To be looking out the window. Space scares me."

"Then you should've joined the infantry, Brumby."

He opened his mouth, then closed it and smiled. "Yes, sir."

I hit the "elevate" button, hydraulics whined, and the fighting chair rose into the blister. We hung off of rotating *Excalibur*'s side belly-out, so centrifugal force still made "gravity" that weighted us toward our own deck plates. That meant that, above my head, *Excalibur*'s vastness curved away in all directions. A hundred yards to either side of me, fighter V-Stars floated at the ends of their docking booms. White missile racks, externally plumbed thruster packages, and Mercury turrets and blisters spoiled their once-sleek lines. A hundred yards ahead of me, *Excalibur*'s Mercury-turret array stretched across my vision like a dull pearl string. Beyond the array stretched space, black and even colder for the icy light-points of stars that punctuated it.

"Jason? Do you see 'em?" Mimi's voice whispered inside my helmet.

"Huh?"

"Straight out across the nose, then left to eleven o'clock."

Barely visible blue smudged space's ebony. I blinked. "I thought I had good eyes, Mimi."

"Punch up your targeting optics. You've got the same magnification available to you that I've got up here in the cockpit."

A sea of never-before-seen buttons, displays, and control handles surrounded me. "I don't want to touch the wrong thing."

"You can't. Unless I activate your controls. Spin the yellow handwheel beside your right index finger."

I spun it and scarlet and green heads-up light reticles traced their way across the inside of the observation dome. At their center, a box labeled "MAG 1000" showed a sea of blue roaches crawling toward us. I blinked.

The Slug armada was closing fast. I had expected them spread out across space, dispersed for protection. Instead they flew a few ship-lengths apart, like a strategic bomber formation close-coupled so the guns of one ship could protect its flanking partners. Golden flashes winked from noses and tails, like aircraft navigation lights.

"Alpha Squadron cast off." The voice was male and metallic. Mimi had left me patched into *Excalibur*'s Combat Net.

To my right and left, the V-Stars' docking booms retracted, until the wedge-shaped fighters floated free, tethered to *Excalibur* only by umbilicals that undulated like silver snakes.

"Alpha One clear."

The report echoed nine times more, then the metallic control voice replied, "You are clear to take the squadron out, Alpha Leader. Godspeed."

The V-Stars formed up an echelon a mile from *Excalibur,* in a silent ballet marked by little thruster puffs visible at their noses and flanks.

They hung static for one indrawn breath, then a noiseless flash made me blink as their main engines lit. In the second it took my vision to clear, Alpha Squadron were specks, visible only as light pinpoints receding into blackness. I breathed, "Damn!"

Mimi chuckled. "Now you know why I fly these things, Jason."

I spun the fighting chair so the magnified reticle rested on Alpha Squadron. Bravo's ten ships flanked Alpha to its left.

Beyond the little knot of V-Stars, and so much larger that they seemed of equal size despite their distance, rushed a Slug-fighter phalanx.

The arms at the Firewitches' noses spread like jaws, then crimson flashes flared at their tips.

"Alpha, we have incoming to you." The control voice elevated an octave.

"Roger. We got 'em. Alpha, on my command, break right. Break!"

The ten V-Stars dodged and a glittering swarm of Slug ammunition sped harmlessly past. Cake. Maybe this wasn't going to be a turkey shoot for the Slugs after all.

All ten Bravos juked left past two Slug volleys.

The combined closing speed of the V-Stars and the Slug vanguard, even slowed down to a relative crawl, had to be ten thousand miles per hour.

I bumped up magnification as Alpha spread into attack formation. The Slugs had formed into a cone-shaped lead pack of Firewitches. The big Troll and more Firewitches followed behind, a protected cylinder of blue streaks, now close enough that they were visible even without magnification.

Our two V-Star formations were juking every second, now. Red flashed as the Firewitches shot volley after volley. Coupled with their steadily winking navigation lights, the scene sparked like a level-six holo-game tank. But this one had no reset button.

"I have target lock." I recognized the voice. Alpha's lead.

"Locked" was repeated nine more times, followed by "Fox One" as each V-Star fired the first of its missiles. Even magnified at max I could see only streaks of rocket-engine exhaust, not the actual missiles.

The V-Stars flashed through the Slug formation like gnats passing skyscrapers.

My mag screen blossomed with explosions, orange as

our missiles struck Slug ships and—ominously—three as green as broccoli.

Alpha's V-Stars bent around and headed back to strike the Slug formation from behind.

"How many we lose?"

"Where's Taylor?"

"Christ."

"There goes Bravo."

"Bravo, adjust your aim points. You gotta hit the Firewitch dead-center between the gun arms. The flanks must be armored."

The trailing squadron shot through the Slug formation with, it looked like, the same result.

Then one Firewitch seemed to boil orange.

I held my breath.

The Firewitch exploded so violently I swore I could hear it across vacuum.

"Yee-hah!" A fighter-jock chorus sang across the combat net.

Brumby tugged my leg. "Sir? What happened?"

I didn't realize I had yelled as loud as the fighter pilots. I glanced down into the bay. "We got a Firewitch."

Brumby pumped his fist and shouted.

I didn't tell him that if I read the green explosions right, we had lost a quarter of our guys on the first pass.

"Jason?" It was Mimi. "Tell 'em to strap in back there. We're losing too many V-Stars too fast. We need to go now."

Ahead of us, Alpha's seven remaining ships made their second run through the Slugs. This time, the Troll was in their sights.

"Jesus! It's like a city!"

"On your left! On your—"

A green explosion flared, then died.

Orange flashes, as our missiles exploded against the Troll's hide, looked like no more than sparks.

"We're not gonna dent the big one, guys."

"We need nukes."

"Get me a count."

"I make us five, skipper."

I glanced at my 'puter. Alpha had taken fifty percent casualties in two combat minutes.

Our V-Star jerked and I bumped my helmet against the fighting chair's frame.

Mimi had shed the docking boom, in violation of Brace's orders. But not in violation of our mission.

She rolled our ship, so the view over my head changed from *Excalibur*'s skin, curving away to its own planetlike horizon, to space's inky darkness.

Ahead of us, the Slug fleet stretched all across my vision field, a sea of winking, iridescent blue. The Firewitches' red flashes now were incoming at *Excalibur*.

"I have targets."

"Are the Mercurys operating?"

No turret in the line that stitched across *Excalibur*'s hull even twitched.

"Something's fucked! Switch 'em to manual!"

"Steady."

"But—"

As one, the turret line swiveled. The six-gun rotating barrels elevated, tracked, then spit solid wands of fire. Thousands of thirty-seven-millimeter cannon rounds ripped through space, their outgoing kinetic energy colliding, as they struck incoming Slug rounds, at a combined speed near twenty thousand miles per hour. It almost didn't matter that our rounds were high-explosive. They hit a Slug incoming round like a penny dropped off the Washington Monument into a cheesecake. The collisions made harmless purple explosions, each volley of Slug rounds painting the sky like a Fourth of July finale as the Mercurys threw up a solid steel wall miles away from us.

I chortled into our intercom as Mimi tiptoed us a mile away from *Excalibur*. "Hooyah, Mimi! At least we don't have to worry about getting shot down."

Mimi didn't answer.

"Venture Star One One Bravo, state your situation." We named this ship for the lowest of the low, an infantry private, Military Operational Specialty 11B.

Our little joke had annoyed Brace no end. I could hear the edge in his voice as he said it, even now.

Mimi answered Brace. "At, we had a short in our docking boom. We had to disconnect or risk being trapped."

Brace's voice was ice. "Ship's readouts don't show any electrical fault. Bring your ship back in."

"At, the squadrons—"

There were no squadrons. There were a handful of V-Stars still flying.

Mimi continued, "—are depleted. Every second counts. We're your reserve. It's time to release your reserve."

"I said, bring your ship back in."

"I've got a stuck thruster. Too hazardous to return. I could damage both ships."

"Bullshit."

Ahead of us, yellow flame lances crisscrossed the sky as Mercury's cannons swatted away swarms of Slug shots. Two huge orange explosions boiled, along with two bright green flashes. The Slugs were paying a steep price, but we would go bankrupt before they did.

Mimi said, "At, drop the rule book! This ship doesn't even carry missiles! We're useless to you."

"We'll refit."

"You don't have time."

Pause.

"Hibble and the others are on board with you. The crew saw them. You're pulling something."

Pause.

"If I don't see your nose come 'round in ten seconds, I'll have you shot down."

I smiled. Ludicrous though Brace's threat was, it wasn't even credible. The Mercurys on auto couldn't fire on a transponder-equipped vessel like us, any more than a vampire could charge at a cross.

All around us, now, V-Stars swooped and explosions flared. The lead Slug ships drew so close I could see their red-flashing gun arms with my naked eyes.

Inside my helmet, Brace counted. "Six. Five. Four." Brace actually sounded like he would shoot down one of his own ships over some pissant turf battle.

"Fire Control, this is Admiral Brace. On my command, switch to manual and engage Venture Star One One Bravo."

Manual? I shouted into my mike. "No!"

"Zero, fire!" said Brace.

Excalibur's Mercury turrets rotated toward us. Black Gatling-gun barrels elevated and zeroed in. Tones, one after another, whined in my headset as Mercury fire-control radars locked on us.

The explosion's flash blinded me.

THIRTY-EIGHT

I HELD MY BREATH and waited to relive my nightmare, tumbling through frozen vacuum, the debris of my exploded spaceship all around me. My heart pounded. I flexed my fingers and felt the stanchion I had been gripping. I opened my eyes, blinked.

Around me arched the Mercury blister's quartz dome. V-Star One One Bravo hovered intact in space.

I focused ahead of me, on *Excalibur*.

Excalibur was gone. A Niagara of exploded debris tumbled toward me. The forward thrusters puffed as Mimi juked us to dodge *Excalibur*'s remains. Pilot that she was, she had reacted even before I knew what had happened.

A rectangle like a taupe-paper funeral announcement tumbled at me. It gonged the blister's quartz dome as I ducked reflexively. The twenty-gauge Plasteel panel floated away. It bore black stenciling "BULKHEAD 104. WATCH YOUR STEP."

Behind the bulkhead flew more debris, flailing. The redheaded 'lock tender who had saluted Jeeb somersaulted slowly as he passed us, his starched coveralls powder-blue in the starlight. His eyes were wide, his mouth open, screaming with no sound. Our eyes met for a breath, then he was gone from sight. And dead a 'puter-tick later.

There in the turret, as debris hurtled away into nothing, I didn't move. My mouth hung open.

The enormity.

When Brace switched Mercury's guns to manual, so he could train them on us, unimpeded Slug barrages tore into *Excalibur* within seconds. Brace, who so prided himself on operating by the book, on caution and precision, had stumbled just for one instant. He had died for his error.

No, it hadn't been just Brace's folly. I had goaded him when I could have helped him. Resisted when I could have cooperated. Our petty clash of wills had snuffed humanity's faint, remaining hope.

The mightiest construct in the millennial history of human ingenuity was now jumbled detritus, destined to float through space until the sun burned out.

The twenty-six human lives *Excalibur* nurtured in her mile-long shell were gone, too, frozen meat adrift upon the cosmos. Because I was a smart-ass. For this destiny, other men and women had died and I had lived.

"Jason?" Something tugged my boot. I looked down and saw Howard peering up into the blister.

"Huh?" Howard's voice seemed like he spoke through a blanket.

"*Excalibur*'s gone," I said.

Howard paused, then said, "We can still follow the plan."

Ahead of us, a few V-Stars jinked and dodged. Fire-witches swarmed around them. For the Slugs, all that remained was a lazy mop-up. Beyond them loomed the Troll.

Mimi's voice twanged in my headset. "Jason? There's not enough distraction. You ready to shoot our way in?"

"That's not part of the plan." Sticking to the plan had just killed Brace. "But what do you need?"

THIRTY-NINE

TEN MINUTES LATER, Mimi twisted and rolled our V-Star among maneuvering Firewitches and V-Stars.

Then, when I looked around, I saw only Firewitches.

So puny were we that the mountainous Firewitches above, below, in front of, and behind us seemed to ignore us. Their navigation lights blinked serenely like fireflies in an ebony meadow. So huge were the Slug vessels that wreckage and interplanetary flotsam gravitated to them and loosely orbited them.

The main engine's vibration stopped. Mimi said, "We might make it by playing dead." A bow thruster puffed and we began a lazy yaw, drifting toward the Troll's mass. We were the last, unnoticed survivors of the resistance that the Pseudocephalopod Empire had swatted like a gnat. But Mimi was making us tumble like we were disabled space junk being pulled in toward the Troll.

Perhaps we weren't the last. Still strapped-in to the fighting chair, I spoke into my helmet mike. "Mimi? Any Maydays on the net? Any chatter?"

She sighed. "There's nobody else, Jason. The rest of the Firewitches are returning and mooring to the Troll."

Our ship rotated so that behind us I saw blue Earth and beyond it the moon, distant, serene, and, now, defenseless. A shadow crossed them. "Mimi, there's one Firewitch that looks interested in us."

The Slug fighter approached us in no apparent hurry. It might be unsure whether we were undamaged, worth expending ammunition on. In minutes, it would be so close that it would know. "Mimi, they're nosy."

"I see. They had a couple pickets out before. That's probably all this is. Just another picket. Wait 'til they're close, then give 'em the gun. Just set it on auto and Mercury will do the rest. I can get us to the Troll if you just disable that one."

Cake. All I had to do was disable a battleship bigger than Fenway Park using a weapon I touched for the first time twenty minutes ago.

Firewitches were vulnerable. We had seen that. The Mercury system I was sitting in could inflict disabling damage. But from the point-blank range we would be at when our V-Star again tumbled into firing position, the Firewitch would present so enormous a target that it would confuse a Mercury on automatic.

"Mimi, how sensitive is the Mercury system?"

"You're right. You'll have to trigger it manually."

Before I could call down to Brumby, I heard him in the troop bay below me, reading aloud from an instruction chip that had been stored in a plastic pocket attached to our Mercury system turret innards. "In most combat situations, automatic mode, or manual mode employing fire-control radar or other ranging device, is preferable."

Below me, Brumby twitched as he read.

"However, in extreme cases the system may be operated in full manual mode."

Howard poked his head under the blister lip. "Jason, you've got three minutes." The edge on his voice cut the cabin air. Howard knew this really was our only chance. The last thing anyone needed to hear from the general in charge was doubt.

"Don't worry, Howard. I can fight this system. It's like Playstation Forty." I ignored the winking control array around me and the fact that Mercury operator school ran eight weeks.

"—is traversed left or right by application of pressure to the respective foot treadle."

I put my right foot down, like a traffic light had turned green. The turret whined, spun right, and the framework nearly decapitated Howard. "Oops! Better stand clear, Howard."

He muttered something.

The Mercury cannon turret now had rotated and sat at an angle on the V-Star's back, like a baseball cap worn sideways for wardrobe effect.

Brumby read ahead. "To elevate the guns, draw back gently on the right-hand pistol grip."

I grabbed the pistol grip, which stuck up above the fighting chair's right armrest, and yanked.

The cannon fired. The V-Star's air frame shook. Hundreds of rounds exploded out of the gun's multiple muzzles. Its barrel assembly spun as fast as a giant dentist's drill. Feed belts clanked as new cannon rounds slammed into the gun's multiple breeches. Hydraulics screamed. Howard yelped.

Brumby read on. "Taking care not to depress the firing

trigger. The firing trigger is the red button at the pistol grip's upper right."

Crap. According to the system readout array in front of me, 612 rounds of Samuel Colt's finest thirty-seven-millimeter high-explosive/armor-piercing mixed ammunition were now hurtling through space in the general direction of Pluto.

"Sir, are you sure you know how to work this thing?"

My chest swelled beneath my armor. If there was one thing the Army had taught me, it was how to fire a machine gun. This was just a big machine gun. With a couple of hundred more controls than I was used to. I made a horizontal smoothing motion with the same hand that had just blundered onto the trigger. "Grease, Brumby. Pure grease."

He frowned. "Sure, sir."

Two minutes' practice later, I was pretty sure I could aim and fire the Mercury well enough to hit a target as big as a Firewitch control room. Which was optimistic since no human being had any idea where a Firewitch had its control room, much less how big it was.

Howard craned his neck to look up at me. "The control ganglion has to be in the front, where the six firing arms intersect."

Mimi whispered to me, "With the firing arms spread, the front end of that thing is like a basket the size of Madison Square Garden. If the control ganglion's where Howard says it is, it will be right where center ice would be for a Rangers game. That's where you shoot. Okay?"

I nodded, invisibly to her. "Okay."

"It's your destiny, Jason."

"Huh?"

"You know. Like Jason the Argonaut. You poke out the cyclops's eye."

I smiled. "Is that Texan mythology? Odysseus blinded the cyclops, not Jason."

"If you get this right, five thousand years from now maybe everybody will remember it was Jason."

Drifting between the Firewitch's firing arms I felt more like Jonah than Jason, like being swallowed by a whale. Curved and iridescent blue, the arms were as large as high-rise apartment towers, alight with window-style openings. I fancied I saw Slugs peering out at us. Unlikely since they didn't have eyes.

At the confluence where the arms intersected rose a dome, smooth and glowing purple. Not so unlike an eye. Mimi didn't dare maneuver our ship obviously, so I rotated the turret and laid the gun on target. I pressed the foot treadle like there was a raw egg between it and my boot sole and I didn't want to break the shell. The apex of the purple dome rose in my sights.

From the corner of my eye, I saw a light wink. The IR sensor on the upper right of my display had flashed. Our V-Star was being painted by active infrared. Slugs saw in the infrared spectrum. They were shining searchlights on us. We were busted.

"Mimi, I have to take the shot."

The Firewitch's arms began to close around us. It might be too close to shoot us, but It could crush us.

The time was now or never. I thumbed the trigger. The fuselage shook and the gun thundered. A stream of yellow tracer stabbed at the dome, dead-center. It exploded. From stem to stern, the Firewitch's lights went out. The outrush of atmosphere from the Firewitch's breached hull blasted past us and buffeted the V-Star like a leaf in a gale.

Mimi muttered in my ear. "Damn, you're good!"

I was. Monsters blinded while-u-wait.

Tugging to unfasten the straps that held me in the fighting chair, I sprained a thumb.

I got the straps loose and swung down into the troop bay like a gymnast dismounting the high bar.

Howard and Brumby, helmeted and armored, jaws tight, turned and stared at me.

I strapped on my rucksack, cross-slung my machine gun over my back, and winked at them. "Now comes the fun part, guys!"

I'd never told a bigger lie.

FORTY

Two MINUTES LATER, I floated in the docking bridge that Howard's Spooks had designed and that Mimi had deployed from the V-Star's back. I pressed my helmet faceplate against the bridge hatch's six-inch-thick quartz porthole. Ahead there was nothing but the Troll's blue vastness.

Mimi slid the V-Star alongside the Troll's skin. Close up, it was seamed and pebbled. Inside the monster's hide beat a heart. The propulsion system. Whatever power could carry an object this big between the stars could surely blow the Troll into rutabagas, and all its Firewitch friends with it.

We faced the minor obstacle that one hundred thousand Slugs inside that skin would be armed, disciplined, and not keen to assist with our plan.

Mimi's voice rang in my earpiece. "Boarding Party, prepare for assault."

My finger trembled, testing my M-20's safety for the hundredth time. We expected close-quarters battle and I had loaded flechette, effectively converting an assault rifle into a shotgun that fired eight hundred shells per minute. Over my breastplate I wore Ord's shoulder holster and

.45. It was loaded with Ord's homemade flechette spe-
cials. But I felt naked without my M-60, which was strung
across my back. Among us we carried all the gear
Howard's Spooks could imagine, since we had little idea
what we might need.

I huffed inside my helmet. The paradox of infantry was
that at the moment of assault, when a soldier most needed
to be quick and nimble, he was loaded like a rented yak.

The V-Star's thrusters rattled my teeth as Mimi eased
us against the Troll.

I turned my head and looked back at Howard and
Brumby. Behind them in zero Gee floated the Bomb, a
tube long enough and wide enough to garage a family
sedan. Once we wrestled the bomb aboard the Troll, in
that inexplicable Slug gravity, it would become a one-ton
handful that we would have to roll through the twisting
passageways to wherever Howard and Brumby decided
was pay dirt.

We were about to worm belly-down through the Slug
ship's twisted passages. The cryptozoologists predicted
Slug defenders would ooze from dark passage walls and
ceilings, knowing what humans would do before we did it.
I knew what we would do before I did it. I was the only
human who had been in a Slug vessel and I didn't want to
go back. I forced myself to exhale and shut my eyes.

A gloved hand fumbled against my shoulder. Howard
flailed beside me. "Jason?"

My eyes snapped open. "Relax, Howard. We're good-
to-go." Commanders are paid to lie at times like these.

"I know, Jason."

"Ten seconds, Jason," Mimi's voice cut in. Cocky and

crisp, the way only a female pilot's voice can be. I'd once asked a pilot like that to marry me.

I shook my head and my helmet scraped against the quartz porthole. No time to grieve.

The hatch grab-bar vibrated in my gloved hands as hydraulics stretched the bridge's docking collar around the Troll's skin.

Thub!

The collar flattened around the alien hull like putty, sculpting a tunnel between the vessels.

My heart pounded out the seconds as Brumby manipulated the bridge's robotic arms. They screeched forward down the tunnel, then stitched breaching charges against the Slug hull, a spider spinning Thermite webs.

I breathed deep. Ozone-tinged air pricked my nostrils and I felt weight on my shoulders, even in zero Gee. History's first clash between ships in space had just been lost by mankind. Was my destiny to survive this long, just to die in the belly of this alien beast?

Brumby called, "Fire in the hole!"

Spider arms jackknifed aside.

Destiny. I had been the first human to board an alien vessel. I had been the first human to contact an alien. And the first human to kill one. I had delivered the first human child conceived and born beyond the Earth. I had commanded the Army that saved the human race. Those all seemed improbable destinies. As improbable as the reality that the next twelve hours would change not just the history of the human race, but the history of the universe.

I squeezed my eyes shut but the breaching charge flashed sun-bright through my eyelids.

FORTY-ONE

JEEB FLEW FIRST DOWN the docking bridge and I floated right behind him, into the purple-lit dimness of the Slug ship. Their artificial gravity tugged me to the deck plates. How the Slugs did that, I didn't know.

There was a lot I didn't know. In front of my left eye, Jeeb's sensors whirled data readouts across the Battlefield Awareness Monocle display. Interior temperature, sixty degrees Fahrenheit. Barometric pressure equivalent to an Earth altitude of fifteen thousand feet above sea level. Atmospheric oxygen fifteen percent, three-fourths of Earth normal, but livable. No atmospheric toxins. So far, Howard's predictions were right. If we could secure this ship, or at least this tiny part of it, we could live and breathe here long enough to save the world. I shut down my oxygen generator.

I glanced over my shoulder. Howard and Brumby swam down the boarding bridge into the Troll, through the enormous yellow donut of the bridge's seal plug, that would inflate and keep vacuum away from us as soon as they got the Bomb past the Plug. The Bomb, leashed behind Howard and Brumby like a chariot behind two-legged ponies, drifted across the threshold from the bridge into the Troll, then thumped onto its wheels as it took on weight. Brumby and Howard twisted around, pulled the synlon ropes that bound them to the Bomb hand over hand, and drew our precious cargo toward us.

Mimi, at the V-Star's controls, spoke in my earpiece. "Disconnecting the docking collar and standing off, Jason."

We had agreed she would stand off because we might need to exit the Troll by another avenue. If so, probably because a thousand Slugs were chasing us. Quick pickup by Mimi could save our hides.

I turned, watched as the bridge tube's snout retracted, and held my breath. If the Plug failed to swell and cork the hull breach, explosive decompression would spit us all out into space. The Plug held.

If Howard's timetable was right, we had three minutes to seal off enough bottlenecks to buy Brumby time to figure out how to blow up the power plant, but still leave us a way to return to Mimi and escape. If Howard's mapping was right we had entered at a main passage that spiraled up near the outer hull at this point. We would hustle the Bomb along it, deep into the Troll power plant's gut. So far, so good.

Brumby, looking past me into the Troll, spoke in my ear on Whispercom. "Which way do we go, sir?"

I spun around. Howard's mock-up said we should see a single passage. Now, in the real world, ahead of us stretched two branching passages. Crap.

Either one would require us to crawl.

That wasn't the real problem.

Brumby said, "Sir, the Bomb won't fit down either of those passages."

He was right. Slug passages varied in diameter, but neither of these came close to being wide or tall enough to swallow the Bomb.

Crap.

"Howard, we're supposed to be in a big passage."

"I know. I'm thinking."

"Can we just blow it here?"

Brumby answered, "We need to confine the explosion, sir. Detonating the Bomb here, just under the Troll's skin, wouldn't do much damage."

Except to us three.

I sent Jeeb winging ahead down the left passage.

He got twenty twisting yards down the passage before the first Slugs hit us.

Slug passageways are twisting cylinders, like purple-lit sewers. The doorways that lead off the passageways aren't doorways. They're four-inch-wide slots. Fine if you're a boneless cousin to an octopus that can squeeze itself as flat as a bad omelette, useless to humans.

For those reasons, the slots make fine ambush points.

At first, the Slugs just poked their odd, curved guns out of the slots and fired wildly at us.

A round grazed my helmet. Slug mag-rail rifles hurl big, powerful bullets. My head rang and I would have sore neck muscles from having my head snapped around, but I had gotten lucky.

We pulled back to our entry point.

Rounds began whizzing past us from the right passageway. They flashed by or pinballed off the passage walls, peeling off wall plates that crashed to the deck.

Slugs had always been lousy shots. Theoretically, the red Eternad armor coating made us look like ghosts to an infrared-sighted observer.

We flattened ourselves on the deck and returned fire. Three M-20s spit a combined twenty-four hundred rounds per minute. Each round blossomed into ninety as flechettes spread. Tracers among the flechette rounds sparked red in the purple light as they vanished into darkness. On full auto, the three of us created a Fourth of July finale.

My rifle bucked against my armor's shoulder cap for less time than it took to breathe before I had to change magazines. I rolled on my belly, one hand snatching a magazine heavy with brass from an ammo pouch on my belt while my other hand flung out the featherweight empty. It was awkward enough with five fingers, two fingers on my one glove just flopped around, empty.

We faced a hundred thousand Slugs. More, if Howard's opposing forces estimate was as wrong as his estimate that we should be in a bigger passage. We had no idea whether our return fire was killing Slugs.

I Whispercommed, probably so loud Howard and Brumby heard my voice right through their helmets without the radio. The Slugs might not be able to see us. But so far we had certainly not seen them. "Switch to semi-auto. At least until they show themselves."

Since we couldn't see them, our rifles went silent.

My heart pounded in my ears.

Cordite smoke fogged my vision.

The fog swirled.

The swirls resolved into solid objects.

Black, armored shapes slid through the gloom toward us.

Boom-boom-boom!

I shuddered at the memory. Slug warriors on the attack beat their weapons against their armor, in unison, the sound still came to me in nightmares.

Brumby whispered, "Hello again, you little bastards." He squeezed off a round and a black ghost reared back, then dropped to the passage floor.

In the instant it took for Brumby's rifle to chamber his next round, the first Slug wave hurtled out of the dimness.

Man-sized, armored except for the green-skinned head-end patch through which they saw infrared light, they snaked toward us like gleaming, black bananas. Each warrior carried a curved mag-rail rifle, its barrel sword-edged. They filled the passage wall to wall and floor to ceiling.

Full auto worked fine.

It was over in thirty-three seconds.

I know that because it takes me eleven seconds to change M-20 magazines and three lay on the deck plates in front of me when we stopped firing.

The leading edge of the first wave lay twenty feet in front of us, Slug slime oozing from armor through flechette-torn pinpricks. The warrior carcasses stacked one upon another to the ceiling plates like flour sacks in a warehouse.

Howard breathed over the Whispercom. "Holy moly!"

Brumby said, "Fuck!"

I gathered up my empty magazines for reloading, from habit.

Alongside the Bomb sat Brumby's containers, no wider than an armored soldier's shoulders. If we didn't just want to sit here taking target practice on Slug warriors, we could haul Brumby's containers with us, even if we couldn't haul the Bomb.

I turned to Howard. "You said you were thinking. Why's your map wrong?"

"We don't understand how the Pseudocephalopod propels its ships. We may be nowhere near the power plant, after all. It was just a hunch."

I slapped my forehead. Well, my armored glove slapped my armored helmet. My palm never got within four inches of my eyebrows. "We bet the future of the human race on a hunch?"

"The future of the human race was only worth a two-dollar ticket, Jason." He paused. "I was counting on you to improvise. That's what you do best."

I shook my head and muttered while I accessed Jeeb.

Howard pounded a wall, and another plate loosened by Slug fire gonged the deck. "This stuff won't stretch. We can't move the Bomb intact. We'll have to dismantle the canister."

Brumby shook his head. "Major, that's three tons of S-51, at Earth-normal. Still a ton in here. We can roll that canister but we're all already toting a couple hundred pounds of gear at Earth-normal."

Jeeb hovered two hundred yards up the tunnel that headed away from the axis of assault of the Slug mob we had slaughtered. In my BAM, I saw what he saw. The passage was blissfully Slug-free. It ended at a sealed Slug hatch, big and different from anything I had seen in my prior travels through a Slug vessel. Was it the kind of hatch an alien, green hive intellect would choose to seal off an engine room? Maybe Howard wasn't as wrong as we thought.

Howard whispered, "Uh oh." He pointed at the dead-Slug pile.

It bulged toward us. Something strong enough to budge a couple hundred Slug carcasses, maybe a couple hundred more live Slug reinforcements, was pushing through to introduce itself to us.

I stared at the Bomb, our ball-and-chain. We had no time to break it down into totable packages.

A dead Slug got shoved out of the jam, bounced over the other bodies, and rolled to our feet. The rest of the pile bulged forward.

I pointed at Brumby's explosives containers. "Grab those. Head down the other corridor."

Howard stared at the Bomb. "What about that? How are we gonna blow up a mountain with no Bomb?"

Another Slug rolled off the moving pile. I hefted a container. "We'll improvise. Move your ass, Howard."

Howard and I had made a hundred yards, panting and cursing the containers we carried, when I realized Brumby wasn't with us.

His voice seeped back over the Whispercom. "Sir, I'm sealing off the branch passages with Megatex as we go. The little fuckers slime through those slot doorways a couple at a time. But if we deny 'em the wide passages they can't come at us hard enough to overrun us."

Megatex was the duct tape of contemporary plastique. A sausage roll of explosives that Brumby could play like a Stradivarius. "Okay. But keep close to us."

Whump!

As if to punctuate our conversation, a muffled but unmistakable Megatex detonation shook the passage. I

smiled. Between Megatex and Brumby, nothing was slim-
ing through *that* passage for a while.

We dropped every Slug that dared to wiggle a green
pseudopod out of a door slot. But there always seemed to
be more.

Howard lurched along just behind me as we ran. "Fifty
yards to go, Howard."

I picked up the pace. Two Slugs popped out of door
slots to my front. Before they could aim their rail rifles, I
snapped off two shots. The beauty of a flechette round is
that aiming becomes a luxury.

Slugs are basically animate fluid sacks. A solid hit pops
them like water balloons. I rounded the bend where those
two lay and slipped on spilled mucus. One foot went from
under me, I crashed down on one armored knee and
gagged. Slug guts stink like rotted mushrooms.

Ahead, the passage branched, again. It wasn't supposed to, again. But this one was big.

Panting through my mouth in the thin air, I Whispercommed Brumby. "Left at the next fork. Stay close."

I kept moving, Howard in tow.

Behind me, firing erupted and echoed up the passage.
Rail rifles whine when they fire, like angry wasps.
Brumby's answering fire rattled. Full auto. That meant
lots of bad guys.

Brumby panted, too. "Sir, fifty of 'em just poured out
from that big passage before I could seal it."

I looked down the tunnel ahead, toward our goal. Beside me, Howard wheezed, his eyes alight with urgency.
Seconds ticked away.

"Close up when you can, Brumby." I stood and ran like
hell to catch up with Jeeb.

I won the sprint to the closed hatch. Jeeb clung shoulder-high to the passage's curved wall, his hide chameleoned purple, so he was invisible if you didn't know where to look. Homeothermic circuits matched Jeeb's temperature to his surroundings, so he was as invisible to the Slugs' infrared vision as he was to human vision. His probes were plastered against the door, reading conditions on its other side.

"Demolition forward," I said.

Nothing.

"Brumby? I need you here *now*!"

A Megatex *whump* shook the floor again.

Thirty seconds later, Brumby brushed past me, panting, his rucksack missing. He already had Megatex breaching-charge plastiques out of his minipack when he came alongside me. He took one breath, hands on hips, while his eyes flicked around, studying the door frame.

My BAM lit with data from Jeeb. The space on the other side of the hatch was vast. What could be vaster than a starship's engine room? Jackpot!

Brumby jumped back from the door and brandished his trigger transmitter. The charges he had placed were generous, as big as bread loaves. I nodded. We didn't have time to try again if he skimped on explosives. He shouted, "Fire in the hole! Fire in the hole!"

Howard and I turned away from the door and crouched.

"Fire in the hole!" On the third warning, Brumby pressed the trigger, even as he ran back down the passage.

FORTY-TWO

HOWARD AND I KNELT CLOSEST to the door, so the explosion flattened us. Air whooshed across us as pressure equalized between the passage and the chamber beyond.

Before the explosion's echoes died, I heard rail rifles zing and felt rounds whiz above my back like swarming wasps.

Brumby's answering fire chattered back.

Pinned down, I twisted my head. Howard lay beside me, eyes closed. Cracks spiderwebbed his face shield and, as I watched, blood trickled from one nostril across his cheek like a tear.

Firing stopped as I switched my BAM display to check his vitals. A green circle indicated healthy, a green blinker meant wounded. Howard's blinker turned solid green.

I touched his shoulder. "Howard?" No answer.

I Whispercommed. "Brumby?" No answer. I switched nets, for the hell of it. "Mimi?" No answer. We had expected hull interference.

My ears rang like firebells. Howard, Brumby, and Mimi could be talking but I might not be hearing.

Beyond the open hatch, through drifting explosion smoke, I saw vast darkness.

I stood and realized I'd sprained a knee. Limping back down the passage, I found Brumby tearing at debris, flinging Slug bodies and twisted metal aside.

It hadn't been fifty Slugs that jumped him, more like one hundred, by my casual body count. Warriors, in that black armor of theirs, and naked ones as well. One of their kamikaze charges, more extreme even than the first one that had hit us. That made me think that whatever was beyond the hatch we'd blown was something they didn't want us to control.

I stood in that passage a long time listening to Slug vital fluids drip. The smell of gunsmoke mingled in my nostrils with the stink of spilled Slug.

Brumby stood and swore.

"What, Brumby?"

"The container I was carrying. I had to drop it to get forward when you called. Then the charges I set blew." He thrust his hands at the mess that plugged the passage, floor to rounded ceiling. "The Megatex. The Microdets. All our best stuff was in there." He shook his head. "It's gone."

We trotted back to the blown door. Howard stood there, peering forward, bent at the waist.

Jeeb stood alongside him, legs extended, tiptoe style, so his sensors could look ahead, too.

Behind us, Brumby had sealed the side passages with explosives, but the way back to the breach where Mimi would pick us up remained open. Theoretically. The Slugs seemed to have abandoned coming at us one by one through their door slots. Slugs were content to sacrifice their buddies, but they knew when to quit a useless tactic.

How long our little armistice would hold I didn't know, but for the moment we could explore the chamber we had breached, unmolested by Slugs.

I Whispercommed Brumby. "Go on back there and see whether you can find the demo pack. Stay ten minutes to see whether that block's gonna hold."

I stepped forward to see what Howard and Jeeb were looking at.

The first thing I noticed wasn't anything to look at. A stench so strong it seemed to knock me back physically rolled out of the chamber.

I said to Howard, breathing through my mouth, "What the hell is that?"

Howard gasped, his palm futilely covering his face-plate. "I've spent time in better outhouses."

I dialed up my oxygen generator and manufactured air replaced the stink. The blackness remained impenetrable. Distant howling echoed from the opening.

I shuddered.

I turned to Jeeb, who stood in explosion debris puddled an inch deep around his six ankles. Nodding at the darkness, I said, "All yours, bud."

He crept through the opening, spread his wings, and flew slowly into the dark. Jeeb's infrared showed a single interior chamber, so vast that neither his visible nor infrared searchlights reached the ceiling or opposite wall. A catwalk or balcony swelled out of the wall fifty feet below our present level. I rigged climbing ropes, rappelled down, then belayed Howard. He twisted, gasped, and swung like a pendulum but I finally got him alongside me.

He turned to the interior wall and his light reflected off it, iridescent Slug blue.

I blinked as he shone his light on me.

Far below us, the howling grew.

FORTY-THREE

THE SLUG CATWALK curved along the chamber's wall and descended. With our headlights and Jeeb showing the way, we followed the catwalk down for twenty minutes, our breath echoing in air that carried the dank feel of something dead.

"Howard, this doesn't seem like an engine room." The Slug walkway—slinkway?—was two feet wide and had no handrail.

We had descended two hundred vertical feet by Jeeb's altimeter when the howling rose to painful levels and I cranked down my helmet-audio amp's gain. We played our lights on the noise and the beams flickered on hundred-foot-diameter drums, rotating in place like gargantuan steamrollers, eternally recycling. Gray glop poured off the rollers and cascaded down into darkness.

Howard, following me down the catwalk, shouted over the din, "It's peculiar. Not the sophisticated drive machinery I expected."

Once the walkway descended below the rollers, it branched and spread out into multiple paths that bridged the interior's open expanse. We descended another hundred feet until, according to Jeeb's sonar, we were one hundred feet above the chamber's floor. I leaned over as far as I dared and shone my light down. Most Slug construction was sleek, but the floor down there was gray, bumpy, and as uneven as cobblestone pavement. And it seemed to ripple like a wind-agitated lake.

When I swung my light back up through the blackness that surrounded us, it flashed over a lump on the walkway fifty feet ahead. When I swung back, it seemed to be one of the floor cobbles.

"Hey, Howard!" I pointed and walked toward it, then readjusted the weight of the M-60 cross-slung on my back before I knelt to examine the object. My pack weighed like bricks so I welcomed taking a knee. I breathed rapidly, and as the air had chilled with depth, my exhalations curled out through my helmet's exhaust valve, so intermittent fogs drifted across my headlight beam.

The cobble was oval and dirty white, like an unbaked bread loaf.

I reached for it. "Howard, this looks like—"

The cobble leapt at me.

I sucked in my breath so hard that the gasp echoed in the chamber's vastness.

It was a miniature Slug. When I recoiled, it flew past me, bounced on the walkway, and tumbled into thin air.

Overbalanced by my gun and pack, I staggered backward and fell over the walkway's edge. I followed the embryonic monster, as it dropped into blackness, and screamed.

FORTY-FOUR

THE CHAMBER FLOOR rushed up at me as I fell head first the one hundred feet toward it. In my headlamp's beam shone writhing, mounded naked Slugs beyond counting or imagination. I twisted in midair and struck them shoulder first. They exploded like stomped tomatoes as they broke my fall. I came to rest ten feet deep in a squirming sea.

Eternad armor is more renowned for perforation resistance than shock absorption, but except for the fire in a banged-up shoulder, I had survived my fall. That was more than I could say for the Slug that writhed and died two inches beyond my helmet visor. Ooze leaked into my mouth under my visor, with the taste of bitter rot and, I imagined, putrid flesh. I gagged.

I thrashed and clawed upward, against the grisly maggots that buried me, until I burst again into open darkness.

One hundred feet above me a headlamp beam hacked back and forth across the dark. "Jason? Are you alright?"

I scrabbled amid the Slugs like a man overboard treading water, then shouted back, "Yeah. Jesus! Howard, it's a nursery!"

"Are they mature? Is there evidence of independent action?"

"Howard! Get me out of here!"

"Well, it's just so fascinating . . ."

"Lower your climbing rope. It's coiled in the long pocket on the left side of your pack."

The scrabbling of gloves against Polyvis echoed above me.

"I dunno, Jason. I'm not sure I can rappel down. This rope is—"

I rolled my eyes. "Not for *you* to come *down*! For *me* to climb *up*! Belay the rope up there, then lower it."

"Oh."

Ten minutes later the purple-braided end of Howard's rope slid down from darkness and wagged above my head. The delay gave me time to imagine that these writhing, mewling monsters were carnivorous. Every time I shifted my weight and something poked me, I figured some slinking Slug had wormed through an armor chink and was chewing my flesh. The truth was that the experience was as pleasant and harmless as doing the backstroke through a stinking pool of maggots.

I caught the rope on the second try, attached a come-along, and began inch-worming back up toward the catwalk. I nearly fell back when I felt something clinging to my boot, shrieked, and my kicking set me swinging like Tarzan. The Slug fell away and I resumed climbing.

An hour after my fall, Howard grasped my pack straps and heaved me the last feet back onto the walkway. I lay there gasping for ten minutes, until I could speak. My forearm muscles quivered, spent, beneath my Eternads.

"What the hell is this place, Howard? What does it mean?"

"Well, it's unfortunate." Howard rewound his rope, using one hand to loop it around his elbow and through the crook of his palm, just like a real soldier. "What I'm going to tell you is disappointing, Jason."

I hissed out a breath. "Howard, giant snails flying through space just bombed the Earth. Three weeks ago I amputated two of my own fingers. I just climbed out of a wriggling monster pit as big as Lake Erie. How much more disappointing can it be?"

He sighed. "While you were climbing, I had Jeeb examine this chamber and the balance of the ship, to the extent he could travel and also by plugging into the Troll's own diagnostics. This chamber is the main tissue incubation center. You were right."

The Spooks figured the Slugs cloned themselves. But I always figured the Slug hatchery would be some giant hospital with rows and rows of zoomy-looking beds hooked up to life-support hoses, or something. "Slugs just grow in a giant fertilizer tub?"

"Simply put, yes."

"If *this* isn't the power plant, where do we go to blow up the ship?"

Howard punched up Jeeb's holotank and his miniature, diagrammatic Troll floated in front of us again. Howard pointed. "Based on Jeeb's explorations, I've revised this." Howard cleared his professorial throat.

I raised my palm. "Does this story end with useful information?"

He nodded. "Both long-term and for our immediate predicament."

"If we don't solve our immediate predicament, there is no long-term."

"We infer that this ship doesn't move by reactive propulsion."

"Because Slug ships can approach light speed."

Howard nodded. We began to climb back up the catwalk with the green-glowing Troll holo floating above the generator Howard held in front of him, like a town crier's lantern.

"The Pseudocephalopod manipulates gravitons."

"Goddammit. Tell me what that means."

"Gravity is the universe's dominant force. It's everywhere, tugging on everything. We hypothesize it's a manifestation of particles. We can't observe them. Gravitons."

Leave it to Howard to chalk up Slug success to particles no one could see. I panted harder as we climbed. "So get these pesky gravitons off my shoulders."

"You're closer to the truth than you know. The Pseudocephalopod *does* keep the gravitons off its ships." Howard pointed at the stinger on the holo Troll's back end. "I think this assembly, and this boom along the left side, generate an umbrella that shields the ship from gravity behind the ship." He wheezed. "It's as though the ship was attached to two rubber bands, stretched in opposite directions. A combination of force tugs equally from all sides on you and on me and on every atom in this galaxy. If you disturb equilibrium by cutting the rear rubber band—"

"The gravity of the entire half of the universe that's in front of the ship pulls the ship forward." I managed a thin whistle. If Slugs could harness half the universe in order to shoot themselves through it, the little worms had impressed me again.

Howard nodded once more. "No fuel required, except to power the gravity-block field generator." He punched the holo generator control and a little Firewitch materialized. He pointed at the arms spread from the smaller ship's front. "These form a basket that scavenges incoming gravitons and converts them to usable energy. Like a Scramjet scavenges oxygen. Elegant."

Howard raised a hand and paused, puffing.

I asked, "Where is this elegant death machine vulnerable, then?"

Howard shrugged. "*If* we could damage the machine, and *if* we could get through the interdicting warrior forces I underestimated at one hundred thousand—"

"Howard, where?"

He popped the Troll holo back up and pointed again. "Ten miles from here as the crow flies. But by the most direct route through the passages Jeeb mapped, forty-two miles."

I looked up. The light rectangle of the open hatch showed far above us. We climbed back above the rollers and heard Brumby calling for us. He would love the news as much as I did. We returned to Brumby fifteen minutes later.

He paced back and forth along the hatch lip, weapon at port arms, glancing back down the passage every other second. "I dunno how long the block will hold, sirs. I don't understand why they haven't busted in already. Is there a fuel tank or something? Maybe I can improvise an explosive—"

I shook my head. We had sealed ourselves in the

Troll's nursery, not its power plant. This ship's vulnerability lay forty-two miles away from us. One hundred thousand Slugs would make it a nasty forty-two miles. Our break-in was like a holotoon where the convict tunnels out of prison but comes up in the warden's backyard. No wonder the Slugs were no longer suicidal about getting to us. If Slugs laughed, they must be roaring.

FORTY-FIVE

I DISPATCHED JEEB TO PATROL so we could circle our wagons.

The three of us sat cross-legged in the dim passage while Brumby laid out the contents of his minipack. A few sausage coils of Megatex, drilled at intervals to take an electric detonation cap or, in a pinch, old-fashioned light-and-run-like-hell detonation cord fuse. We had a tubful of Thermite sticks, great for burning holes in spaceship hulls, not so good for blowing spaceships to pieces. A roll of high-temp, magnesium-impregnated det cord, great for setting off Thermite, overkill for detonating Megatex.

Brumby surveyed his meager arsenal and sighed. "Sirs, they say you can make a bomb out of almost anything. But we need a big bomb. If we can't blow this ship, shouldn't we just leave? Do we leave?"

It was a fair question. If we returned to the hull breach and called Mimi to return and pick us up, there was the slimmest chance we could get back to Earth and die like infantry with our boots in homeworld mud. Otherwise, eventually the Slugs would breach our barricades or infil-trate a significant force through their door slots. We would buy the farm actively or they could starve us or suffocate us, passively. If they assaulted, taking lots of them with us was little satisfaction, because down below us the Slugs were replicating faster than bathtub scum.

But cutting and running wasn't my style.

I looked at Brumby. "What would you do?"

Brumby tipped his head. "Not much waiting for me back home, sir. I'd just as soon buy it here as in a jail or a VA hospital."

I turned. "Howard?"

"If there were a reason to return to Earth, a chance to win the war, I'd take it. What we've learned here about near-light-speed propulsion would have incalculable impact if mankind could survive. But once this vessel disembarks troops on Earth . . ."

It was unanimous. We would go down swinging, right here. I reached for my M-60 and began to field-strip it for the last time.

Two hours later, Brumby and Howard dozed, Brumby tortured and thrashing, Howard serene. I ran and reran holo'd Troll diagrams, looking for something, anything.

Behind me metal scraped metal. I stiffened. The little bastards had found a way in that we hadn't thought of. They always seemed to be a jump, a nanosecond ahead of us.

My machine gun was laid out on its bipod, loaded and ready, aimed down the passage, the most likely axis of Slug approach. Too far from me.

I reached for Ord's Colt .45 automatic holstered on my chest. Ancient, but reliable and with stopping power to drop an armored Slug.

I drew the Colt, spun, and squeezed off the grip safety.

Jeeb reared back. Not that a bullet would have fazed him.

I relaxed. "Any luck?" Talking to a 'bot about luck was as silly as talking to a 'bot.

But I swear Jeeb nodded.

Howard opened one eye, then sat up and stretched. "Let's download him."

Twenty minutes later, the Chipboard in Howard's hands trembled, as did the leads that hardwired it to Jeeb's belly.

Howard said, "Precognition! That's the key!"

"Precognition? Fortune telling?" I shook my head.

We were surrounded by enemy legions bent on killing us. Yet the professor in Howard took over. "We believe the Pseudocephalopod originated outside the Solar System."

I nodded.

"Any other planetary systems are light-years away."

"Yeah."

"So interstellar travel is infeasible. Because nothing can travel faster than light."

"My fist can, if you don't get to the point, Howard."

He rolled his eyes. "The Pseudocephalopod has solved the puzzle of interstellar travel. We've thought for decades that there are places where space and time as we know them curve back on themselves, touch." He folded a ration wrapper, then pointed to a place where it touched. "Quick hop from here to here." Then, he traced around the wrapper with his finger. "Compared to the long way around."

"Shortcuts."

He nodded. "A logical place for a shortcut is the point where something has tacked the folded temporal fabric together. Only something massively attractive can fold space and time and tack them together."

"What's strong enough to fold the universe?"

"When matter comes together, its gravity attracts more matter. The more matter collapses together, the more attractive the mass becomes. Consider the Sun's mass compressed until it was no larger than a single electron."

"A black hole."

"So attractive that nothing, not even light, can escape."

I stared ahead. "This spaceship falls into something smaller than a golf ball. It gets squashed so small that it'll take an electron microscope to find what's left of it."

"Technically, you couldn't find it with an electron microscope. It becomes packed so densely that light couldn't escape to reflect back."

"Whatever."

"But for the Pseudocephalopod, that black hole is just a cosmic traffic circle. The ship whirls around it and gets slingshot out the other side."

"The other side being . . . ?"

"A long way from home."

Howard leaned his elbows on his knees and cupped his chin in his upturned hands. "You know what I'd really like to know?"

"How any of this helps us blow this ship up?"

"Well, that. But what puzzled me until now was how the Pseudocephalopod overcame the paradox of relativity."

"That one's kept me awake for years."

He sighed. "E equals MC squared. You do know *that*?"

"Okay."

"As matter approaches the speed of light, time slows down relative to matter moving slower."

"Sure. The space traveler returns home a year older but his twin has aged twenty years."

He nodded. "Postulating a quick transit of the black hole, with rapid acceleration inward, followed by corresponding deceleration as the ship exits, because the hole tries to suck the ship back in. Time dilation would be insignificant except at velocities that would only be attained for a few minutes, measured in what would incorrectly be called absolute time. I'd guess an object would lose weeks or a year on a given transit, no more."

"I thought that was your big puzzle?"

"That's not the paradox that puzzles me. The Theory of Relativity also predicts that at relativistic speeds mass increases. Mass accelerated to the speed of light becomes infinite."

"So, for a few minutes, this ship is as big as Jupiter, relative to the rest of the universe? But the Slugs don't feel it? Then they shrink back?"

"Not exactly. It's more that the amount of energy required to move the mass approaches infinity, you see?"

I didn't. "So?"

"Other matter is being sucked in from the opposite side of the displacement at similar velocity. The collision odds of this ship hitting golf-ball-sized debris traveling through the emptiness of space are tiny. At additive speeds faster than light, in the constricted corridor this ship has to transit, the collision odds of two objects—that may have increased masses—are reversed."

"Boom!"

"Big boom."

"But we know the Slugs do it. They beat the odds, Howard. They must have radar or something."

He shook his head. "Radar—all remote sensing—is based on something reflected back from, or at least something emanating out from, a detectable object. Nothing—not light, not radiation, nothing—reflects back or escapes from a black hole."

"But Jeeb's readouts tell you how the Slugs do it?"

Howard stared up at the ceiling and squinted. "Broadly speaking, yes. Ever swat a fly?"

"Sure. I miss them sometimes. They're quick."

"Insects, arachnids even more so, sense future events by means that laboratory experiments have been unable to link with sensory mechanisms tied to measurable physical phenomena."

"Spiders have built-in crystal balls?"

"Precognition. Even if it's measured in nanoseconds."

"This is big news?"

"Coupled with what we learned about gravity propulsion, it could provide mankind with the key to interstellar travel. We could carry the battle to the Pseudocephalopod. Fight it at arm's length."

"One small obstacle to mankind flying to the stars, Howard. In a week mankind will be history."

"Not if you just blow this ship to pieces."

"If I could blow this ship to pieces, I would have done it already!"

Howard's absentminded professor act amused me most of the time. Not now.

I pointed at Brumby, who rubbed his eyes, awakened by my yelling. "Brumby doesn't even have enough fucking explosives to sink a rowboat! I sent Jeeb patrolling because we're out of ideas, here. In twenty minutes of downloading, what have you done that can help us blow this ship to pieces?"

Howard paused, then tugged his lip. "Actually, nothing."

"Goddammit, Howard. I hijacked a spaceship. I violated every oath an officer can take. I got another spaceship blown up because of my stupidity. Forty-six people died out here in space. I did all that because you said you could figure out how to blow this ship up. But after a fucking lifetime studying fucking extraterrestrials, the best you can tell me is we're sitting on a fucking fertilizer mountain?" I leaned against the Slug metal bulkhead, arms extended, head down, like I could push the bulkhead away with my palms, and let my anger drain away.

Brumby cleared sleep from his throat. "Fertilizer, sir? Would that be ammonium nitrate?"

I sighed and pointed at Howard. "That's what he told me, Brumby."

Howard smacked his forehead. "Of course!"

FORTY-SIX

HOWARD JUMPED UP AND DANCED, arms waving over his head.

Brumby blinked furiously. "Oh, baby!"

My outburst had driven them around the bend, too.

I turned and faced them. "What?"

Howard grinned. "N-H-Four, N-O-Three!"

"Brumby? In English?"

"Ammonium nitrate makes bombs."

"Real bombs?"

Howard stopped dancing. "In 1947 a ship cargo of ammonium nitrate fertilizer caught fire. The explosion and tidal wave destroyed the port of Texas City and broke windows in Galveston, ten miles away. It raised a mushroom cloud a half mile high. The ship's anchor weighed a ton and a half. It buried itself ten feet in the ground two miles away."

Brumby said, "You mix it with diesel oil."

"Brumby, I don't think starships carry diesel oil."

"It doesn't have to be mixed. It's stable against impact. You can hit it with a hammer, even shoot it. But heat it above its slow-decomposition point, 393 degrees Fahrenheit"—

Brumby raised his arms like a symphony conductor—"and up she goes."

"How big a bomb can you make with this stuff?"

"How much ammonium nitrate you got, sir? Texas City was twenty-three hundred tons."

Hair rose on my neck. And my forearms and everywhere else.

"What do we have to do?"

Brumby reached for a Thermite stick. "Thermite burns at over two thousand degrees. Stuff Thermite all through the fertilizer pile, at intervals. Light the high-temp fusing. Run like hell."

I rubbed my chin. "How long can the fuse be?"

Brumby picked up the det-cord reel and peeled off lengths he measured by arm spans, like a tailor. Then he counted the Thermite sticks. "Allowing for some fuses to be longer since you gotta light them first, then run and light the others, ten minutes, tops."

I frowned. "It took me almost an hour to climb out of that pit."

Brumby pointed at Jeeb. "Let the 'bot do the work, sir. He can fly away."

Millions of Jeeb's mass-market cousins had been vacuuming floors, pruning shrubs, and painting walls since the turn of the century. Jeeb could fly like an eagle, crack codes, translate every known human dialect in real time, and track every soldier in an infantry division, but his current appendages and programming were adapted for locomotion, self-maintenance, sensing, and data assimilation. I shook my head. "Jeeb can't even light a match, Brumby. Much less dig holes and plant bombs."

Howard asked, "Can't we just chuck 'em down there? Like throwing dynamite sticks?"

Brumby shook his head. "You can drop a lit match on paper and not burn it. The heat's gotta be confined." He waved his hand over the few Thermite sticks. "And it's not like we have spares to practice with."

Cold settled in my gut. Knowing the right thing didn't make it easier to do it. "So we have to go down there and set this bomb off. And we won't be able to get away."

We stared at one another.

Brumby raised his hand. "I'll do it, sir. I'm the logical one to work with the charges and det cord."

I shook my head. "Commanding officer's prerogative, Brumby. I can light a match with the best of 'em."

Howard said, "Look, this whole thing was my idea. I can do it."

Brumby said, "Maybe we all stay and do it, then."

Howard got to his feet and paced. "No. Somebody needs to get the drive-system information back. If the bomb works, we win this battle. If we also bring back that information, humanity might win the war."

Brumby gathered up the Thermite sticks and stuffed them in his minipack. "Send the 'bot back."

I grabbed for the pack, but Brumby jerked it out of my reach. I said, "Mimi won't know to come get just Jeeb. Besides, there's no sense you two getting yourselves killed, too."

Unless I pulled rank, this had the makings of a three-way brawl for the privilege of getting onself blown to smithereens. Not to mention a philosophical debate over the nature of heroism and sacrifice.

In the breast pocket inside my armor, Jeeb's holo-cube

link vibrated against my chest. I paused and looked over at him.

Jeeb was facing up the blocked passage, pogo-ing up and down on all six legs and whistling audibly.

The passage wall where he had pointed himself began to glow, a ring on the metal as big as the end of a tanker truck, first red, then orange, then white-hot.

FORTY-SEVEN

I LOOKED FROM THE WALL to Howard to Brumby. "Looks like the Slugs brought their own version of Thermite." I pointed up the passage, past the impending Slug breach point, where Mimi would dock the V-Star. "Howard, you go. Jeeb, too. Now. Before the Slugs burn through."

The wall ring was white from top to bottom now. A molten lump oozed, fell to the passage deck, and sputtered.

"Brumby, you and I'll plant the Thermite."

Howard said, "Jason—"

I pointed at Jeeb. "Take care of him."

"You got it."

Jeeb hovered, wings extended.

Molten metal slid down the passage-wall face in rivulets.

Howard turned and jogged past the Slug breach point, ducking away from sparks.

I turned to see Brumby already stepping through the open hatch into the incubation chamber. I ran after him as a gong and hiss announced the fall of the molten-edged passage-wall cutout.

A second later, a mag-rifle round ricocheted off the bulkhead just above the open hatch I ran for.

I dove through the hatch, rolled to my feet, and followed Brumby down the spiraling catwalk, his headlight and mine bouncing zigzag in the darkness as we ran.

A bumblebee whirred past my ear, then another.

I switched my optics to passive infrared and looked up. Hundreds of feet above us, purple Slug infrared searchlight beams crisscrossed, hunting for us. Rail-rifle rounds rained down, more random than aimed. The Slugs couldn't see our visible light beams and their own lights didn't reach far enough to pick us out, infrared. They moved slowly through a space that was as dark for them as for us. We had a three-minute start, I guessed.

I caught up with Brumby at the wide spot on the walkway where I had found the larval Slug. He stood bent over, hands on knees, panting, the minipack of Thermite sticks and det cord slung across his armor. An entrenching tool, for digging in the charges, dangled from his belt.

"We have to rappel down from here, Brumby."

He looked up, swiveling his light to catch my face. "Yes, sir."

I glanced back above. Up the spiral walkway, the Slugs had stopped wasting ammunition, but their light beams still swung to and fro, searching.

"Look, Brumby. There's maybe a dozen of them up there. We can see them with our headlights before they can see us. They can't handle any GI one on one and our armor's better than theirs. There's no need for two of us to stay here and plant the charges. You fight your way out." I held out my hand toward his minipack. "Give."

"Sir? Seems to me the general's better qualified to fight Slugs and I'm better qualified to plant charges."

He straightened, but made no move to hand over the pack.

I lifted the climbing rope coils over my helmet. "Brumby, this is the Army, not a debate club. Give me the pack."

A Slug beam swept purple across the chamber wall, just above our heads.

Brumby shook his head, light wagging in the dark. "What's at home for me, sir? Jail? A VA bunk? I'll go making a difference, thank you very much."

The fact that Brumby's analysis was right didn't make it right for me to let him plant the charges. The stupid thing about leadership is that leaders have to do stupid things. "Brumby, I order you to hand over those charges."

Spang! A Slug round thudded into the deck a foot from us.

Brumby hooked a thumb in his minipack strap as he looked me in the eye. "Yes, sir. You know the last thing I would do as long as I live is disobey an order."

And then Brumby stepped backward into thin air and fell serenely into the dark.

FORTY-EIGHT

I STARED INTO DARKNESS, the space before me empty.

The wet thud as Brumby fell into gelatinous Slug larva and ammonium-nitrate soup echoed across the vast chamber.

Slug lights jerked and arrowed, closer now. Slug shots spattered the walkway.

"Son of a bitch!" Brumby's voice rasped over the Whispercom.

"Brumby? You okay?"

"Nothing broken, sir."

I swallowed back tears. "Brumby, what you just did—"

"With respect, sir. It's done. What the general needs to do now is keep the Slugs off my butt so I can get my digging done down here."

I turned back and headed up the walkway as the first Slug infrared beam swung across my armor. A three-round burst from my gun sent the light and its owner toppling into the pit.

One sighted GI against a squad of blind Slugs is hardly a fair fight. Twenty minutes later, I stepped back into the passage that led back to Mimi, Howard, Jeeb, and, perhaps, home.

"Brumby?"

"Just dug in the last charge, sir. Should be a great finish. I'm gonna light the first fuse now. Ten minutes, sir. You take care."

I drew a breath and my lip quivered. In ten minutes, Brumby could have gotten back to the walkway, but he would still be a half hour from rescue. "You, too, Brumby."

As I came abreast of the Slugs' breach in the passage wall, ten squirmed forward from their passage, firing. I snatched up the cut-metal wall section for a shield, knelt behind it, and gun-fought them until the last one dropped. I used up the last M-60 ammunition and left the gun behind with a pang.

If I was going to keep the Slugs away from Brumby, the best way was to blow this passage shut with the remaining Megatex, then set up shop back at the breach point, where we had bottlenecked the Slugs before. As I ran to our breach point, I heard the charge I had set crump the passage closed. I chinned my radio to Command Net. "Mimi? Howard? Over."

If Howard had made it, my ride would be long gone, racing to beat the blast upon which the future of the human race depended.

I tried squad net. That would just reach Howard, who probably didn't have his radio on and wouldn't know how to answer it, anyway.

Nothing.

A Slug wave surged at me. I dropped Slugs with M-20 flechette until I ran out. My ammo pouches were bare. Three more surged forward. I drew Ord's .45 and hit all three, but one got off a round that whacked my thigh. But for my armor, it would have torn my leg off.

I rounded the last bend, limping. The yellow plastic plug that sealed the six-foot-diameter breach point remained in place. That proved nothing. The docking procedure left it in place, whether Mimi had rescued Howard and Jeeb or not.

I drew up to the breach point, panting, rested my shoulder against its pillow, and read my 'puter.

If Brumby did his job, he and I had five minutes to live. And if Howard and Jeeb had done theirs, the human race might have forever.

I glanced down at the deck plates and my heart skipped.

FORTY-NINE

I KNELT AND PICKED UP A SQUARE of paper a bit bigger than an old postage stamp, but nothing else.

I smiled. The paper was a Howard Hibble nicotine-gum wrapper. He and Jeeb had made it this far, in fact had paused long enough for Howard to have a chew. If Slugs had caught up with them, there would be spent brass on the deck, if not blood or a body. Howard when cornered became a wildcat with 20-200 vision. He wouldn't have gone down without firing a shot.

So they had made it.

I popped the magazine out of the pistol butt, awkwardly, since I had to do it three-fingered. Then I reached for a fresh magazine and found nothing. I tried Brumby on squad net and got nothing, which I expected, considering the interference between us.

Debris from the earlier fighting still littered the little chamber where we had entered this ship and begun this battle. The Semtex canister we had left behind was gone. Slugs weren't stupid. Without ammunition, the best I could do to delay any Slugs that tried to get to Brumby was barricade the passage. I dragged debris and flung up a ratty barrier.

I slumped, and slid down the plastic plug until I sat on the deck plates, sprawled my legs and rested my head against the plug's cushion. I turned the .45 to hold the barrel in my good hand, to tomahawk Slugs with the gun butt. Why I bothered, I didn't know. The Slugs and I would be tiny bits of interplanetary flotsam in four minutes. Or not, in which case, with odds of one hundred thousand to one against me, I wouldn't last long anyway.

It had, all things considered, been a fine twenty-five years. I had known my parents, though not for so long as I would have liked. I had grown up. I had known good people. The best, in fact. I had experienced the one great love of my life, albeit for just 616 days. Oh, and, depending on which version of history one read, I had saved the world.

My 'puter beeped. Three minutes.

They say contemplation of death comes in phases: denial, anger, some other stuff, then, finally, acceptance.

A mile beneath me was Brumby, too, taking the opportunity to accept his death?

Maybe that was the thing I had been luckiest about, compared to the other orphans I had known. It is a soldier's destiny to die young and unexpectedly. They may die for noble causes. They may die for others' hubris or stupidity. But it is rarely a soldier's destiny to have the time to accept his death.

That, I supposed, was the thing that would stand clear to me for what remained of my life.

"—stand clear."

My own thoughts echoed in my helmet. In my last moments, I had begun talking to myself.

"Jason? Come in. There's no time to dock this thing." Mimi squawked inside my helmet. "I'm just gonna poke the docking bridge through the plug. Stand clear, then dive in through the bridge hatch fast. 'Cause I gotta reverse out in fifteen seconds."

Across the chamber, my debris barrier fell.

Slugs boiled through, so thick I couldn't count them.

I scrambled to my feet and spun around.

The plug bulged inward, like a giant, yellow bubble-gum bubble.

Blam!

The explosion as Mimi stung the docking bridge through the breach hurled the plastic plug and me, somersaulting like a crimson bowling ball, twenty feet back down the passage. Slugs scattered like tenpins.

"Jason, I hope you heard me. 'Cause if you're not inside that bridge when I pull out, explosive decompression will shoot you into space like a watermelon seed."

I kicked the plug off me like blankets on Christmas morning and scrambled to my knees.

Slugs swarmed around me. I pounded one, pistol-whipped another, and wondered why I hadn't been shot a dozen times already.

Slugs ignored me as they surged around and past, headed toward Brumby and our makeshift bomb. They ignored me because I couldn't kill their invasion. But they had figured out that Brumby could.

The bridge hatch beckoned, twenty feet away.

I crawled forward. And my web-gear harness caught on

the plug's torn surface. I tugged and dragged the plug behind me.

Ten feet to the bridge hatch.

Beyond the hull breach, I heard thrusters fire, their sound conducted through the contact between the hulls of the V-Star and the Troll.

The gap between me and the bridge hatch widened to twelve feet as Mimi backed the V-Star away.

My 'puter beeped. Two minutes to detonation.

I popped the buckle on my harness. It fell away from my body and flopped to the deck, along with the deflated plug.

I dove for the bridge-hatch handle, caught it, and got dragged toward outer space as the V-Star backed away from the Troll. I twisted my body and the hatch fell open. I scrambled in, the hatch snapped shut behind me, and the rush of atmosphere exploding out of the open breach thundered against the docking bridge's skin.

Armored Slugs got sucked out through the breach into vacuum like spilled black marbles. The passage became impassable. The Slugs couldn't cross vacuum and get to Brumby in time to prevent detonation, now.

I lay there in the docking bridge's white metal tube and just breathed, listening to thruster nozzles fire as Mimi rotated the V-Star so she could fire the main engine.

I weaseled around inside the docking bridge and pressed my helmet faceplate to the quartz porthole in the hatch.

We were five hundred feet from the Troll's vast surface, and backing off fast.

"Jason? You in?"

"In."

My 'puter beeped. One minute.

"Hang on."

Mimi lit the main engine and acceleration crushed me against the docking bridge's rear hatch like a musket ball rammed down a flintlock's muzzle.

I don't know how many Gees we pulled, but my helmet faceplate got measled red from my nosebleed.

I was jammed against the rear inspection plate, a quartz port like the front hatch porthole. Behind us, the city-sized Troll already looked as small as a basketball. I chinned my faceplate dark.

My heart beat and I thought of Brumby.

The Troll seemed to wiggle, growing smaller by the second, then it turned into a miniature sunrise.

The yellow explosion raced at us.

In my helmet, Mimi muttered, "Go. Go, you mother!"

Flame engulfed us in seconds. The ship rocked and spun. Debris banged against us like the start of a rain.

I tumbled inside the bridge as the ship yawed.

Then space was black again. The roar of the main engine cut off and weight lifted off my chest as the V-Star coasted through space.

"Jason? You okay?"

"Bruised. But glad to be here. I owe you."

Mimi asked, "Howard?"

"Holy moly!"

I dragged myself through the inner bridge hatch and floated in the troop bay, where Howard was strapped in, helmet off, his head poking up out of his armor like an undernourished turtle's. I popped my helmet and let it float in the bay.

Mimi Ozawa wormed her way back from the flight deck. This time I watched.

She drifted into the bay, tugged off her own helmet, and smoothed back sweat-plastered hair with both hands. It struck me that she had never looked more beautiful.

She said, "This thing flies itself."

Howard narrowed his eyes until she smiled at him. "But can we get home in this thing?"

"We're pointed in the right direction and close enough that the Earth's gravity will help reel us in after about three days. If you mean all that un-aerodynamic thruster piping and tankage? Easy on, easy off." She pointed at a mushroom-shaped red button, shielded and mounted alongside the backup gauge panel set in the forward bulkhead. "Before we insert into the atmosphere, we hit that. Explosive bolts blow it all off and we're clean as a whistle for reentry."

She said to me, "General Wander, this is the second time you've been late for a bus I was driving." Then she grinned again, as warm as pre-war sunshine.

"Nice driving, too, Major. One invasion transport the size of Toledo blown to pieces. Not to mention one hundred twenty-one really ugly fighters."

While I spoke, she swam herself up into the Mercury system's crystal blister and let herself spin slowly, enjoying a non-viewscreen look out at space.

Her next words rang cold. "Make that one hundred twenty."

FIFTY

"Huh?"

Mimi scrambled down from the observation blister and dog-paddled along handholds toward the flight deck. "Firewitch Alpha. Dead astern and closing."

"But—"

Howard said, "Most of the Firewitches had docked with the Troll. It had pickets out. One must've survived."

The survivor would be very grumpy.

I called to Mimi. "We've been coasting. Can we outrun it?"

She called back as her boot soles wriggled at us from the flight-deck access tube, "Not likely. Even if we had fuel to spare. Which we don't."

Howard drifted alongside the redundant gauge bank set in the forward bulkhead. He looked at one, then tapped it with his finger. "This says eighty-five percent."

"You're looking at the auxiliary maneuvering-thruster fuel. That's no help. If we burn the main engine too much, when we reverse we won't be able to decelerate. If we can't decelerate, we enter the atmosphere too fast. Either we skip off and slide out to an orbit beyond the moon, where we suffocate, freeze, or starve, or we plunge right on in and burn to cinders."

I tugged my helmet back on. "So, what do we do?"

"You game to shoot 'em up with the Mercury again?"

I heard no other option. I swam up into the blister again and twisted into the fighting chair. It seemed like home, now. I flipped the power-up switch and the cage whined and vibrated around me. I hit the foot treadles, swinging left, then right and elevated, then dropped the chair relative to the horizon. I spun the turret rearward and punched up magnification. I didn't need to.

Blue against space's blackness, its navigation lights flaring in patterns only a Slug could decipher, the Firewitch had already closed to firing range and its ordnance arms spidered open.

Up front, Mimi had to be looking in her rearview. "Jason?"

Range was really not an issue with ballistic weapons in space. For practical purposes, the Mercury's cannon rounds wouldn't slow down. Aim wasn't a factor either, with a target as big as the closing Firewitch in my sights.

I depressed the trigger. The gun shrieked. Flame spit from a half-dozen rotating barrels.

And stopped.

Yellow tracer flew downrange and a hundred 37-millimeter rounds exploded in a hundred harmless orange-poppy blooms on the Firewitch's nose.

"Jason? Why'd you stop?"

"I didn't!" I looked down. My gloved thumb pressed the trigger so hard it shook. I ran my eyes across the gauge bank, then groaned at a flashing red light. I had ripped away, trigger-happy, on the first Firewitch we disabled.

Now I wished I had a few of those rounds back. "The ammo light was green. But we only had a hundred rounds."

The Firewitch snapped off a first round. It burned toward us like a crimson comet, then passed over my left shoulder, a hundred yards away.

"They won't take long to target us."

We shot through space at ten thousand miles per hour. The Firewitch pursued even faster. It was occupying the space we were in mere seconds later. It would all be over in moments.

I pounded the cage frame with my three-fingered hand and yelped. We had come so far! Beaten such impossible odds! I had given up a literal piece of myself. Brumby had given up his life.

Brumby, who could make a bomb out of nearly anything.

I paused and stared at my reflection in the dome, then asked Mimi, "What's the auxiliary thruster fuel?"

"Why?"

"Goddammit, what's it made of?"

"Liquid hydrogen and liquid oxygen."

"Is it explosive?"

"Yeah."

"How much we got?" I was already unbuckling from the fighting chair.

"Four, five thousand pounds."

Another Firewitch round bore in on us and shot past. It screamed above me, noiseless, but so close that I saw Slug hieroglyphs etched on its blue, spinning side.

I looked up. The Firewitch's arms twitched small adjustments. The next salvo would be "fire for effect."

I slid down into the troop bay and launched myself at the redundant gauge bank, floating, it seemed, as lazy as a Thanksgiving-parade balloon.

I tore open the safety cover and punched the red JETTI-SON button with my bad hand. Weightless, my fist didn't strike the Earth-standard spring-loading hard enough to depress the plunger.

What idiot engineer didn't think about that?

I pulled myself against the panel, braced my feet, and swung again.

Click.

The explosive bolts thumped, not all at once, as piping and tankage peeled away from our skin, piece by piece, and drifted back into our wake.

I made it back up into the dome as the silver tangle of discarded equipment tumbled toward the Firewitch's vulnerable, cyclopean, purple eye.

"Mimi, better spend a little juice, or we'll blow ourselves up, too."

But the Firewitch didn't explode like the Troll had. The eye exploded satisfyingly, then the ship's lights went out in a finger snap and it slowed and drifted.

Howard poked his head up into the bubble and looked back as the derelict began to tumble, its momentum carrying it slowly behind us, toward Earth. "Holy moly. Jason Wander, the three-fingered buccaneer."

"Huh?"

"You just captured our first capital prize of this war."

Howard wedged himself into the fighting cage alongside me and I rotated it so we faced forward.

Earth hung peaceful and blue in space, the moon silver,

and off her shoulder, the Milky Way's swath powdering the blackness behind them.

I pointed toward the stars. "We're not alone in this galaxy. Is our destiny out there?"

"You mean 'destination.'"

"No, I don't."

FIFTY-ONE

"GENERAL?" My command sergeant major knocks on the hatch frame of my stateroom as he opens the hatch.

"Time, Sergeant Major Ord?"

"Yes, sir."

I stand up at my desk and rub my hand. "I already knew." Organic prosthetic fingers are indistinguishable from original, they say. But the change in atmospheric pressure when a Metzger-class cruiser accelerates to make Temporal-Fabric Insertion always makes mine throb.

The swabbies don't really need the embarked-division commander on the bridge at insert. It's routine now. But it's also tradition. And tradition counts with Space Force as much as it did with the old wet-Navy.

Ord strides beside me, holding a Chipboard for me to sign, clicking from document to document as we walk. Genius may be ninety-nine percent perspiration but commanding a division is ninety-nine percent paperwork.

Ord snaps off the board. "That's all the business for now, sir."

I smile. The real business that this ship—this fleet—will do remains months and light-years away.

I pause at the bridge hatch. The swabbie rating with his little manual whistle spots me.

He snaps to, skirls out a call, and misses a note.

I squint at his chest. His ribbon row is as short as his skin is baby-pale. But he wears the blue-and-gold *Rodger Young* ribbon.

First of the gravity-shielded Corvette-transport fast-movers, crewed with bright kids, the *Young* exploded on her maiden voyage before she ever got out of Earth orbit.

In the best military tradition, those kids who never saw it coming got posthumous medals because somebody made a mistake.

The *Young*'s orphaned survivors had been distributed among other ships. He's probably never played a manual bosun's whistle before.

He calls, "Attention on deck! The embarked-division commander is on the bridge!"

I step around the master holo and salute the captain. Admiral, actually. "How we doing?"

The admiral points at the frontscreen. "Nothing unusual. The fast-movers made insertion two days ago. Those new ones fly."

In the frontscreen's green glow, I see wistfulness in her eyes. "You miss flying fast-movers, don't you, Mimi?"

She smiles. It would be unprofessional to mention it on the bridge, but as lovely as the day we met. She says, "I'd trade the Metz for a Brumby-class command in a heartbeat."

"And miss the fun of keeping peace between your squids and ten thousand mudfeet?" The Metzger class may be slower than the Corvette transports, but each ship can haul a full division.

The three "P"s that dog theater-grade commanders are paperwork, personnel, and politics. That was the best part of Insertion. Once you popped out in new space, you were light-years away from the politicians. No armchair quarterbacking until you came home.

If you came home. Not that politics offers safe harbor in the Slug War. Jeeb and I visit Ruth's grave when we're dirtside. We both cry.

I bitch a lot—only to myself and my Significant Other—about the three "P"s, but the fact remains that ten thousand kids bet their lives on my ability to juggle all those things and still be a better soldier than any of them.

In the viewscreens, the space ahead of us darkens first, as all light gets sucked into the ultradwarf core of the Insertion Point.

The kid with the whistle stares, bug-eyed.

I lean toward him, hands clasped behind my back. "First Insert?"

He nods. "Yes, sir."

"And you worry why you get to see it while your buddies on the *Young* never will?"

His jaw drops. "Uh, yes, sir."

I shake my head. "Don't worry. Live the best life you know how. The rest is destiny."

I point at the sidescreens. "Watch. First the stars stretch out like taffy, when their light gets bent. Then their light turns parallel to us and they go out altogether. It's really wick!"

He looks at me oddly. They tell me nobody has said "wick" since before the war, but the only way I throw my rank around is to choose my own slang.

A 'puter voice, throaty and feminine, chimes. "Insertion in five."

There was a time when I giggled every time I heard that.

The stars go out.

Acknowledgments

Authors like reissues because others do the heavy lifting. Rarely, those others lift extraordinarily well, and Orbit's reissue of *Orphan's Destiny,* like its predecessor, *Orphanage,* is such a rarity. Therefore, my special thanks to Orbit publishing director Tim Holman and editor Devi Pillai for vision and drive; to Calvin Chu for a sparkling new cover design; to Alex Lencicki for imagination; and, to Jennifer Flax for keeping them all on track.

Thanks, too, to my agent, Winifred Golden for unflagging enthusiasm and savvy, and to Mary Beth, for everything.

extras

meet the author

ROBERT BUETTNER is a former Military Intelligence Officer, National Science Foundation Fellow in Paleontology, and has published in the field of Natural Resources Law. He lives in Georgia. His Web site is: www.robertbuettner.com.

author's note

Orphanage: A 2004 take on
an evergreen story
by ROBERT BUETTNER

On January 29, 1898, the *Saturday Review* gasped at a new "romance" that had "hit upon a subject so far from experience and completely outside common expectation" that "our readers must buy it and alarm themselves with it at their leisure." Readers did.

A century after H. G. Wells' *The War of the Worlds*, we still snap up Alien-war tales. Those tales have evolved to match the *zeitgeist* of the world in which each was written.

Wells' story reflected Victorian fears of massive, mechanized war that would torture all of Europe.

Wells was right, but he won no sympathy for Aliens. In 1993, Sir Arthur C. Clarke stopped short of "blam[ing] Wells for all the later excesses of interplanetary warfare," but Sir Arthur complained that Wells laid it down that "anything Alien was likely to be horrible." Nowadays, we prefer our Aliens warm, fuzzy and politically correct.

Fortunately for those who like good yarns, writers didn't write all *Mork-from-Ork* since 1898, probably because the world they wrote in was no sitcom.

In Cold War 1959, Robert Heinlein won a Hugo with *Starship Troopers*. As Uncle Sam drafted even Elvis Presley to repel the Commies, Heinlein penned a tale of noble battle against city-nuking spiders commanded by fat, Nikita Khrushchev brain bugs.

Post-Vietnam, Joe Haldeman exposed a never-ending war, started by our side for no good reason, waged by cynical conscripts, in his own 1974 Hugo-winner, *The Forever War*.

So, why the *Orphanage* books, a fast, darkly funny, re-told tales of a young man-become-soldier amid interplanetary war? Because *Starship Troopers* and *The Forever War* marvelously embraced the *zeitgeist* in which each was written, but each suffers for it in a post-9/11 world.

Starship Troopers glorified a neo-facist future where only soldiers earn voting rights and we flog criminals publicly. Dialogue often echoes '50s TV. Women pilot Heinlein's starships, but they are perfumed and mystical, like aproned '50s moms flying Frigidaires.

Vietnam-vet Haldeman expressly rewrote Heinlein and scorned *Starship*'s Cold War jingoism. Haldeman embraced the '60s' "emerging truths." The war is our fault. All officers and politicians are sadistic fools. Soldiers get pot rations and bunk co-ed, rotating sex partners nightly.

Orphanage and *Orphan's Destiny* avoid politics. It was written to say one true thing to a population that has been blessed by scant military experience but that, post-9/11, finds soldiers again relevant. That thing is: soldiers fight not for flags or against tyrants but for each other. Combat soldiers become one another's only family. Strip away politics and, wherever or whenever, war is an orphanage.

Orphan's Destiny was written to explore the challenges soldiers face when they survive.

Orphanage and *Orphan's Destiny* engage readers in a future just forty years distant, where space shuttles and television are antiques, not ancient artifacts. Any passion and humor they muster, compared to Heinlein's and Haldeman's classics, grows from affection for foot soldiers, an affection those books share.

Readers familiar with Heinlein will detect a few covert tributes, as will Haldeman fans.

Orphanage and *Orphan's Destiny* aren't anti-communist or anti-war like their predecessors. They are just pro-foot soldier.

introducing

If you enjoyed ORPHAN'S DESTINY,
look out for

ORPHAN'S JOURNEY

Book 3 of the Jason Wander series
by Robert Buettner

"TEN YARDS SEAWARD from where I stand on the beach, the new-risen moons backlight our assault boats, outbound toward six fathoms. Beyond six fathoms lies hell.

Wind bleeds oily smoke back over me from lanterns roped to a thousand gunwales. Fifty soldiers' churning paddles whisker each boat's flanks. The boats crawl up wave crests, then dive down wave troughs, like pitching centipedes. For miles to my left and right, the lantern line winds like a smoldering viper.

I'm Jason Wander. Earthling, war orphan, high school dropout, infantryman, field-promoted Major General. And, on this sixth of August, 2056, accidental Commander of the largest amphibious assault since Eisenhower hurled GIs across the English Channel.

New century. New planet. Old fear.

An assault boat's Platoon Leader stands bent-kneed amid his paddlers, waving his boat's lantern above his head. He shouts to me, "We gladly die for you!"

I salute him, because I'm too choked to shout back. And shout what? That only fools die gladly? That he'd better sit down before his own troops shoot him for a fool? That someone should shoot me for one?

At my side, my Command Sergeant Major whispers, "They won't shoot him, Sir." I blink. Ord has read my mind since he was my Drill Sergeant in Basic.

The Bren may not shoot one another tonight, but the first Bren proverb we translated was "Blood feud is bread." For centuries, Bren has suffered under the thumb—well, the pseudopod—Slugs are man-sized, armored maggots that have no thumbs—of the Pseudocephalopod Hegemony. Still, every Clan midwife gifts every male baby with a whittled battle axe. Not to overthrow the Slugs. To whack human neighbors who worship the wrong god.

But if the newly unified Clans fail at sunrise, the Slugs will peel humanity off this planet like grape skin. Because we four Earthlings arrived.

Did I say "unified"? Ha. We should've segregated every boat. Mixed Clans may brain each other with their paddles before the first Slug shows. The final toast at Clan funerals is "May paradise spare you from allies."

Packed into twenty square miles of beach dunes, the Second and Third Assault Waves' cook fires prick the night. Smells of wood smoke and the dung of reptilian cavalry mounts drift to me on the shifting wind, along with Clan songs.

Yet twenty-two miles across the sea, the Slugs sleep.

Actually, no human knows whether Slugs sleep. But I have bet this civilization's life that tonight the Slugs have left the cross-channel beaches undefended. It seems a smart bet. No boatman in five hundred years has crossed the Sea of Hunters at full moons, and lived.

I chin my helmet optics. Two heartbeats thump before I get a focus. A mile out, faint wakes vee the water. The first kraken are rising, like trout sensing skittering water bugs.

Sea monsters mightier than antique locomotives are about to splinter those first boats, like fists pounding straw. But troops that survive the crossing should surprise the Slugs. Surprised or not, the Slugs will still be the race that slaughtered sixty million Earthlings, as indifferently as mouthwash drowning germs.

Waves explode against boat prows. Windblown brine spits through my open helmet visor, needling my cheeks. My casualty bookie says that, even before the moons set, four hundred boats and crews will founder. Because I ordered them out there. The brine hides my tears.

Is my plan brilliant? Hannibal crossing the Alps? MacArthur landing at Inchon? I swallow. "What if I blundered, Sergeant Major?"

Ord nods back his helmet optics, then peers through binoculars older than he is. "Sir, Churchill said that war is mostly a catalogue of blunders."

Ord told me exactly the same thing as we lay in the snow of Tibet, three years ago. If I'd listened, this ratscrew could've been avoided.